PERSONS OF RANK

A clever and witty historical romance.

Eleanor and Beatrice dream of love matches but the Dowager insists romantic love is for housemaids, not for the Graceover women. Beatrice, despatched to London at the Dowager's behest to look over the current crop of eligible bachelors, is unimpressed by the frivolities of the season, while the beautiful and headstrong Eleanor is up to mischief of her own which is guaranteed to earn the disapproval of her grandmother. Will her secret be discovered? After a desperate struggle in the potting shed at midnight, not only does love triumph but the Dowager is not displeased.

PERSONS OF RANK

by

Anna Jacobs

Magna Large Print Books
Long Preston, North Yorkshire,
BD23 4ND, England.

British Library Cataloguing in Publication Data.

Jacobs, Anna
    Persons of rank.

    A catalogue record of this book is
    available from the British Library

    ISBN   978-0-7505-3326-3

Published in Large Print 2010 by arrangement with
Sherry-Anne Jacobs, care of Wade and Doherty Literary
Agency

LP

Magna Large Print is an imprint of Library Magna Books Ltd.

Printed and bound in Great Britain by
T.J. (International) Ltd., Cornwall, PL28 8RW

To David
my beloved best friend and husband

ONE

'Persons of our rank,' declared the Dowager, quivering with outrage at the mere thought, 'do *not* fall in love! They may, if they are that way inclined, come to feel some affection for their spouse – I have known it to happen, even in the best of circles, though I myself consider it extremely vulgar – but – are you listening to me, Eleanor? Beatrice? – I repeat, persons of rank *do not, under any circumstances, fall in love!*'

She rapped her cane on the floor by her chair to emphasise this point and added, with monumental scorn, 'Nor do they read puerile tales in half-marble covers about the sort of low-bred persons who *do* indulge in such habits! They leave such absurdities for menials and governesses who know no better!' Her eyes flashed with anger as she surveyed her niece Beatrice and her granddaughter, Eleanor, both in severe disgrace for being caught reading a novel together.

Lady Eleanor Graceover's bright blue eyes were still sparkling with indignation at seeing her enthralling tale thrown on the fire. Now she and Beatrice would never know whether poor Melissa managed to escape from the toils of the evil Count and be reunited with Gervaise, her childhood sweetheart! But she had more sense than to defy or contradict her grandmother, in whose charge she had been for ten of her nineteen years. One did not get one's own way by outright opposition to her ladyship. In fact, poor Beatrice rarely got her way at all, but Eleanor was never quite sure whether that was because she was submissive by nature or because she did not care enough about what happened to dispute Lady Marguerite's authority or judgement. There had been one or two occasions when Bea had dug in her heels about something and then nothing had been able to move her.

She herself was cast, Eleanor felt complacently, in a more resolute mould. She had learned the trick of dealing with her grandmother over the years and had no intention of allowing Lady Marguerite to plan her whole life for her, let alone choose her husband. It would be just like Grandmama to try to marry her off to some knock-kneed idiot, because of his family connections. Why, she had spoken approvingly only last week about Eleanor's second cousin Maria's engagement to a quite elderly nobleman, who was thirty-two if he was a day. Just because his family had come over with the Conqueror!

Eleanor knew that her own future was presently under consideration, because she just happened to have overheard her grandmother talking to the family lawyer recently about marriage settlements. She bent her russet curls over her clasped hands and tried to look as if she were listening meekly, for Lady Marguerite did not like to be interrupted when she was delivering a peroration.

'Pray tell me, Beatrice, since you are the elder, why you were reading such – such vulgar inanities?'

Eleanor sighed as she watched an agonised expression creep over Bea's face and her hands twist together.

'We only wanted to see what they were like, Grandmama,' she volunteered, seeing that an answer was expected. Poor Beatrice had never been able to fabricate a convincing tale. 'How is one to know about love and – and such things, if one cannot discuss them or read about them?'

'You have only to ask me. I can always tell you exactly what is or is not suitable for a

Graceover of Satherby Abbey. And rubbishy novels are highly *un*suitable!' She shuddered in disgust and added sharply, 'I forbid you, do you hear, absolutely forbid you to read such housemaids' trash again! Love! Pah! Love is only for the lower classes, who can afford to become quite ridiculous under its influence! Or for those fools who have forgotten their station in life. Fools like my younger brother Warren.'

Eleanor smothered a sigh. This was one of her grandmother's favourite cautionary tales and was regularly trotted out and held before them as a warning.

'Look what happened to him!' continued the Dowager. 'Married for love, dead in a year, wife and child left living in poverty. It's I who have had to provide for poor Beatrice! My brother's fate is a lesson to us all to remember our station in life and maintain our standards accordingly!'

She breathed deeply to calm the anger that always boiled in her, even so many years later, at the memory of her favourite brother's defection. Like their father, she had never forgiven him for marrying the daughter of a low-born apothecary. A disgusting misalliance! However, her doctor had forbidden her to fly into rages, on pain of bringing an apoplexy upon herself, so she managed to swallow her temper. She needed desperately to go on living for a while longer.

She continued more temperately, 'That is why I have never encouraged Beatrice to get married. My father quite rightly cut my brother off without a penny when he made a runaway marriage. She therefore has no money – and to marry without money is the height of improvidence, as I have told her many times. Have I not, Beatrice?'

Beatrice nodded, her eyes shaded with pain, but said nothing.

'Not,' continued the Dowager, determined to be fair, 'that Beatrice could not have found herself some curate or gentleman farmer who would not care about her lack of dowry. She's a Dencey, after all. And she's pretty enough to attract some gentleman's attention, were she to set her mind to it. She takes after her mother there, more's the pity! Fortunately, she also takes after our side of the family in her common sense. And it is this which has saved her.'

They both turned to study Beatrice, who sighed and picked up her embroidery with fingers that trembled slightly. Like Eleanor she had heard all this before and over the years she had learned not to let it upset her. Well, not much. Lady Marguerite had taken her in when she was Eleanor's age and could well have afforded to provide her niece with a modest dowry, but it had never been forthcoming. And Beatrice, who had seen her mother cough her life away in a damp cottage, had at first been too relieved at being given a home to do anything that would upset her ladyship.

As she grew older, she had gradually grown accustomed to the role as the Dowager Lady Graceover's unpaid companion, and had developed a genuine affection for her aunt; but once in a while she could not help thinking wistfully how pleasant it would be to marry and have a home of one's very own – and even, perhaps, to have a family. She had always loved children, which was why she had welcomed the chance to help raise Eleanor, also orphaned, but it was not the same as having a child of one's own.

'In future, kindly do not forget what you owe to the Family!' continued the Dowager, her anger subsiding. 'I have better things planned for you, Eleanor, than falling in love! You'll be the last of the Graceovers, more's the pity, but you're rich enough to seek a husband among the True Nobility.' Her ladyship had no opinion of newcomers whose families had only been ennobled in the past hundred years or so and, in the days when she still moved in society, had been known to snub them directly if they approached her unbidden. For the past few years, however, arthritis had chained her to her chair, and county society, what little there was in the neighbourhood of Satherby Abbey, had had to come to her.

Eleanor risked rekindling the wrath. 'What have you got planned for me, Grandmama? May I not know?'

'No, you may not, miss! I'll tell you what you need to know when the time comes. In the meantime, you may go and practise your music. I want a word with Beatrice.'

Eleanor picked up her embroidery (for her ladyship could not abide people who left their things lying around in a slovenly manner), curtsied to her grandmother (who had some very old-fashioned ideas about young ladies' behaviour) and made her way to the Blue Salon, where her favourite piano had been placed out of her ladyship's hearing (only inconsiderate persons inflicted the sound of their practice upon the ears of their families). She was quite happy to do this, for she loved music and could lose herself in it for hours.

Once the two women were alone, the Dowager rapped her cane sharply on the floor. 'Put that sewing down and pay attention to me, Beatrice! This is important!'

Her niece did as she was told and sat with her gentle brown eyes fixed on her aunt, awaiting an explanation.

Lady Marguerite studied her for a minute before speaking. She very much approved of Beatrice's quiet self-containment. 'You're not to encourage the chit to think about love and romance and such vulgarities!'

'No, Aunt. Though it's only natural at her age.' And how anyone could stop Eleanor from doing something upon which she'd set her mind was more than Beatrice knew. It was, of course, Eleanor who had acquired the novels, but Beatrice had to admit that she too had enjoyed the improbable adventures of their intrepid heroines. She sighed. She sometimes feared what would happen if Eleanor and Lady Marguerite ever crossed swords about something they both considered important, for Eleanor had all her grandmother's determination and spirit.

As she waited patiently to be given her

orders, she was surprised to see that her aunt was groping for words. A slight frown creased her forehead. It was more common for Lady Marguerite to unleash a torrent of commands, and even abuse if her joints were hurting, than for her to hesitate like this.

Bang! went the cane again. 'It's time we were thinking of the chit's future.'

Another pause. Beatrice saw that her aunt was chewing her lip and scowling down at her twisted hands and her interest was piqued.

'I'm out of touch with the younger set,' the Dowager announced at last. 'Don't know who's who any more.'

Beatrice frowned. 'I don't understand. Why should you have kept in touch with the younger set, Aunt Marguerite?' Her aunt did not seem to care for anything save her own family and the respect she considered due to her rank?

The Dowager continued to scowl at her niece. 'And I'm too old to do another Season, more's the pity.' She glared at her twisted hands. 'So *you* will just have to go up to London for me.'

'Me?' Beatrice sat bolt upright on the edge of the chair.

'Yes, you, ninny! Who else is there? No men left in the family now. Only ourselves to rely on. Ah, we women are weak vessels!' The Dowager attempted to look frail and ill-used, but only succeeded in looking even more ferocious than usual. 'And here's me with the chit's whole future to settle. So I'm going to need you to go up to London for me.'

'What about Johanna?' ventured Beatrice. Her ladyship's only surviving daughter was a wealthy widow, who lived in London and was a devotee of its pleasures. They had occasionally visited her in town until the last few years, though they had never gone about much in society during those visits. More often, it was Johanna who came to Satherby, descending on them in a flurry of presents and luggage and servants, and rarely staying above a day or two. However, she regularly sent her mother long screeds from London about the doings of the ton, which the Dowager pretended to despise, but which she read with visible enjoyment.

'Surely Johanna would be the best person to deal with any business you wish conducted in London?' repeated Beatrice. 'After all, she lives there.' Her face cleared. 'And she knows everyone.'

The Dowager's scowl deepened. 'Johanna's a fool! I shan't trust *her* judgement when it comes to finding a husband for Eleanor.'

'Finding a husband for Eleanor!' Beatrice clutched the arms of her chair, finding comfort in its solidity. Somehow she had thought it would be years before the Dowager allowed Eleanor to marry.

'Stop repeating what I say! Makes you sound like a sheep.' She looked down at her cane for a moment, her wrinkled claw of a hand trembling on its silver handle. 'What else d'you think I'm talking about when I mention the chit's future? And I won't ask Johanna to do this for me! Look at the sort of men she allowed *her* daughters to marry! Johnny-come-latelies, both of them. A mere baronet! And a nabob! What's the world coming to when a direct descendant of the Graceovers and the Denceys marries a tea-merchant!'

She fell silent and her breathing deepened for a moment or two, for this connection had rankled for several years. 'Though you'll stay with Johanna when you're in London, of course. You'll need her as a chaperon, and she'll be able to introduce you to the right people. She knows everyone, whether they're worth knowing or not.

I'll write and tell her what I want and to whom you're to be introduced. Then you can do the Season and look 'em all over for me.'

By now, Beatrice was feeling quite bewildered. 'Look who over, Aunt?'

'I've been telling you! Young people don't know how to listen to their elders any more! Why am I always surrounded by ditherers and half-wits? I'm talking about the younger set! Persons of rank, mind, not tea-merchants! You'll have to go and look 'em over for me! How else can we find a husband for Eleanor.'

Beatrice looked horrified. 'But I can't...'

'Of course you can! I'll give you a list of acceptable families, though few of them can match up to the Graceovers in their lineage. *We* have not married out of our rank, except for your father, of course. Then you'll only have to sort out one or two possibles and invite them down here to meet Eleanor. I'll do the rest. We should be able to get the knot tied before the end of the year – if *you* will only bustle around a bit, that is!'

The room reeled around Beatrice. 'But Aunt, really, I couldn't possibly...'

The old face grew grim. 'I'm not lettin' the chit loose on the town without me to keep an eye on her. She's far too rich for her own good. And too innocent.'

Beatrice wondered what her ladyship would say if she knew some of the exploits which the innocent chit had been up to lately, the little excursions unescorted, or the way Eleanor would talk to anyone – gipsies, shopkeepers, farmers' boys. She tried desperately to reason with the Dowager. 'But surely, Aunt Marguerite, Johanna could – she could…'

'Johanna could not! She encourages the attentions of upstarts and mushrooms! I want better breeding than that for my girl's husband. When you're my age, you'll realise how much that sort of thing counts.' She bowed her head for a moment, then looked at Beatrice and for once there was no hauteur in those knowing old eyes. 'The doctors don't think I'll last much longer, Bea. Get a pain in my chest if I do much nowadays. He says there's nothing he can do about it. A year at most, he thinks.'

'Oh, Aunt, I'm so sorry!' Beatrice moved across the room to kneel by her aunt's chair and clasp her hand. For once, her overture was not rejected. The bond between the two of them was a strange one. Love was something her ladyship affected to despise, but she had grown to respect her niece, in spite of the bad blood she carried from her mother's side. For her part, Beatrice felt enormous gratitude for having been taken in and given such a comfortable home. She might not have been helped to a suitable marriage, but she had been well cared for and treated in every way like a daughter of the house. Affection had been demonstrated a thousand times, if rarely expressed.

The hand let go of hers. 'I believe you meant that, for which I thank you, Bea, but I'm five and seventy, so I don't need anyone to feel sorry for me. I've had a good long life and I'm not complaining. I've seen most of the people I've loved die and – well, it gets a bit lonely at times.'

She sighed and looked across the room into some distance only she could see. 'The pity of it is that with two healthy sons I didn't get even one grandson to carry on the name. That idiot, William Herforth, will inherit. No, he died, didn't he? I keep forgetting. All the fault of that stupid will! How my husband came to write it, I'll never know!' She sat still for a moment, her eyes half closed, then jerked upright. 'What was I saying?'

'You were talking about the Herforths, Aunt.'

'Yes, so I was. You grow forgetful as you get older, Bea, however hard you try to remember things. It's Herforth's son who'll be inheriting. What's the fellow's name again?'

'Crispin.'

'Yes. Crispin! Did you ever hear such a ridiculous name? No one with Graceover blood in him should have been so lacking in sense as to christen his heir Crispin!'

'It's only a name,' Beatrice said softly.

'It's not a Graceover name! We call our sons Paul and Simon and William.' There was a minute's silence, then the Dowager's mouth worked, as if she were swallowing something distasteful. 'I swore that Herforth fellow wouldn't set foot across the threshold till I was gone, but I've changed my mind, had to change my mind. He'll have to come and stay for a while, because he needs to learn how to manage the estate. Got to make sure he looks after it properly when I'm gone.' Her voice trailed away again and for a moment or two she dozed, as old people will.

Beatrice remained quiet. She had noticed that her ladyship was beginning to show her age, but it still came as a surprise to see the redoubtable Lady Marguerite Graceover succumbing to any normal mortal weakness. She had seemed invincible for as long as anyone could remember, terrifying her children and her servants, arrogant and capricious, but surviving every other family member of her own generation and most of the next generation as well. She had also endured stoically through a series of tragedies that had wiped out her menfolk and would have broken a lesser woman.

Now, if her heart were indeed failing, she had some reason to be worried about Eleanor's future. Her husband, who had died twenty years before, had left his wife life-long use of and control over the Grace-over properties, which would then pass to the next male heir. With two sons living, he could be forgiven for expecting that one of them would inherit, but although both had survived him, neither had lived beyond the age of thirty and neither had sired a living son.

The Dowager woke up with a start, coughed and spluttered for a moment, then reverted to her topic. 'Have to settle you both, but Eleanor's more of a worry, d'you see. She's a considerable heiress, even if she don't get this estate. Her mother had pots of money and inherited a good deal more. That's why I chose her for my Paul. Pity she was such a poor breeder!'

'Yes, Aunt.' Beatrice had heard all this many times and needed only to murmur suitable sounds at intervals to show that she was paying attention.

'Still, it's only fair to leave you properly provided for as well, Bea, and don't think I've forgotten you.'

She was talking to herself and Beatrice let her run on. Somehow she had never doubted that she would be provided for.

'You've been a good girl, Bea, put up with my megrims, not fussed over what couldn't be helped. Needed you to help me bring up the chit. Too old to do it all myself. And you did a good job, too, young as you were.'

'That was a pleasure for me, as you know.'

'Yes. You're a born mother. You should have had your own family by now. But it's not too late.'

Beatrice flushed. 'I'm nearly thirty, Aunt.'

'Twenty-eight last month. Don't exaggerate!' Rap! went the cane. 'Now! Hold your tongue and listen! It's not too late at all! I've settled enough money on you to get yourself a decent husband, one whose breeding we needn't be ashamed of.'

Beatrice's face flushed and she spoke up with a vehemence that was unusual for her.

23

'I don't care to have you buy me a husband, Aunt!'

'Hoity-toity! You'll do as you're told, miss!' Then the Dowager sighed and her face softened. 'You'll do as you're told, because it's my dying wish to see you settled. And because I know you'd like to have a family of your own.'

Beatrice choked back the indignant words she longed to utter at this cavalier disposal of her future, but shook her head still.

'If I have to beg you, I will.' The thin old voice paused, then her ladyship spoke in tones of desperation unusual to her. 'I can't go in peace if I'm leaving you two girls to be turned out of your home by those Herforths. I'd hoped to last out for a bit longer, but I know now that I won't. *Please,* Beatrice! I beg of you! Please do this for me!'

Beatrice could only gape at her in amazement. Never once in the past ten years had she heard this autocratic old termagant plead with anyone for anything.

'But Aunt, I...' Her voice tailed away.

The sunken eyes stared at her unwinkingly. 'Didn't think to hear me plead, did you? And I didn't think I'd have to do it, either. Just goes to show. Death is a great leveller.' She paused, then asked sharply, 'What's got into you, girl? You've shown nothing but good sense since you came to live with me. Never been any trouble since the day you arrived. What've I asked you to do now that sticks in your gullet?'

'I don't – I cannot like the idea of – of having a husband bought for me. Someone who will only be interested in my money.'

Her ladyship cackled loudly! 'Is that all?'

'Isn't it enough?'

'No! It ain't enough! What other way is there for persons of our rank? Whether you admit it or not, marriage is a business transaction like any other. You're a Dencey, after all, in spite of your mother. And my family, apart from your father, has always known its own value. Good Saxon stock. The original English. Then a bit of Norman blood to leaven it. *We* have never needed a title. Always loyal to the Crown. Always respected. Besides,' she glared at Beatrice, angry for being made to continue pleading, 'I can't die with you on my conscience, girl! Should have found you a husband years ago. Selfish of me not to, but I needed you. Eleanor needed you.'

Beatrice shook her head. 'I– Aunt, I just can't like the idea!'

The old eyes narrowed in cunning. 'Eleanor will need you even more once I'm gone! And you'll be able to look after her much better if you're a married woman, not to mention looking after yourself! Single females have no status, no freedom. Don't deserve it, either, if you ask me. A woman's business in life is to marry, and marry as well as she can.'

Beatrice went back across the room to stare at the embroidery. Anything to avoid those sharp old eyes. She saw nothing of the rich silks she had sewn into her tapestry. 'I – I shall need to think about it, Aunt. I can't just – just – snap up your offer straight away. I *can't!*'

Her ladyship nodded. 'Don't object to that. It's a big step, marriage. We're not talking of vulgar things like love matches, you know, but of sensible arrangements between persons of breeding. Yes, you go and have a think about it. In fact, you *ought* to take the time to think about something so important. It's what I'd do myself in your place. Come here, first!' When Beatrice approached her chair again, she pulled her niece's head down towards her own and planted on the soft cheek the first and last kiss she would ever give her. 'You're a good girl, in spite of your mother. It's the Dencey blood. Quality will always tell.' She patted her niece's cheek, then pushed her away again. 'Go and do your thinking! But send Lippings in to me first. And not a word about this to the chit, mind!'

Beatrice's thoughts were in a turmoil as she went to summon her ladyship's maid and then take refuge in her own bedchamber. She locked the door, then plumped down in front of the fire. One of the few indulgences she allowed herself was to sit on the rug and toast her toes. The Dowager would have been horrified at such undignified behaviour, but Beatrice had long ago found that staring into dancing flames was a good way to sort out one's thoughts. She had needed to do that many times when she had first arrived at Satherby Abbey, a grieving and inexperienced girl of seventeen, with no understanding of her father's world and only a lawyer's assurance that she would find a home there.

Her Aunt Marguerite had not been overtly kind – that was not her ladyship's style – but she had taken her niece in without hesitation and had looked after her well, in her own way, teaching her with surprising patience the manners and tricks of polite society, with which most young women of her age were already familiar. And she had allowed Beatrice to love and mother Eleanor for most of those years. That had made it all worthwhile for Beatrice, that and knowing her Aunt did not mean to upset her when she spoke slightingly of her mother. It was just her way. She spoke slightingly of most people, including her own children.

And now the Dowager was expecting Beatrice to repay her by getting herself into a position where she could continue to look after Eleanor. It was not an unreasonable expectation. Although Beatrice spent over an hour staring into the flames, she had to conclude that there was really no choice. Her ladyship was acting in a sensible manner by anyone's lights, and was offering generous provision for the niece whose maternal family she considered to be so unworthy of alliance with the Denceys.

Well, Beatrice had come to terms with many things she disliked since she had come to live at Satherby Abbey. She could come to terms with this as well, no doubt. But, she thought, frowning into the embers, although she might not be able to find a husband whom she could love (and unlike her aunt, she did believe in love, for her mother had loved her father's memory all her life and taught her to do the same), she would insist on having some say as to whom she married. That would be her one condition in agreeing to her ladyship's last wish.

With a shock she realised that she had allowed the fire to burn down low and that she was feeling thoroughly chilled. She reached out to put on some more wood, then lit the candles. She had long ago found that she disliked having a personal maid-servant, so now she changed her clothes quickly and tidied her hair in time for the dinner gong.

'I'll have to do it,' she told her reflection in the mirror, 'but if there's any choice of husband to be had, it'll be mine, not my aunt's!' Two clear hazel eyes stared back at her in a face anyone else would have considered remarkably pretty, but which Beatrice rather despised, for the full redness of her lips and the slumberous beauty of her eyes were, to a mind schooled by long years with the Dowager, rather theatrical in appearance.

She smoothed the creamy skin of her cheek with one fingertip and turned to study her profile in the mirror, then shrugged her shoulders. She supposed she'd have no trouble in finding some sort of husband if she had a dowry, but she rather suspected that she was too fastidious in her tastes to make a marriage of convenience to someone she did not respect.

As she had never yet met a gentleman to whom she had been particularly attracted and as she did not hanker after a fashionable life, she had been quite happy to stay on at the Abbey with the Dowager. She enjoyed the beauties of the changing seasons in the country. She enjoyed the power she had to improve the lot of the poorer tenants on the estate. She was the one to whom the upper servants referred their everyday queries. In fact, her life was very satisfying in many respects.

She stood up and smoothed her full silken skirts, shaking the frills around her feet into place, then picking up a warm shawl to counter the draughts that abounded in that aristocratic residence. No use worrying about the future now, when she had not even sealed her bargain with the Dowager.

TWO

The carriage was luxurious, if a trifle old-fashioned, with heavy fur rugs and enough hot bricks to keep several travellers warm, for the weather in March could be bitter. Her aunt's under-housekeeper sat stiffly in a corner, to lend her young mistress respectability, though it had seemed a pity to drag poor Ruth along.

Beatrice nodded to the other woman, who said in her soft country voice, ''Tis mortal cold, Miss Dencey.'

'Yes, isn't it?' Beatrice tried to relax. She could not rest easy, however, for all the luxury that surrounded her. In the fading light, she studied once again her aunt's list of acceptable families and shuddered at the thought of the task she had been given. She had the names off by heart now, but they would mean nothing to her until she met the gentlemen bearing those names in person. But how was she to set about choosing a suitable husband for Eleanor from among them? And how, in heaven's name, did you tell a complete stranger that he was considered husband material by the Dowager Lady Marguerite Graceover and that he was to present himself at Satherby Abbey for inspection?

And then there were Eleanor's tastes to be considered. It had been extremely difficult not to betray Lady Marguerite's plans to her, for Eleanor obviously suspected something. A girl with her spirit would not agree to marry someone whom she disliked! So it would be up to Beatrice to choose someone Eleanor *could* like, or else a battle royal would rage at Satherby – and that must not happen, for it might kill the Dowager.

Beatrice shuddered every time she thought about what lay ahead of her. She wished desperately that she was more like her enterprising young relative, that she had even half of Eleanor's confidence. Her only hope was that her cousin Johanna, who was twenty years her senior and who had married off her own daughters to men of large fortunes early in their first Seasons, would know how to deal with such delicate matters.

It was dusk and threatening rain when the chaise reached Preston Gardens, but the house before which the coachman stopped was glittering with lights and had attracted a small crowd of onlookers. Beatrice's coachman had to wait for two ladies and a gentleman, all very lightly clad considering the inclement weather, to descend from another carriage before he could pull up to the door.

Beatrice drew in a slow, painful breath at the sight of their elegant appearance and confident demeanour, and pulled her travelling cloak more closely around her, feeling very dowdy and countrified. As the elderly footman, who had journeyed with them and who had served the Graceovers all his life, handed her down, he said quietly, as if he understood how she felt, 'She always did like company, Miss Johanna did. Her ladyship, I should say.'

It was an ordeal for Beatrice to climb the steps to the front door and face a houseful of strangers, even supported by Ruth, but the butler greeted her with a bow and a friendly smile and that gave her a little confidence. As he took her cloak, she murmured that she was not dressed to meet company, and he nodded instant understanding and showed her into a small parlour away from the noise. Ruth followed him to the servants' quarters without being told, exhaustion written all over her face.

Servants were always so kind, Beatrice thought. With a sigh of relief, she sank into a chair. Then she realised that a gentleman was already occupying the high-back arm-chair on the other side of the fireplace and she started up again. 'Oh!'

He rose and bowed with a flourish, elegance personified. Beatrice blinked at this apparition. His black pantaloons displayed shapely, but muscular legs, and his coat, black also, was stretched across shoulders that needed no padding to give them a fashionable broadness. The coat's raised collar and revers framed a shirt collar which was gleaming white, but only moderately high, and which was embellished with a cravat tied in a neat Irish knot and fastened by one small gold pin. Even the Dowager could not have objected to his appearance, as she did to that of most of the younger gentlemen she met. They appeared, she was wont to declare, often to their faces, to have bandaged their throats or to be wearing horse blinkers, so high were their collars and so bulky their cravats.

'I must apologise for startling you, ma'am. Permit me to introduce myself. Justin Serle at your service. Are you also seeking refuge from the merrymaking?'

She was quite tall, for a woman, but he was much taller, which made her feel at an unusual disadvantage. She looked up at dark hair, neat side-whiskers and a long aristocratic nose. Strong features, not exactly handsome, but forming an attractive whole, or would have done, she thought, if the expression in his grey-blue eyes had not been so aloof.

She realised that she had been staring at him like an idiot at a fair, and first blushed, then took an involuntary step backwards as the name sank in. Oh, good heavens! Serle! He was at the top of the Dowager's list and he was one of the few individuals specified by name. 'I – I beg your pardon? What did you say, sir?' she stammered, feeling stupid.

'I merely wondered whether you too were seeking refuge from the merrymaking, ma'am.' He sounded bored, not really interested in her answer, and that made her feel worse.

He stared back at her openly, somewhat annoyed at the way she had been scrutinising him. Who was she to stare so? Quite pretty, if you liked rosy-cheeked brunettes, which he did not, but with country manners and wardrobe to match. Not at all like Lady

Johanna Ostdene's usual guests, in fact.

'Er – no. I'm not escaping anything. I've only just arrived. From – from the country.' She could hear how flustered she sounded and she saw a look of weariness flicker across his face. That made her feel worse and she began to feel angry. How dared he behave so arrogantly? Who did he think he was? Lord of all he surveyed?

A voice interrupted them unceremoniously. 'Serle! Are you in hiding already? I vow I'll not invite you to one of my parties again. Go back at once and talk to Mary.'

He gave an exaggerated sigh and flourished a bow. 'Must I, Lady Ostdene? She has the most foolish laugh it's ever been my misfortune to hear!'

Beatrice could not help staring. What an ill-mannered way to speak about a fellow guest! She did not, she decided, like the looks of this Lord Serle, even if he did come from a noble and ancient line! She listened to the rest of their banter with growing disgust.

'No, no! You're quite wrong there, Serle. It's Isabella Mardsley who has the silliest laugh of anyone in town.'

They both chuckled at that, then Johanna continued, 'I don't think you've met my cousin Beatrice, have you?'

'No. We were just introducing ourselves.'

'Beatrice Dencey – Justin Serle.'

They nodded to each other, neither making the effort to shake hands.

Johanna turned back to the gentleman, 'Well, Serle, we had an agreement about tonight, did we not?'

He sighed. 'To my great dismay, yes! I shall keep my word, at whatever cost to myself.' He bowed languidly to them both and turned to leave.

Johanna chuckled as she watched him saunter out. 'What a wretch he is! I knew poor Mary – she's my god-daughter, you know – would not take his fancy, but he absolutely promised to give her a little attention tonight, for my sake, and I'll hold him to that. Where Justin Serle shows an interest, other men do not disdain to follow.'

She came to present a perfumed cheek for Beatrice's kiss, then held her at arm's length to study her. 'So you're here to find yourself a husband at last, are you? Not to mention one for Eleanor as well! Mama wrote me a long letter explaining all her plans.' She grimaced. 'Typical Mama! Full of contradictory orders. But I couldn't be more delighted to give you a Season, Bea! Truly, I couldn't! I've been suggesting it for years. It was such fun getting my girls married off that I wish I had a few more daughters to bring out. And now I have my wish granted.'

Beatrice smiled wearily. 'It's very kind of you to say that, Johanna.' She wished that she could share her cousin's enthusiasm. Or her confident elegance. Plump as she was, Johanna always made her much younger cousin feel ill-groomed. Her curls might be greying now, but they were dressed in an elaborate style which flattered her still-pretty face. Her smooth white throat and soft hands sparkled with jewels and her gowns were miracles of the modiste's art. But most attractive of all was her lively personality, which made her such fun to be with.

'She's a happy soul, my Johanna,' the Dowager had once said. 'Married well, lives in comfort, has two perfectly satisfactory daughters – bore 'em without the slightest trouble, of course – and didn't long mourn that nonentity of a husband when he died young and left her a fortune. Can't ask for much more in life, can you?'

Beatrice would have asked for more. Love such as her parents had known might not come to many people, but to seek affection,

38

between oneself and one's spouse, did not seem to her to be an unreasonable aspiration.

Johanna hugged her again. 'You poor lamb, you look tired out! Did you travel down from Leicestershire all in the one day?' She linked arms with Beatrice. 'Let me show you to your room. You'd be welcome to join the party – it'll go on for hours yet – but I can see that you're nearly asleep on your feet. This way! I've given you Penelope's old room. It's got a fine view of the square and the most comfortable bed in the house. People always sleep well there, I don't know why. And how's Mama?'

'Oh – er – much as usual.' The Dowager had strictly forbidden her to divulge anything to Johanna about her state of health.

'And Eleanor? Is she still as pretty? It must be a year or more since I've seen her.'

'Oh yes. Very pretty. At least, I think so. And with very lively taking ways.' Though a little rash at times, she added mentally, already starting to worry about what Eleanor would do, now that she was left to her own devices.

'Then we should have no difficulty finding her a husband, should we?' Gossiping all the way, Johanna escorted Beatrice up the stairs, waving to several people en route and promising to introduce her cousin to them another time. Anyone less like her formidable mother would be hard to find, thought Beatrice. Johanna was always so affectionate and so comfortable to be with!

Left alone at last, Beatrice sighed and sat down on the edge of the bed. Noise and laughter floated up from below and she wondered despairingly how anyone could possibly expect her to sleep with a party going on. Within half an hour, however, she had allowed a young maid to unpack her travelling case, drunk a glass of hot milk and eaten a piece of cake, and had proved her hostess's point that it was, indeed, the most comfortable bed in the house.

When she woke up the next morning, it took Beatrice a minute or two to remember where she was, then she sat bolt upright in the bed and gasped. She was in London already and rushing towards a fate she was not sure she relished. What sort of man would want to marry a woman as old as she was, and one, moreover, whose family connections were not all they should be? An older man, of course! A widower, probably.

Her imagination ran riot for a few minutes, picturing a series of elderly gentlemen creaking down onto their knees to propose to her, then she gave a shaky laugh and banished the images from her mind. She would take one day at a time. First, she must grow accustomed to London ways, for her Aunt Marguerite had never gone about much in society on their occasional brief visits to town, confining herself to receiving, in much state, those whose ancestry she did not despise.

Beatrice stared across at her trunks, remembering the elegance of the people she had seen the previous evening. She must purchase some more stylish clothes. She smiled at the thought. That prospect, at least, was a pleasant one. Who would not enjoy buying a completely new wardrobe? She took a deep breath. Not until all that was accomplished need she think of the other thing. Not for another week, at least.

Her determined expression faded slowly as she remembered the arrogant gentleman in the parlour. Oh dear! It had started already, without her wishing it to, for she had met one of the Names within minutes of entering the house. Justin, Lord Serle, of Melbrough Park, the list said, with a mark beside the name to indicate that he was a highly preferred candidate. She could still see his handsome disdainful face looking down at her with controlled politeness and she blushed as she remembered how she had stammered and stuttered in reply to his questions. How stupid she must have appeared to him! And how very arrogant he had appeared to her!

She gasped aloud and giggled suddenly, as it occurred to her that he exactly fitted the description of the villain in the novel her grandmother had burned. The Conte di Maggione! Oh, she would definitely purchase another copy and find out how the tale had ended, ridiculous as it was.

A knock on the door heralded the entrance of the same small maid who had helped her unpack the night before, this time come to light the fire. 'Shall I fetch your hot water up yet, miss? And would you like a tea tray? And if you please, her ladyship says to tell you that I'm to help you get ready and look after your things until you find a lady's maid of your own.'

'I don't need any help, thank you.'

The girl's face fell so dramatically that Beatrice was moved to ask her what was wrong. The Dowager frequently grew angry with her for paying so much attention to servants, but it was one thing she refused to change. Servants were people with the same feelings as anyone else and one of the few powers she had was to make their lives a little more pleasant by showing her appreciation of their services.

'Please miss, I know I'm not a real lady's maid, but Sarah, what maids for her ladyship, she's been giving me lessons and she says I have a knack with hair and that I'm good with the ironing and mending, too. I won't let you down, honest I won't!'

Beatrice realised from this that she would be blighting the young maid's big chance in life if she refused her help. She was too kind-hearted to refuse such a plea. 'Very well, then.'

The thin face was instantly radiant. 'Oh, miss, you won't be sorry! I'll be ever so careful. You'll see. Now, I'll just go and fetch you a tray, then I'll get your hot water, and then I'll come and get your things ready. Sarah's shown me 'zactly what to do.' The words poured out in an enthusiastic stream.

'Just a minute!'

'Yes, miss?'

'You haven't told me your name.'

'Ooh, so I haven't! Sorry, miss! I'm Lizzie.'

So Beatrice submitted to the first of her London ordeals and allowed herself to be attended by the eager Lizzie, who would not let her do a thing for herself, but who really did have a deft touch with hair and who absolutely radiated happiness as she reverently performed her duties.

Breakfast was not until nine and Beatrice, an inveterate early riser, felt the day was half gone by the time she made her way down to the breakfast parlour. She was already at table when Johanna floated in, still dressed in a chamber gown.

'Ah, there you are, Bea! Did you sleep well?'

'Very well.'

'Of course, you did go to bed much earlier than I did. But then, I've never been much good in the mornings. How dreadfully energetic you look!' She yawned again and languidly helped herself to a piece of toast. 'Did Lizzie look after you all right?' Sarah thought we might give her a try-out, but if she's not suitable, you must tell me. In any case, we'll soon find you a proper lady's maid.'

'Oh, no!' Beatrice exclaimed involuntarily.

'Why, whatever do you mean?'

'I – I prefer to look after myself.'

'Well, you can't do that in London, silly, whatever you do at Satherby. Why, I daresay

I change my clothes four or five times a day, and you'll be doing the same. You're going to *need* someone to look after your things. Mama said I was to find you the best lady's maid to be had, and never mind the expense. In fact, we're not to consider the expense of anything. What delicious fun!'

'Oh, dear!'

Johanna grinned at her. 'Has she been laying down the law to you about what you're to do and not to do?'

'Well – she has, rather. And I've no ambitions to look like a fashion plate. I like to feel comfortable. A real lady's maid would be sure to despise me! Your Sarah does!'

Johanna burst out laughing. 'No, she doesn't! She wouldn't dare! That's just her way of maintaining her dignity.' She studied Beatrice carefully. 'You know, if you don't mind me saying so, I think you're shyer than either of my girls were, Bea, and they were years younger than you when they came out. You shouldn't be so modest! I prophesy that you'll take very well. Any maid would be pleased to look after you. They have their pride, you know, and you're prettier than I remembered, or you will be, once we've got you properly gowned and your hair dressed to better advantage. Besides which, you have a very substantial dowry, and that's sure to...'

'Beatrice dropped her knife. 'I have what?'

'Surely Mama told you how much she's decided to settle on you?'

Beatrice's cheeks were burning. 'No!'

'Didn't you even ask?'

'No!'

'Well, isn't that just like her? She adores making mysteries. Don't colour up, you silly goose! In my opinion, a woman should know her own worth to the penny. Why, my girls knew exactly what they would bring to their husbands before they were even twelve years old!'

Beatrice was speechless. Aunt Marguerite always said that marriage was a business, but to calculate the exchange rates so openly filled her with embarrassment. A very substantial dowry might buy her a husband whose birth did not displease the Dowager, but would it bring her one whom she herself could respect and like?

'Anyway,' Johanna went on, not noticing her guest's utter demoralisation, 'Mama's decided to settle twenty thousand pounds on you. That should give you a good range of choice, once the word gets about.

Beatrice! Beatrice, where are you going?'
She stared open-mouthed at the half-open
door. The sound of her cousin running up
the stairs floated back.

'Well, Mama said you were nervous about
all this, but she didn't tell me you were so
touchy!' she said aloud. 'No wonder she left
it to me to tell you about the dowry!' After a
minute, she smiled to herself. 'Still, such
modesty might set a new style, if I play it
well.' She reached for another piece of toast
and smeared it liberally with butter and
blackberry conserve, her thoughts busy with
plans for launching her cousin. An evening
party first, with a full-scale ball later. A few
dinners and visits to the theatre. What fun it
would all be!

Upstairs, Beatrice was staring unhappily
out of the window, breakfast forgotten.
'What am I to do?' she whispered to herself,
pressing her palms to her burning cheeks.
'How am I to face it all? Twenty thousand
pounds! It's far too much! No one'll care
what I'm like – they'll just be interested in
my money! And Aunt Marguerite knew, she
knew perfectly well, that I'd have to accept it
after my promise to her!' It was over an hour
before she could calm down enough to face
Johanna again. The only thing which kept

her to her promise of finding herself a husband was the thought that as a married woman would she be better placed to protect Eleanor. And Eleanor's happiness mattered very much indeed to her.

Lizzie came to find her eventually, to let her know that her ladyship was nearly ready to go out shopping. Beatrice asked automatically for her cloak, but Lizzie shook here head. 'Cloaks isn't worn for shopping, miss. I'll unpack the rest of your things for you while you're out, but perhaps you can tell me if you've got a pelisse or spencer you like to wear with that dress? If it needs ironing, I can easily run down to the maids' room and smooth it over.' She was obviously bursting to help and was as good as her word, running up the back stairs within minutes carrying Beatrice's perfectly-ironed pelisse reverently across her arms. 'Here you are, miss,' she said, before she had even closed the door behind her.

She smoothed the pelisse with tender hands as it lay on the bed and Beatrice watched her thoughtfully. She hated the idea of having her life invaded by a starchy lady's maid, like the one who served Johanna. The majestic Sarah ruled her mistress with a rod of iron where her appearance was concerned. That would not at all suit Beatrice. Perhaps, though, if she could persuade her cousin that Lizzie would be able to cope, things might not turn out too badly. She was already growing to feel comfortable with the girl, who was cheerful and willing. 'Is it your ambition to become a lady's maid?' she asked casually as she prepared to go downstairs.

'Ooh, yes, miss! And Sarah says I may just do and she's been giving me lessons for ages now. I'm to be available to help guests, and I'm to get an extra guinea a year if you're satisfied with me this time.'

She looked so anxious about it all that Beatrice smiled and said in her gentle way, 'Well, you're doing an excellent job so far, Lizzie.'

She was rewarded by another beaming smile.

Beatrice nodded as she studied her reflection. If I really do have to have a maid, she thought, watching Lizzie's still-smiling face behind her in the mirror, I think I'd much prefer a cheerful young girl like her. Did Johanna say we'd have to change our clothes four or five times a day? Oh dear! How tedious! However many clothes will I need for that?

Johanna looked her cousin over critically when she came downstairs again, then nodded. 'Not the height of fashion, but a neat enough turnout. Trust Mama to find a good country dressmaker. Anyway, we'll soon remedy that and have you cutting a dash.' She hesitated before adding, 'Are you over the shock of finding yourself a rich woman, yet, love?'

Beatrice shook her head ruefully. 'I'm sorry if I seemed rude, but Johanna, I still can't believe it! How can I accept so much money from your mother? I have no right to it!'

'Just say thank you and be grateful. Mama's extremely rich, you know, and she never does anything she doesn't want to do. And look how you've put up with her for all these years. We all know what an autocrat she is.'

'She's been very kind to me – in the circumstances.'

Johanna screwed up her nose. 'Well, I think it was quite gothic to cut your father off without a penny, like that!'

Beatrice shrugged. 'That was all over and done with long ago. It still doesn't entitle me to such a – a fortune!'

'Well, I think you've *earned* every penny of

the money, I promise you. Now, let's forget about all that nonsense and go to Odette's. She's been my modiste for years. She charges prodigiously, but she's a genius, my dear, an absolute genius. You'll soon be setting the fashion if you put yourself in her hands. And Mama said to spare no expense.'

Beatrice sighed audibly.

'Don't you like clothes?' Johanna's tone was incredulous.

Beatrice grimaced. 'Well, I do normally, of course I do, but at the moment I feel like an offering being prepared for sacrifice. I – I daresay I'll grow used to the idea.' She smiled bravely.

Johanna roared with laughter. 'Oh, Bea, you'll be the death of me yet! Grow used to it, indeed! You should revel in the idea of being worth twenty thousand pounds. Mama's kept you too quiet, but don't worry, I'll teach you how to enjoy yourself.'

Wisely, Beatrice did not try to contradict her, but she rather doubted whether she would enjoy city life among so many strangers. She allowed Johanna to gossip about fashions all the way to the modiste's, but her own thoughts were still in turmoil. Twenty thousand pounds! she kept thinking. Too much! She could not help remembering the hardships she and her mother had suffered and the thought occurred to her that only a fraction of that dowry disbursed earlier would have made them both comfortable and perhaps kept her mother alive. Life could be so unfair! She took a deep breath and reminded herself, as she had many times before, that the Dowager had not known of their circumstances, and thus could not be held to blame for their difficulties.

The two ladies were granted the honour of an immediate interview with Mademoiselle Odette herself, and Johanna explained her cousin's needs and aspirations so frankly that Beatrice was soon blushing again. Odette nodded briskly and turned to study her new customer. Even Johanna's tongue was stilled, as she watched the modiste.

'Will you please stand up and walk about, Miss Dencey? Yes, now sit down. Stand up again. Turn round. Hmm! Let me think. Do please sit down again!'

Beatrice sank gratefully onto a spindly gilt chair and stared at the carpet, feeling more than ever like a sacrificial victim.

After a few minutes, during which Odette moved to survey Beatrice from several angles, her impersonal fingers turning her new client's head first one way, then the other, the modiste nodded. 'We shall set a new fashion with Miss Dencey, I think, your ladyship. Restrained, ladylike elegance. Simple, but exquisite. The shyness will enhance this. Quiet colours, wonderful fabrics, no fuss. You'll see.' She began to take Beatrice's measurements, nodding in approval as she called them off to an assistant.

When that was over, Johanna nodded to her in a friendly way. 'I'll leave it all to you, then, Odette. How soon can you have something ready?'

'Which garments would you like made up first, Lady Ostdene?'

'Something for paying morning calls, something for walking in the park – oh, and an evening gown, of course.'

'I'll send them round as soon as they're ready, your ladyship. A fitting tomorrow, if you please, Miss Dencey, to give us the exact sizing, then we'll make up a dummy for everything but the final fittings. Price?' She cocked her head on one side like a bright-eyed bird.

Beatrice just looked confused, so Johanna intervened. 'The price is irrelevant, Odette. As long as you live up to your usual standards. I wish my cousin to be noticed.'

Odette's eyes gleamed. 'Have you ever known me to fail, your ladyship?' Especially when I'm given carte blanche with such a good subject, she added mentally. This one will be a pleasure to dress.

Johanna was admiring herself in a mirror. 'No, you don't normally fail. This is quite one of my favourites, Odette.'

'It does look well, your ladyship.'

Johanna turned her attention to Beatrice. 'But you must admit that my cousin is a little different from your usual clients.'

'Colours will make a nice change from whites and pastels, your ladyship.'

'Yes. Warmer colours, I do agree. Please let us have the samples as soon as possible, so that we can purchase accessories.'

'Certainly, your ladyship.'

Beatrice was determined to have some say. 'I don't like fussy garments.'

Odette drew herself up. '*I* do not make fussy garments, Miss Dencey.'

Johanna poked Beatrice in the ribs and she fell silent.

Odette, having made her point, did not prolong her displeasure. One did not quibble when one had been given carte blanche to dress someone, especially someone who would do her modiste so much credit. 'If I may say so, your ladyship, Miss Dencey may be older than the usual young lady making her debut, but she's also more interesting than an ingénue. She has character and resolution in her face. With her height and figure, we cannot fail.'

By this time, Beatrice was again scarlet with embarrassment. She felt as if she had done nothing but blush and stutter since she arrived in London.

'Anyway,' Odette became brisk and businesslike again, 'I'll visit the silk warehouses immediately myself. I shall want special fabrics, something out of the ordinary for Miss Dencey.'

As they settled back in the carriage, Johanna sighed happily. 'Now, accessories. Stockings, gloves, shawls, bonnets. We'll go and inspect a few things today, but we won't buy much until we have our sample swatches. Oh, what fun it will all be!'

'Don't we have *any* choice – about the colours and materials, I mean?' ventured Beatrice.

'Choice? With Odette? I wouldn't *dare* tell her what to use! She's a genius, my dear, a pure genius! Just leave it all to her!'

They spent a busy morning shopping, first

at the premises of Harding, Howell and Company, a most amazing emporium, situated in Schomberg House in Pall Mall. It actually consisted of several shops all under the one roof, each separated from the others by glazed mahogany partitions, and to Beatrice's dazed eyes, it seemed enormous.

The shop was spacious and dignified, and it even contained a refreshment room upstairs, where customers could be served with wines, tea, coffee and sweetmeats. Johanna confessed a weakness for the pastries there and consumed three of them before they continued on to Grafton House in New Bond Street. This was so crowded that they had to wait for fifteen minutes before they could even be attended to. At both shops, Johanna introduced her cousin to a bewildering number of ladies whose names she was sure she would not remember. By the time they left, her head was spinning with names and elegant trifles and the extravagance of it all.

As they were walking out towards their carriage, there was a small commotion. A haggard-looking man with one arm missing, who had been begging near the corner, collapsed suddenly in the street. Before Johanna could prevent her, Beatrice had rushed across to his aid and was actually kneeling down to help him sit up, ignoring the dirt on both the ground and his person.

Johanna, horrified, remembered her mother complaining that if Beatrice saw an injured bird, it had to be brought home and tended. Well, she would not be able to tend all the beggars in London! And this one appeared to be as dirty as the rest of them.

'Bea!' she gasped. 'Bea, come back!'

She was ignored.

The man apologised for the trouble he was causing, and staggered to his feet, but even then, Beatrice could not leave well alone. While her cousin watched in horror, she commanded a small boy loitering nearby to fetch something hot to eat and drink, held out a sixpence and promised the same as a reward for himself if he carried out the errand swiftly.

'Give that man some money and come away!' hissed Johanna, twitching at Bea's sleeve. She glanced around, terrified that someone would see them.

She was again ignored. Within minutes, Beatrice had found out that the man was an ex-soldier and without means of support, also that he had been ill for the past week and had had little to eat. Not content with giving him money, she quickly found out that his ambition was to become a pie-man, but that he lacked the capital to launch this business venture. She tipped the change out of her purse and provided him with enough money on the spot, together with some sound advice and her name and address. He was to come and let her know how things went.

Only after this was all arranged, the boy had brought back some food and the man had promised to keep in touch would Beatrice consent to return to the carriage.

'You really shouldn't hand out money to such people, you know,' Johanna protested, once they were safely out of sight in the carriage. 'And just look at the dirt on your dress!'

'That man lost his arm defending his country and no one seems to care. What does a bit of dirt matter?'

'You'll never hear from him again.'

'I think I will.' She stared at her cousin. 'I can remember myself what it's like to go hungry.'

Johanna fell silent. A few minutes later she asked in hushed tones, 'Did you really go hungry, Bea? Actually not have enough to eat?'

'Many times. My mother and I had very little money and you know how food prices rose during the war. We weren't the only ones to suffer.'

'Goodness, why have you never said anything about it before?'

'What was the point? What's past is past and can't be changed. Even my aunt didn't know till afterwards how bad things had been for us. My mother had her pride, too. It was only when she was dying that she wrote to your mother's man of business. And by the time he replied, she was dead.'

Johanna could only pat her hand. It was beginning to occur to her that Bea might not be quite as meek and amenable as she had expected. Then, putting such an unwelcome idea from her mind, she quickly recovered her good humour. She leaned back in the carriage and smiled. 'Spending someone else's money is such fun, Bea, even better than spending one's own. I'll send out to a Domestic Employment Agency when we get home and tomorrow we can start interviewing lady's maids.'

Beatrice screwed up her courage and shook her head firmly. 'I don't wish for a lady's maid, Johanna. Not at all! Couldn't I – couldn't we, I mean – just – well, see how

Lizzie goes on?'

'Lizzie? She's a nice child, but you'll need more help than *she* can give you.'

'Johanna, please believe me when I say that I dislike the idea of having a personal maid! I don't enjoy having someone fussing over me.' She took a deep breath and said in a voice that was a little unsteady, 'It's Lizzie or no one!'

'Nonsense! You can't mean that!'

'I do mean it! I'm not used to all this.' Tears gathered in her eyes. 'Please, Johanna, let's just try Lizzie for a few days. That can't do any harm, surely.'

Johanna eyed her shrewdly, realised that her cousin was genuinely upset and capitulated. 'Oh, very well!' After all, Sarah would be there to help out, and Sarah was obviously enjoying training Lizzie. It had put her in a good mood for weeks now. 'But she's only on trial, mind,' she added. 'Don't say anything to her about a permanent place till we see how she goes!'

'Whatever you say, Johanna.' Beatrice sank back in relief.

When they got home, it was to find the house in an uproar. A carriage stood at the door and there were trunks and parcels all over the floor.

A head peered over the banisters. 'It's me, Mama!'

'Jennice! What are *you* doing in town?'

Her younger daughter chuckled naughtily. 'Fleeing, Mama.'

'What on earth do you mean by that? And come down, will you? I'm getting a crick in my neck talking to you like this.'

A very pretty young woman descended the stairs. Beatrice stared at her. How Jennice had changed since her marriage! She was plumper than she had been, but Beatrice wished she could walk as lightly as that. And she could never imagine herself looking even half as assured and elegant. In that, Jennice took after her mother. The pair of them made Beatrice feel very dowdy.

Jennice planted a hearty kiss on her mother's cheek and a fleeting one in the air above Beatrice's ear. 'So nice to be here safely!'

Johanna swept them both into her own small sitting room, calling out to the butler to send them some refreshments. 'Now, young woman, kindly explain yourself!' she said with mock sternness as she sat down. 'What exactly are you fleeing from?'

Another chuckle. 'My husband, Mama!'

'Oh, that's all right, then. What's he done

this time?'

'Threatened to keep me at Lymsby for the rest of the year.'

'Goodness, what a dreadful fate! Why does he want to do that?'

Jennice smiled smugly. 'Oh, just because I'm about to make you into a grandmama!'

'What!' When the shower of hugs from Johanna was over, Jennice explained how excited Boris had been at the mere suspicion of a child, and then how unbearably despotic he had become once its existence was confirmed. 'As if I were ill or something! I told him that childbearing is a perfectly natural thing and that common women continue working until the very last minute.'

'And what did he say to that?'

'He turned up his nose and said that *his* wife was neither common, nor required to work for her living, and would be looked after as befitted her station. So there was nothing for it but to show him how silly he's being. I waited till he went over to a friend's to look at some horses – I'm fed up with him going out and leaving me alone! – and then I left straight away. I just hope nothing sends him home early. He shouldn't get back to Lumsby till after dark, so he won't set out tonight, but I daresay he'll be here tomorrow, breathing fire and brimstone. I'll soon bring him round, you'll see – at least I will if you'll only help me by telling him how dangerous it is to thwart a pregnant woman's wishes.'

Johanna threw back her head and laughed. 'You never change, Jennice! Very well, I'll help you. But when you get bigger, I do think you should retire to Lymsby and set poor Boris's mind at rest. Husbands are always so much more fussy with the first child. He'll probably leave you in peace with the others – at least, he will if this one's a boy. And you *will* have to cosset yourself a little more than usual, you know.'

'Well, of course I'll retire when I grow bigger! You don't think I wish to be seen in public looking like a – a cow in milk! You know how gigantic Penelope got and I daresay I'll be the same. But first I have a million things to do, buy all the latest novels to keep myself entertained during my incarceration, arrange for some new clothes to be made – oh, do all sorts of other things that one can only do in town!'

She turned to Beatrice. 'And I must apologise, Bea, for ignoring you like this. What are you doing in London? Have you fled from Grandmama?'

THREE

Two days after the visit to Odette, the first of Beatrice's new clothes arrived, thanks to the efforts of three seamstresses who had stayed up until late each night sewing. Odette herself came to supervise the final trying-on, a rare attention, but the modiste was rather pleased with what she had created and wished to see that her efforts were properly appreciated.

Lizzie stood in awed attendance as Odette's assistant helped her mistress don a soft apricot-coloured street dress with a high waist. Beatrice studied herself in the full-length mirror, her eyes shining with wonderment. Two lines of simple tucking gave body to the fabric just above the scalloped hem, and the long full sleeves ended in tucking, too, with narrow cream lace ruffles. These were matched by a soft lace frill rather like a ruff around the high neckline. To wear with the dress, there was a pelisse in a deeper colour of apricot velvet. She had never possessed anything which suited her half as well.

She turned to Odette first and reached out to clasp the modiste's hands, 'Thank you!' she said, with a catch in her voice. 'I never dreamed I could look so – so elegant!'

Johanna noted in amusement that Odette was completely won over by this egalitarian treatment and watched her press Beatrice's hands in return, before releasing them and stepping backwards. 'You will set a fashion, Mademoiselle,' Odette prophesied. 'I shall make sure of that. And, if I may suggest, to go with this dress, a simple poke bonnet with a full brim and very little trimming. Perhaps *un tout petit peu de dentelles,* not too much lace, mind! And one spray of flowers in a colour to match the pelisse?'

'Whatever you say.' Beatrice turned next to her cousin. 'I – I don't know what to say, Johanna.'

Her cousin's eyes softened. 'You don't need to say anything, Bea. I'm thoroughly enjoying all this. And you look lovely. Now, try on the balldress! I think Odette has excelled herself with that.'

Beatrice retired behind the screen with Lizzie and the assistant in attendance and Odette stood there, a small smile curving her mouth. Success was sweet. When her newest customer emerged like a butterfly from its chrysalis, she made no attempt to moderate her delight.

The dress was in a soft creamy silk which glistened slightly. It was trimmed above the one frill which graced the hem with three rows of narrow satin ribbon just a shade or two darker. At one point the frill rose to a high point and the ribbon curved upwards a few inches to meet a near-flat spray of delicate silk rose, also in cream. These were echoed by a matching spray on a satin fillet for the hair.

Beatrice's delight in the dress lent a sparkle to her eyes and soft colour to her cheeks. She had been dreadfully afraid that the dictates of fashion would force her to dress in multiple flounces and gaudy trimmings or fussy strands of artificial flowers like the pictures in *La Belle Assemblée* and *The Ladies Monthly Museum* – Johanna's favourite reading material. Odette had captured her own wishes exactly in this elegant simplicity.

'I have just the thing to wear with that!' said Johanna and left the room, to return with a huge shawl, two and a half square yards of fine satin-striped Lyon silk, with scalloped edging. 'There! You'd think we'd matched the colour of the ribbon purposely, wouldn't you? Drape it round your shoulders, Bea!'

She stood back to gauge the effect and was rewarded by another nod of approval and complicity from Odette, who was becoming more French by the minute in her excitement. *'C'est parfait,* your ladyship. *Absolument parfait!* I know that I can rely on your good taste not to spoil the effect of the other dresses which I shall create by purchasing fussy accessories. Everything should be of the purest lines for mademoiselle, but of the very finest quality. *Très simple, mais très chic.* I've found some materials which are rather special. I think, *non, j'en suis sûre,* that you will be pleased with them.'

Johanna nodded. She would not have dared to disobey Odette's commands, even if her own fashion sense had not told her the same thing. 'That's exactly my opinion,' she agreed, 'but it won't do for the court dress.'

'Certainly not!' Odette's eyes gleamed. 'For that, we shall need more elaboration, or it will be taken as a lack of respect for Her Majesty.'

'Do I *have* to be presented?' pleaded Beatrice, though she knew she had little hope of escaping this.

Two shocked faces were her only answer.

She sighed. 'I shall feel so ridiculous! Hoops! And feathers on my head! I shall seem six feet tall! I can't bear it.'

Johanna shook her head. 'My dear, we all go through it and we all survive. And hoops are not nearly as much trouble as you might expect, especially since you won't be sitting down in them. Now that really is difficult to manage elegantly.' She saw Beatrice's mouth open for another protest. 'No! Not another word! Odette, we shall leave the design of the court dress entirely up to you. White, of course.'

'*Bien sûr.*'

Beatrice sighed again. She had forgotten about being presented in her anxiety about her aunt's list of eligibles. Now it loomed before her as yet another ordeal to be faced.

The next day she wore the new apricot dress as she sat with Johanna in the salon, it being her ladyship's day to receive visitors. Her natural serenity lent her the gentle dignity which best suited both her looks and nature, but she was completely unaware of how well she looked, for she was concentrating on trying to remember people's names and on learning what sorts of things ladies discussed when they went out in society. All the older ladies who met her commented later about how refreshing it was to meet a young woman who did not put herself forward and who was such an attentive listener.

Justin Serle arrived just as the last visitors were leaving. He was apparently a frequent caller, being a cousin of Johanna's son-in-law. An expression of obvious surprise crossed his face as he gazed at the transformation of the foolish woman in crumpled travelling clothes whom he had met a few evenings previously and whom he had dismissed out of hand as a pretty nonentity.

Beatrice did not miss his look of surprise and she felt her indignation rise. How dared that man judge her by appearances! What a frivolous creature he must be! She gave him only the tips of her fingers to shake and removed her hand from his as quickly as politeness allowed, giving him no encouragement to linger by her side.

When he crossed the room to sit next to Jennice, who was in high fettle today, Beatrice retreated to sit in the bay window and stared down at the street. She had found the last hour or so rather tedious. Did no one talk about anything but parties and fashions and the latest gossip here in London? The sun was shining outside, but no one seemed to wish to go out and enjoy it. Poor men from Manchester were so hungry that a group of them had tried to march on London to demand help, but no one cared. The newspapers seemed glad to see the Blanketeers dispersed by troops, but the poor fellows had all her sympathy.

The doings of Princess Charlotte had been the main topic of conversation for several of the ladies that day. Beatrice had already seen Her Highness in the distance, driving past in a carriage, plump, with yellow hair and un-distinguished features, and had been extremely disappointed by the appearance of the much-fêted Heiress of England.

Justin did not miss the look of disapproval on her face as she took his hand and he decided that even if his first impression of Miss Dencey as a country dowd had been wrong, he had not been mistaken in her character, which was serious to a fault. She would definitely not take in town, with that sour expression, and she was certainly not to *his* taste, however well she looked. He put her out of his mind and began to flirt outrageously with Jennice, whom he had known all his life and who therefore knew better than to take him seriously.

'So, Justin, how do you find this year's

crop of débutantes?' Jennice said, lounging back on the sofa in a manner which the Dowager would have condemned instantly as hoydenish.

He pulled a face. 'Much the same as last year's. Sweet, innocent and deadly dull.'

'I vow, you're too demanding. The poor girls haven't got a chance with you! It's time you took a wife, for you're past thirty now. 'Tis your duty, sir, your solemn duty!' Her laughing eyes belied her words.

He bent his head for a moment in mock acceptance of her reproof. 'I admit it, and I have tried, believe me! But if a girl possesses one good quality, she inevitably possesses two bad ones. And surely, it's not too much to ask that a wife should be pleasant in appearance. You note, that I do not stipulate beautiful. That would be to ask too much of Providence.'

'Well, there are any number of pleasant-looking girls for you to choose from!'

'Yes, but I require one or two other qualities. Absolutely insist, in fact.'

'Such as, sir?'

'A soft voice, a modicum of intelligence and the capacity to act as my hostess and châtelaine without tittering like a laundry-maid.'

Beatrice watched enviously, admiring the dexterity with which Jennice handled the light-hearted repartee and wishing that she were similarly skilled. She could maintain a conversation, it had been part of the Dowager's training, but not with such verve and lightness. Indeed, she felt herself to be extremely dull and prosaic by the standards of her cousin Johanna's set.

In the middle of Serle's visit, Lord Boris Newthorpe arrived at last to confront his errant wife, and, since he was boiling with rage and related to all the persons present, he did not scruple to start a quarrel in front of them. 'So, madam,' he declared, striking a pose in the doorway, 'I find you here at last, do I?'

Beatrice could only gape, for she was not aware that Lord Newthorpe was given to a melodramatic turn of phrase when his ire was roused.

Jennice tilted her nose upwards and said sarcastically, 'Since I left a note to tell you that I was coming to visit Mama, and since I was with you only two days ago, I cannot understand either your difficulty in finding me or your tone now, sir!'

He ground his teeth. 'You know what I mean, madam.'

'I'm sure I don't! I never do when you get on your high horse, Boris! *And* – if you're so concerned about me – why has it taken you two days to get here?' She tossed her head at him.

'Majesty had sprained his fetlock! I had to see that it was properly tended. You know how ill-tempered he is with anyone except me.'

'I'm well aware that that horse is more important to you than I am!' She stood up, turned her back to him, and pretended to study her reflection in a mirror, patting a curl into place while watching him from beneath her eyelashes.

He glared at her and turned to bow coldly to his mother-in-law who took the opportunity to re-introduce Beatrice to him, but his thoughts were clearly not on the introductions. As soon as he had bowed over her hand, stared blankly at her and said through gritted teeth how delighted he was to see her, he turned back to his wife. 'Kindly instruct your maid to pack your things, madam!'

Jennice spun round. 'Certainly not!'

'If you don't,' he was growing redder in the face by the minute and rapidly losing his dignified tone, 'then I shall give the order myself.'

Jennice's dignity also began to slip. 'Well, she won't obey you, so there! She's *my* maid and she answers only to me!'

'Then I shall be compelled to turn her off and find a maid who *does* recognise her master, shall I?'

Jennice lost all her elaborate poise abruptly. 'You wouldn't *dare!*'

'I dare do anything to protect my unborn child!'

'My dears, pray calm down!' murmured Johanna, who was finding it hard to conceal her amusement. Neither of the combatants paid her the slightest attention.

'I never heard of anything so mean in my life!' declared Jennice, hands clasped at her bosom. 'Threatening to turn away Susan, who has been with me for years, just because you're miffed! You're a beast, Boris Newthorpe, an absolute beast! What sort of a father will *you* make? Oh, my poor baby!' She pressed her hands protectively over her stomach.

Boris grinned nastily. 'You have only to obey your husband's lawful commands, madam, and the woman may stay!'

'Obey your commands! *Obey your commands!* I never heard anything half so gothic! And that from a man whose horse is more

74

important to him than his wife!'

'Dash it all, I explained about that. If it had been any other horse than Majesty...'

She sniffed scornfully. 'Anyway, you deserved that I should leave. Ordering me about like that and then going off to look at horses! What sort of husbandly care is that, I ask. And who do you think I am – your slave?'

'You're my wife and have promised to obey me.'

'Oh pooh, who ever means that! It's just words.'

'Madam, I insist that you do as you're told!'

'Well, I won't! And if you *dare* to even *begin* to carry out your threat about Susan...' Jennice was unable to think of anything dire enough to threaten him with in return, so she hid her dilemma by bursting into tears, which usually brought him to heel.

This time, however, all that the tears elicited from her husband was a scornful, 'Hah!' and another dramatic pose against the mantelpiece, this time with arms folded.

Beatrice, scarlet with embarrassment at the public nature of their altercation, felt a gentle touch on her arm. Serle was standing beside her. 'May I suggest that we leave them to their quarrel and go out for a stroll round the square?' His eyes were brimming with laughter as he kept an eye on the tragi-comedy being played in front of them, but he had noticed that it was really upsetting Miss Dencey. 'We're certainly in the way here.'

'Oh yes! They must wish to be private!'

He rather doubted that, since both the Newthorpes loved playing to an audience, but he did not voice his disagreement.

Jennice sobbed twice as loudly when Boris did not rush to her side and, after looking at him covertly, sank gracefully onto the sofa and demanded that someone bring her a vinaigrette before she fainted quite away, 'Oh, how did I come to marry a monster like you?' she declaimed. 'What a father for my poor children! He will care more for his horses than for my poor babies!'

Beatrice moved rapidly towards the door and Johanna turned her head away for a moment as her shoulders shook with suppressed laughter.

Justin went across to whisper in his hostess's ear and Johanna nodded permission. She knew that it would be a while before Boris could be brought to heel and Jennice calmed down, and although she thoroughly enjoyed watching the minx's antics, she could see that her young cousin was suffering from acute embarrassment. Poor Bea had always been over-sensitive about quarrels, while Jennice and Boris enjoyed theirs thoroughly – not to mention the reconciliations that followed them!

Beatrice waited in the hall with Justin for her new velvet spencer to be brought down. When Lizzie had assisted her mistress to don it and a simple straw bonnet, and had stood back to admire the effect, the butler stepped forward to open the door for them. 'I think,' Justin told him quietly, 'that your mistress will not wish to receive any other callers this morning.'

Jennice's sobbing was quite audible even from the front door. A shriek of rage punctuated it suddenly, making Beatrice gasp, but the butler did not flinch. 'Quite so, sir,' he said. 'Miss Jennice does get a trifle upset at times. Lady Newthorpe, I should say.'

'We'll just take a walk round the gardens here in the square. You can send someone out to fetch us when the fireworks are over.'

'Certainly, my Lord. Fine clement weather we are enjoying, is it not, miss? The spring flowers are just coming out nice in the gardens. I fancy you'll enjoy the displays.'

Not until they were outside in the weak spring sunlight did Beatrice realise that Jennice's quarrel with her husband had thrown her into close proximity with someone who was almost a complete stranger and to whom she had taken a strong dislike. She stopped abruptly. 'I – er – should we be...' and could not think how to phrase her question without sounding as if she wished to reject his company.

'If you mean is it proper for us to be out walking together without a chaperon, yes, it is, that is, as long as we keep to the public gardens here. I'm sure you'd prefer to be out of the house while those two continue their quarrel. Boris can be a trifle arrogant at times, but I think he's more than met his match in Jennice. Do you know why he's so eager to take her away from town? I had thought they were planning to come up here for the whole season.' He offered her his arm.

'She's expecting a baby,' Beatrice replied without thinking, then flushed and stopped dead just as she was about to take his arm. 'Oh dear! I'm not sure whether I should have told you that! Pray don't tell them. I mean...' Her voice faded and she could only study the flowerbed to her left in an attempt to hide her blushes.

He began to feel bored, but offered her his arm again. She was acting as foolishly as she had done the other night. 'You needn't worry about discussing it with me, Miss Dencey. Boris is a cousin of mine – we more or less grew up together – and I'm bound to be one of the first to know. No wonder he wants her to return home! They've been married for four years without a sign of the precious heir.'

His voice had become a little scornful during this last sentence, so she said quietly as they strolled on, 'It's only to be expected that he would wish for children. It's one of the main purposes of marriage, isn't it?' Apart from the money aspects, a voice said inside her head. 'Besides, what woman does not wish for children!' Her own longing echoed clearly in her voice, and which made him stare at her in surprise. 'Jennice was delighted about it, I think, though not about Boris wishing her to stay in the country.'

'I'm not an expert on children. Most of the women I know complain loudly of the tedium of the breeding process and then leave their offspring to the care of nurse-maids. Jennice won't enjoy being cloistered at Lymsby, nor can I see her devoting

79

herself to her children, not once the novelty has worn off.'

She was not to know that he and his younger brother had rarely seen their own mother, and had been raised by their nurse. Fortunately, that redoubtable woman had furnished them with the permanent affection all children need, and as well, they had had each other's company. There being only eighteen months difference in age, they had been as close as many twins.

The same nurse was now in charge of the housekeeping at Melborough and had lately taken to scolding Justin whenever he visited his country estates about the shameful and selfish way he had remained single for so long and thus omitted to provide an heir for the Serle line. If he were not careful, Mrs Powis had told him bluntly only a week previously, his unmarried state would become a habit and he would end up a crab-tempered old bachelor, with no one to love him in his declining years.

She was more successful in persuading him to consider his duty when she reminded him that the lack of an heir would also mean that his cousin would inherit the title and properties. And what would become of all the tenants then, she added ominously?

Had he thought about that, eh? If not, he had better start doing so at once! Master Luke had already gambled away most of his own inheritance and would like as not waste the Serle fortunes as well if given the opportunity, for a more reckless spendthrift creature she had yet to meet. He should have been spanked more soundly as a child.

The matter of an heir had not been as important while his brother was alive, but Peter had been killed at Waterloo nearly two years previously. Justin still missed him desperately and was quite aware that he had grown cooler with the world since his brother's death, for he had no one to make him laugh now, or to tease him out of his dignity.

So unremittingly had Mrs Powis scolded him during his recent visit that in the end he had cut it short and returned to London. She was the only person left who could get beneath Justin Serle's smooth surface and the only one who could make him do things he did not wish to do. His mother, a fashionable beauty, had died when he was twelve, and his father, a bluff man more interested in breeding horses than raising children, when he was twenty-two so there had been no one else close to him but his brother, Mrs Powis and, in a less important way, his cousin Boris.

This time, Mrs Powis's words had been reinforced, unknown to her, by the fact that his cousin Luke had recently been hinting at the need for a loan to cover his gambling losses, if the heavily mortgaged Mendleton estates were not to be sold. Justin had refused to supply that loan. Even as a boy, Luke had never returned things he was lent; as a grown man, he had turned into a loose fish, and had even tried to pledge Justin's name to certain debts, though Justin had soon put a stop to that.

Justin was now trying to steel himself to the idea of marriage, but was not at all enamoured of the prospect. Every year the new crop of hopeful misses seemed to get sillier, like Johanna's god-daughter, Mary. There was no way he could live with a laugh like that! And how boring it would be to face the same empty-headed woman every morning over breakfast and then again in the evenings! He shuddered at the prospect.

In fact, he had never met a woman he did desire to face every day. He had had a mistress or two, of course, like most men of his class, older women usually, ones who had a bit of common sense about life, were not rapacious and had no illusions about the strength of his feelings for them. They had departed from his life amicably when he tired of them, as he always did within a few months, and none of them had complained about his generosity. The main thing now stopping him from marrying was a private worry, which he was unable to discuss with anyone, as to whether he could actually bring himself to make love to a silly young chit who did not attract him, purely for the sake of begetting children. The mere thought of failure to do so made his blood run cold.

He and Beatrice walked round the square in silence for a time, each busy with thoughts that were developing into serious worries.

'I couldn't leave *my* children to be brought up by servants like that,' Beatrice said after a while, voicing her thoughts aloud. Was that the sort of behaviour that a gentleman of rank would expect of his wife?

Justin made a non-committal noise, not at all interested in what she, or anyone else, intended to do with their as-yet-unborn children. At least her soft voice did not grate upon his ears, so it was no great trial to walk with her; though it was a pity she had that tendency to grow flustered for no reason.

'I think children need as much love as you can give them,' Beatrice added, sighing as she thought of dear Eleanor, whom she was missing dreadfully.

'And are you – er – an expert on child-rearing, Miss Dencey?' he asked, beginning to be somewhat amused, for he knew she was a spinster well past the usual age of marrying.

She flushed at the mockery in his voice and said quietly, 'I've had the pleasure of bringing up a young relative from the time she was nine until now, and Eleanor is eighteen, so I *do* know a little about such things, Sir.'

Her gentle dignity made him feel ashamed, which further irritated him, but one could not show that to a lady one was escorting. 'I cry pardon, Miss Dencey. I didn't mean to mock you. I was unaware of your exact circumstances.'

She bowed her head in a dignified acknowledgement of his apology, but her expression told him plainly that she did not really care what he thought and he was rather surprised at that. 'Do you mean to make a long stay in London?' he asked idly, it being a standard question to put to a newcomer.

'I suppose I shall have to stay for the whole Season.' Her tone was despondent.

The unexpectedness of this answer made him look at her in surprise. 'You don't sound very enthusiastic about that. Most young ladies can't wait to have their London Seasons.'

She spoke impatiently, her mind still on Eleanor. 'Well, as you've no doubt noticed, Lord Serle, I'm not exactly young and I'm not particularly thrilled about doing the Season!' Nor about being thrown into the company of an arrogant person like you, nobleman or not, who spends his time making trite meaningless comments or else being sarcastic! Why, you'd make Eleanor's life an absolute misery! she decided indignantly. I shall cross your name off my aunt's list the minute I get back to my room!

'Might one ask why?' He smothered a sigh and glanced furtively at his watch.

She thought he was now turning his mockery onto the lateness of her debut and replied quite sharply, 'I'm here at my aunt's behest, not by my own choosing, believe me, Sir. And I'm not at all sure that I shall enjoy spending so long in the city. I much prefer life in the country.'

He did not really believe her. So many

people said such things for effect, especially those trying to sound blasé. What woman would not relish the opportunity to buy a wardrobe full of new clothes and to sample all the pleasures of the London Season? That was all women seemed to care about.

After another awkward pause, he began to speak of the parties planned by his friends, assuming that she would be attending them all with her cousin and she dutifully followed his lead, thinking how tedious all these festivities would become, crammed one upon the other as they seemed to be. She wondered whether the wildflowers were out in the woods and whether in London she might sometimes be allowed to go out for proper walks, not like this boring dawdle round and round the square. The spring flowers were certainly out in the gardens here, four narrow flowerbeds full of stiff rows of plants. Poor little things! She had a fellow feeling for them. Already she was feeling restless and penned up.

Justin, dutifully continuing his attempts to entertain her, found to his pique that his companion was not really paying him much attention, and as this was a new experience for him, he fell silent and walked beside her in bafflement. Unlike other ladies of his acquaintance, Miss Dencey did not rush to fill the subsequent silence with inane chatter; indeed, she did not even seem to notice that he had stopped speaking.

On their next circuit Beatrice paused to stretch out a hand and caress a frond of soft spring foliage on one of the bushes. 'The young leaves are so beautiful,' she murmured. 'But everything's all caged up here in London, isn't it?' She resumed her walk and her silence, and he realised with surprise that she was just as happy to study the beauties of the garden as to indulge in polite conversation.

In fact, he thought, smiling wryly, he rather got the impression that she preferred the flowers to his conversation. Which was unusual for a lady favoured with his attentions. He walked in silence for a while, determined to make her furnish the next topic of conversation, and was amazed when she suddenly stopped and exclaimed. 'Oh, there's Tom! Would you mind, Lord Serle, if I just had a word with him?'

She left his side without waiting for his permission and he turned to see who this Tom was. To his utter astonishment, Tom was a haggard-looking man who was lacking an arm and had a rather grimy sleeve pinned up across his chest. An old soldier, from the looks of him. The streets were still full of them, though the war had been over for nearly two years. Intrigued, Justin followed Beatrice across the square.

'Oh, Tom, I'm so glad to see you looking better!'

The man touched his cap, as if saluting an officer. 'Came to show you me tray, miss.'

'Oh, it's exactly right! Now, you must be sure to keep it clean. That makes *such* a difference, you know.'

Justin watched in amazement as his erstwhile tongue-tied companion, who seemed to have completely forgotten his presence, laughed with Tom over some escapade or other and then questioned him closely about the details of his business. When her face was animated, as it was for this shabby creature, she was quite startlingly lovely. Tom's business appeared to consist of selling hot pies from a tray slung around his neck to people he met in the streets, and the whole contraption seemed to have been recently funded by Miss Dencey.

It was Tom who, after a while, ahemmed and begged the gentleman's pardon for taking up the lady's time.

Beatrice's animation vanished abruptly.

'Oh yes, I had quite forgotten. I beg your pardon, my lord! I was just so glad to see Tom looking better. He's been very ill, you see. You be sure to keep your chest warm, Tom! I shall keep an eye open for you when I'm out shopping tomorrow.' She watched as Tom touched his cap and walked away, then turned back to Justin, her expression schooled to that of a dutiful listener once again.

'He's a strange kind of acquaintance for a lady!'

She coloured slightly, knowing how annoyed Johanna would be at this encounter. 'I saw him collapse in the street a few days ago from hunger and was able to help him. All he needed was a little assistance and he was quite capable of earning himself a living. It's shameful the way these old soldiers are abandoned by their regiments. The government ought to do something about them, if no one else will! He lost his arm at Waterloo, poor fellow.' She dropped her eyes. 'I'm sorry. *You* cannot be interested in Tom. You were saying...' Her eyes became glazed as she waited for him to take up his conversation again.

At this, Justin felt indignation surge up within him so strongly that he almost allowed himself the pleasure of being rude to her. Here he was, honouring this non-descript female with his company for over half an hour, and she could hardly be bothered to listen to him! Then she became animated at the sight of a shabby old ex-soldier, a mere ranker! His expression was for a moment so savage that she stared at him in astonishment.

'I can be very interested in anyone who was at Waterloo,' he said, more sharply than he had intended, 'since my own brother was killed there! And I applaud your generosity in helping that man, Miss Dencey. I do, indeed.' I shall keep a better look out myself in future when I'm in town, he added mentally. Peter would not have liked to see his men in trouble. He thought the world of them.

She flushed. 'Oh. Well, I thank you for the compliment, but it's – it's a pleasure to help them.'

They were both relieved to se a footman coming across the square and to be told that her ladyship was waiting for them with a light luncheon as soon as they were ready to return. Well, Justin was certainly ready to eat! Miss Dencey was not at all a comfort-able companion. And the memory of her laughing face as she spoke to Tom still rather piqued him, if truth be told. Few ladies were so transparently impervious to his charms and no lady had ever before shown herself to be actually bored by his polished conversation.

Beatrice stifled a sigh as they turned back towards the house. 'It seems a pity to be indoors on such a lovely day.' Forgetting her London manners, she walked back with what could only be described as a stride, and he noticed that she turned at the door to look back longingly at the sunny sky.

They found Johanna waiting for them alone, her eyes still crinkled in amusement.

'Has the battle been won?' asked Justin lightly.

Beatrice frowned to hear him talk so flippantly about something as serious as a quarrel.

'It has indeed. The combatants are indulging in a very touching reconciliation at this very moment.'

'And who won the engagement?'

'Who do you think?' she countered.

'Jennice, of course. I'd back her any day.' There was a tinge of scorn in his voice. That's what you got for marrying. A wife who wheedled and wept, did anything, in fact, to get her own way.

'Correct! Jennice is to stay in town with me for a month or two before returning to Lymsby.'

Beatrice occupied herself with her food as the other two joked about the Newthorpes. Would she ever grow used to the way people poked fun at serious things here? A quarrel between husband and wife was no laughing matter. Nor was the prospect of a child. If *she* were expecting a child, the last place she'd want to come to would be London and the last thing she'd wish to do would be to run away from her husband and home.

'And did you two enjoy your walk?' Johanna asked, intrigued to find out how Justin, who usually bestowed his attentions only upon spirited ladies of dashing habits, had coped with a quiet serious-minded companion.

'Very much!' he said automatically, inclining his head towards Miss Dencey.

'Beatrice?' Johanna asked, for her cousin was avoiding her eyes.

'Oh, the gardens are very pleasant, Johanna, and it was very kind of Lord Serle to escort me. Though I prefer real walks in the countryside. One is so restricted in the town.'

Johanna raised her eyebrows in surprise at this lukewarm statement. 'You'll have to grow used to taking the air in such a way, I'm afraid,' she said. 'I'm not one for long walks myself, and certainly not brisk ones. I much prefer shopping.' Her grin at Justin showed him just how amused she was by his failure to charm the lady.

Beatrice kept her mouth resolutely closed on the truthful answer she would have liked to give. 'Shopping can be very, um, pleasant,' she murmured, unable to think of a better response.

'Did you not enjoy his company?' asked Johanna curiously, once Justin had taken his leave of them.

'Whose?'

'Whose do you think? Serle's, of course!'

'He was, umm, very polite.'

'He's accounted very good company by most young ladies, not to mention good-looking. Why, he's one of the most sought-after bachelors in town!'

'Well, I'm not a young lady and if you really want to know, Johanna, I prefer people whose conversation is less frivolous, and who don't spend their time mocking other people.' Her tone was severe and dismissive. She had definitely decided that

Justin Serle would make the worst possible husband for Eleanor. Dear Eleanor needed someone more serious-minded, someone who would counter her impulsiveness. But not someone stuffy. That would be just as bad! Oh dear, this was all going to be so difficult!

FOUR

Within a few days, Beatrice had grown used to her cousin's indolent habits and to the patterned behaviour of the upper classes in town, and had decided that such a life would never suit her. She had suspected it on their brief shopping visits to London, before the Dowager grew too frail to travel; now she was absolutely certain of it.

Back at Satherby she had had a myriad occupations to keep her busy, what with visiting the tenants, helping the sick, managing a large household for her aunt, sketching, talking to Eleanor and walking in the woods. Johanna's house ran smoothly without the need for much attention from its languid mistress. And no one Beatrice met in London ever seemed to say what they meant, or to discuss anything interesting.

Worst of all, no one seemed to care that there were still limbless soldiers starving and begging in the streets, even two years after the defeat of that monster Bonaparte. She could not be prevented from stopping to talk to them or from giving them largesse, although her cousin scolded her for this foolhardy behaviour.

To avoid upsetting anyone, Beatrice developed the habit of walking out with her maid early in the morning, when Johanna and the others were still in bed. She would visit her favourites, like Tom, and help them in any way she could. She loved to watch the street life that teemed in London, once one got away from the calm oases inhabited by the rich.

Johanna expostulated with her in vain. 'But such creatures are *dirty!*'

'So would you be if you had to share a water pump with a dozen other streets!'

'Well, don't let anyone see you on these expeditions – and for heaven's sake, take a footman with you!'

Beatrice ignored this instruction. A starchy footman would drive away the people she wanted to talk to. Lizzie was quite enough company, thank you.

Unfortunately, this innocent desire to help her fellow creatures led her into trouble the week after Jennice's arrival. One morning, she was watching with amusement an old woman buying a pie from Tom and making a big fuss about which one to choose from his tray. The two of them had already had sharp words because he refused to let her feel all his stock, to see which was the warmest, and they were now vigorously debating which was the plumpest pie. Beatrice wished she had her sketch book, for she would have loved to try to capture the old woman's expression and the way her whole body was absorbed in the choosing of that one pie.

Then Lizzie screamed and shouted, 'Stop thief!' and Beatrice realised with a shock that a boy had cut the strings of her reticule and was even now darting through the streets with his booty. If it hadn't been for Lizzie's quick eye, he would have got away unnoticed, for she had felt nothing.

Angry at being caught like that, she started to run after him, following him round a corner off the main street. Although he was still ahead of her, she saw him turn another corner and increased her pace. Lizzie was soon left behind, not having expected a lady to chase after someone like that, nor indeed, to be able to run so fast. Beatrice, who had spent most of her youth roaming the countryside, fending for herself and her mother, had reverted instinctively to the same mode of behaviour in this crisis.

Suddenly, she felt herself falling and was unable to stop. As she thudded to the ground and lay there, half stunned, a figure loomed over her and reached out towards the simple gold chain around her neck. 'Tut! Tut!' said a hoarse voice. 'Very careless of me to trip you up like that! What a pretty chain, my dear!'

Beatrice slapped his hand aside and tried to cover the chain with her own hand. When she tried to roll away from him, however, it only brought her into contact with another pair of legs clad in ragged fustian trousers. Another man was barring her way on the other side, and another grimy hand was reaching down towards her. She was being attacked and robbed! How was that possible so close to the busy streets?

A voice screamed. 'There she is! Help!'

Beatrice's new assailant cursed and tried to grab the gold chain. She fought him off, but then something struck her head and pain exploded around her. The world receded into a red mist and it was a time before she came to her senses. Through a blur of noise and pulsating colour, she gradually became aware that she was leaning against a man's chest, with Lizzie fanning her face.

'What – happened?'

'Oh, miss! Are you all right? Oh, miss, you gave us such a fright!'

'What on earth were you doing, chasing someone down these unsavoury lanes?' demanded a furious voice above her head. 'Had you taken leave of your senses, Miss Dencey?'

'I was … they'd stolen my reticule,' she said, her head still swimming. She fumbled at her neck. 'And my chain.'

'And could as easily have stolen your life! These are the back streets of London, not come country village! Those men would cut your throat as soon as look at you!'

'It's Justin Serle,' she said, not realising she was speaking aloud. 'How did he get here? And why is he so angry with me?'

'I don't think she's come to herself proper yet, m'lord,' said Lizzie. 'I saw him kick her in the head, the villain! An' she's that pale!

I've never seen her so white.'

'She'll probably be sick in a minute,' he said, still sounding angry. 'People often are when they've been hit on the head. Can you run and find us a hackney cab?'

'I don't think I ought to leave her,' said Lizzie dubiously. 'If she's sick, she'll need me. And what if they come back?'

'I, at least, can defend her if those villains return.'

Lizzie stood up, uncertain of where her duty lay.

'Lord Serle has a very strong heartbeat,' announced Beatrice. 'I can hear it quite clearly.' She nestled against his chest.

Justin jerked his head in the direction of the main streets. 'On your way, girl! I want to get Miss Dencey home as soon as possible. The best way you can help your mistress at the moment is to find us some transport!'

Footsteps clumped up to a point behind Beatrice's head, but she could not summon the energy to turn round and see who it was. Tom's voice announced gruffly, 'They got clear away, sir, I'm sorry to say. Look, I can go an' get you a hackney, sir.'

'I'd prefer you to stay here with me, Tom, in case we're attacked again. Move yourself,

Lizzie! Tom, stand on the corner and watch her to safety.'

Lizzie bowed to the voice of authority and moved. The footsteps returned.

'I doubt I'd be much help to you in a scrap, sir,' Tom said in a tight angry voice.

'You've still got one hand and two feet, haven't you?'

The voice cheered up. 'Well, I'd certainly do my best, sir. Nicest lady I ever met, Miss Dencey is. Lucky day for me when I collapsed in front of 'er, I can tell you.'

Justin stared down at the pale face so close to his. He had not realised how long Miss Dencey's eyelashes were, or what a pretty colour her hair was when the sun was shining on it.

Beatrice looked up at him for a minute, then grimaced. 'I feel sick.' She was finding it hard to form the words. 'But I can't – can't sit up.'

Deftly and with a surprising lack of embarrassment, Justin moved her into a sitting position and held her until she had finished, then lifted her a little distance along the street and wiped her mouth. She leaned against his chest again, sighing. The world was beginning to make a little more sense. 'I'm sorry – to be so much trouble.'

'You were quite feather-brained to take such a risk!' He glanced around, alert to the possibility that the thieves might come back with reinforcements. Then he looked down and saw tears come into her eyes. 'I'm sorry. I shouldn't be scolding you now. You must be feeling dreadful.'

The world was still hazy around her, but she felt a need to explain. 'Didn't like to – to be robbed.'

'He dropped your chain when I hit him with me tray, miss,' volunteered Tom. 'I've got it here safe for you.'

'Oh, Tom! Thank you so much!' She tried to turn her head towards him, but winced and stopped as a pain shot through her.

Lord Serle's voice was severe. 'You should be resting, Miss Dencey, not trying to talk.'

'Yes.' Her eyelids fluttered and closed, but she could still hear what they were saying, as if it were at the far end of a long tunnel.

'Remind me to reimburse you for the pies you lost,' said Justin. 'Miss Dencey is very obliged to you. As am I. You bore into those villains like a good 'un.'

'Ah, you should 'ave seen me when I 'ad both me arms,' said Tom regretfully. 'I'd ha' caught one of 'em for sure in those days. Nor I don't need payin' to 'elp a lady like

Miss Dencey.'

'You've more than earned it.'

'I wouldn't take nothin' at all, sir, only I need the money for more stock, you see. Mine got spilled, full tray, it was, too, an' it'll all 'ave been picked up and et by now. I ain't got nothin' saved yet, you see, me only just starting like.'

The chest behind Beatrice was warm and comforting, and she gave in to the temptation to snuggle more closely into the crook of his arm. 'You're stronger than you look,' she murmured. 'Not just a dandy.'

Justin, who prided himself on his sporting prowess, stiffened and exclaimed in astonishment, 'A dandy! Is that what you think of me?'

'Always talking about fashions and parties and things,' she explained, still feeling light-headed and more than half convinced that this was just a dream, and a bad one, at that. It did not really matter what she said in a dream. She would never dare say such things to anyone in real life, but she had often longed to.

Serle's lips tightened and Tom hid a grin.

'Not interested in real things,' she continued. 'Always immaculately dressed. That's a dandy, isn't it?'

The rattle of wheels and the sound of Lizzie's voice interrupted Beatrice's ramblings, and she found herself being lifted up and settled in a vehicle which smelled of stale sweat and mouldy straw. She could not help crying out, for being moved made her head stab with pain, but a gentle voice promised she would soon be safe in her bed, so she subsided against Serle, clinging to him with her free hand. 'Feel safe now, with you,' she said, 'Don't let them hit me again!' She could feel herself drifting off. The dream must be coming to an end. She would be glad to wake up. Her head was hurting so much she could not think properly.

He stared down at her beautiful hair, feeling an urge to stroke it. Like burnished beech leaves, he thought. He could feel her breasts rise and fall against him. She had a woman's figure, warm and soft, not a slight girlish frame, like most débutantes. Strange, how he had not fully appreciated before what an attractive woman she was. Perhaps that was because she did not set out to attract. His expression became forbidding again as he remembered what she thought of him. A dandy, indeed!

Another period of jolting was followed for

Beatrice by a chorus of voices and by more movement and light, which hurt her head again. She could not help moaning and was relieved when a man's deep voice told the voices sharply to be quiet and ordered someone to show him where Miss Dencey's bedchamber lay.

'You're breathing very deeply,' she told the man who was carrying her. 'Where are you taking me? Oh!' For as he started to climb some stairs, her head began to throb again. She clutched his shoulder tightly.

'Is that hurting you?'

'Yes.' Her voice was a mere thread of sound.

'I'm sorry. But see, we're here at your bedroom now.'

As he laid her on the bed, she opened her eyes, only to see the room spinning about her. With a sigh, she let herself spiral down into the darkness, glad to leave the pain behind.

When she awoke, it was dark and Johanna was sitting by her bed. There was a rustle of silk, then, 'Bea?'

'Johanna,' she managed. 'What happened?'

'At least she seems to be in her right senses,' Johanna commented to someone invisible beyond the pool of light thrown by a single candle.

Beatrice frowned. 'Of course I'm in my senses? But why am I lying...? Oh!' Memories came flooding back.

'You were attacked.'

'It wasn't a dream!'

'No. Fancy running after a thief like that. Don't you know how dangerous those alleys are?'

A cool cloth was laid on her forehead and she sighed. 'Nice,' she managed, closing her eyes.

'Does it help?'

'Yes. Head's aching!'

'I'm not surprised! Those villains kicked you! Such people should be hanged!'

'Probably hungry.' She gasped as her head throbbed in protest against even a slight movement.

'Never mind that! Just try to rest, Bea! The doctor said that nothing is broken and that you'll be all right in a day or two.'

'Yes. Rest.' There was a fire flickering in the grate and she found its cheerful flames tugging at the corners of her eyes. She could not keep them open. She could not...

It was light when she woke again, and this time it was Lizzie who was sitting beside her.

'Lizzie,' she said aloud, pleased to find herself in her own bedchamber.

'How do you feel, miss? You look a bit better now, I must say. Got a bit of pink in your cheeks again. You slept for most of the night though you was a bit restless just before dawn.'

Beatrice's head was still aching, but she could think more clearly. She gasped as she started to remember what had happened and tried to persuade herself that it was just a dream, but somehow, her memories seemed only too real. 'Lizzie!' she said, after a minute or two.

'Yes, miss?'

She had to find out whether she had really spoken her thoughts aloud and been so rude to poor Lord Serle. 'Did I – did I say anything – er – anything impolite – yesterday?'

Lizzie giggled. 'Well…'

'Tell me!'

'Well, miss, Tom says you told Lord Serle he was a dandy an' not worth talkin' to, an' that he wasn't best pleased with that.'

'Oh dear!'

'Don't you worry, Miss! He'll soon forget it, his lordship will. He knows you was out of your senses. Concussion, the doctor said.'

Out of her senses or not, she'd been extremely rude! How would she ever face him again? What must he think of her? Especially as, dandy or not, he'd come to her rescue. She lay there for a minute or two, then tried to turn her head to look at Lizzie. The effort made her head throb again and she cried out.

'Just you lie still, Miss. I'll go an' tell them you're awake.'

Bea dozed off after that, until she became suddenly aware of a debate between Johanna and Lizzie as to whether the doctor should be summoned again. 'I'm all right,' she managed and opened her eyes. 'Johanna!'

Her cousin leaned over her. 'How are you, love?'

'Thirsty.'

'Lizzie, get your mistress a drink of that barley water the doctor ordered. Afterwards, we'll sponge you down, Bea, and make you feel fresher.'

'Yes. Yes, I'd like that.' Almost before they had finished their ministrations, she could feel herself drifting into sleep again. 'So tired,' she sighed.

By the following day, apart from a slight residual headache, she felt well enough to be helped to a couch by the fire in her room.

Jennice came to visit her, but she could not seem to concentrate for long on what her young relative said. Jennice's cheerful voice and lively conversation hurt her head. Johanna was a more comfortable companion, because she talked quietly and softly, not demanding answers. Lizzie was best of all, because she said very little.

Lord Serle had sent her a huge bunch of hothouse flowers, which gazed accusingly down at her from a wooden plant stand. In the end, she told Lizzie to take them away, pretending that the perfume made her headache worse.

It was several days before Beatrice felt strong enough to go downstairs again, days in which she worried about the fact that she had insulted Lord Serle and must apologise to him as soon as she possibly could. During those days, she was fussed over by every servant with a claim to serve her.

From the start of this visit, Johanna had watched with wry amusement as Beatrice gradually won over *her* servants and had them eating out of her hand, even Moreton, who was famous for being one of the most supercilious butlers in town. But not with Miss Dencey. With her, Moreton was fatherly and helpful, especially since her accident. For her, he would unbend amazingly and the two of them would hold long conversations about the manners of the ton nowadays and those in his youth, or the difficulties of maintaining standards during the recent war, with prices so high and food and goods so scarce.

While Miss Dencey was ill, there was distinct rivalry between the various servants as to who could do most for her, and it was noticeable that Moreton found several excuses to visit her upstairs, even carrying up the notes from well-wishers himself. Lizzie had become very possessive of her temporary mistress and Johanna could see that there would be no chance of hiring a more experienced lady's maid after this. Even that man Tom had appeared at the kitchen door every day, begging for news of Miss Dencey.

Once she had recovered, Beatrice resumed her social engagements again, somewhat embarrassed by the notoriety she had acquired because of her adventure. Justin Serle, she found, was cast in the role of the hero rescuing a poor foolish heroine. It was even worse than in the novels, for people spoke of his bravery in the most extravagant terms as if expecting her to swoon away at the mere thought of it. No one seemed to give her any credit for trying to fight off her attackers, but rather, hinted at how foolish she had been to try to follow the thief. She had to dig her fingers into her palms several times to prevent herself from answering sharply, but thanks to her years of training with the Dowager, no one suspected how angry she sometimes felt.

Serle came to call upon her as soon as he heard that she was out and about again and, though she had been dreading this meeting, she could not refuse to see him. When he had sat down, and Johanna, whom she had fore-warned, had tactfully gone into the next room and left them alone, she began to speech she had prepared.

'I wish to tell you that I – I'm grateful to you, Lord Serle, for – for rescuing me from those men.' She knew that her voice was stiff, the words coming out woodenly, so that she sounded insincere, but she could not help that.

'I am happy to have been of service to you, Miss Dencey.' His voice was just as stiff, his expression cold and accusing. He must still be angry at what she had said. She found it even harder to broach that subject. 'I believe,' she said, fiddling with the fringe of her shawl, 'that I owe you an apology as well.'

'What on earth for, Miss Dencey?' he asked languidly.

She could not now imagine this man holding her so carefully in his arms. The memory of the way she had nestled against him had made her blush several times, not to mention haunting her dreams. 'I'm sorry for – for saying things. About you. Things I had no – no right to – to…'

'There is no need to…'

But she could not leave it at that. She knew she had to make him understand. 'I didn't realize, you see. I thought I was dreaming.'

If that was how she dreamed, she must have a very low opinion of him, he thought, trying to contain his anger. He could not understand why he was still so annoyed with her. What did her opinion matter, after all? 'Pray give it no more thought,' he said, his voice tight and angry. 'Your wits were wandering after the blow. I can assure you that no one could possibly take offence at what you said in that condition.'

'You still sound angry, though.' She looked at him uncertainly.

His face was quite expressionless. 'I repeat, pray give the matter no more thought. We shall blame it on the blow to the head. And you said nothing to which I could take offence, after all.'

She knew this for a lie. She had been extremely rude to him. In spite of his gracious words, he was furious. But she could not think what else to say, how to mend matters between them. In the end, she was glad when Johanna returned. The conversation turned to the social inanities she so despised and thereafter she made little attempt to join in.

He was more aware of how foolishly he was behaving than Beatrice would have believed, and yet, he could not think of anything conciliatory to say to her. Her ladyship's return had made him feel even worse, for she knew him only too well, being a sort of honorary aunt. If he behaved differently towards Miss Dencey than towards other young ladies, Lady Ostdene would notice and wonder why. He was not sure what she might wonder about, but he knew that he did not want it.

Just before he left, he remembered something. 'I've seen Tom once or twice,' he said abruptly. 'Kept an eye on him for you. He's doing well with his pies. He's found a better supplier and is becoming quite popular in certain streets.'

'Oh, I'm so glad! Thank you for that, Lord Serle!' Her voice was warm again, as if she had forgotten their differences.

'I was pleased to help. He's a decent sort of fellow.'

They parted on a more friendly note.

Afterwards, Johanna, who had been eavesdropping unashamedly in the next room, insisted on knowing what her cousin had said to Justin that required an apology, and she roared with laughter when Beatrice confessed. 'Well, that's probably the biggest set-down Serle has ever received in his life,' she said, wiping tears of laughter from her eyes. 'Calling him a dandy! Justin, of all people! Oh dear, I wish I could tell our friends, but of course that would be unpardonable when he so kindly rescued you. Besides, I have some fondness for Justin myself.'

'Well, I thought, I mean, he's always so well-dressed!' muttered Beatrice defensively. 'And – and I've apologised to him about it. I don't see what more I can do!'

Johanna, still chuckling, informed her cousin that Serle was a noted Corinthian, a famous sportsman and rider, and in no way a dandy. 'A dandy, my dear, is likely to lisp at you, to wave his hands when he speaks and to breathe perfume all over you.'

'Oh dear! Why did I not know that?' Serle had smelled of some crisp cologne. She had found it very attractive.

'Fancy thinking it in the first place!' Johanna could not stop chuckling. She wished she had been there to see Serle's face.

'Well, he puts other men quite in the shade by the way he dresses. He always looks so elegant.'

'That's because he's *not* a dandy! Simply a gentleman of exquisite taste.'

'Ought I to apologise to him again?' Beatrice frowned and added, 'But that still doesn't explain. Johanna, why does he behave so languidly? He seems so frivolous.' And yet he had rescued her and held her in his arms and carried her up to her room. And she was no fragile flower. She remembered the way his chest had moved, labouring under her weight. And he had held her when she was sick, and been very gentle with her afterwards. She remembered it all quite clearly now.

'By no means must you apologise again! I told you, it'll do him good to know how others see him sometimes. I'm very fond of Justin, but he has lived behind a barrier since his brother's death and has hidden his feelings from the world. He does have a serious side, you know; he just doesn't care to broadcast it. He sits regularly in the House of Lords and he takes a keen interest in improving his estates. His tenants and employees are very well looked after, I assure you.'

'I'm glad of that.'

Johanna saw that Beatrice was still looking thoughtful and began to wonder about the two of them. It was not like Justin to show that he cared about someone's opinion and it was not like Bea to worry on about something. She would, she decided, keep an eye on them the next time they met and see how they behaved with each other.

During the following few days, for someone who affected indifference to his lordship, Beatrice mentioned his name a surprising number of times. And for someone who had been insulted so greatly, Justin paid an amazing number of visits to check on Miss Dencey's progress and to report on Tom! Was it possible, Johanna wondered, that her quiet young cousin was proving attractive to Justin, Lord Serle, the man of whom matchmaking mamas had despaired for years?

However, Justin was not the only one to show an interest. Beatrice might underrate her own charms and talk of finding a husband for Eleanor, but she was a very pretty young woman and she was attracting some interest among the ton in her own right.

Only the previous evening, Lady Clayre had commented on it to Johanna. 'That cousin of yours has got good manners, better than most young folk nowadays. She got cornered by St John Hardinge at Amelia's rout. I tried to rescue her. Felt guilty, him bein' a connection of mine. You know what a bore he is.'

Johanna raised expressive eyebrows. They had all been cornered by St John Hardinge at one time or another.

'Well, I couldn't get across the room, so I watched your cousin listening to him, and you'd have sworn from her expression that he was a wit, instead of a half-wit.' She guffawed so loudly at her own joke that she choked and by the time she had recovered, she had found another subject to pursue, to Johanna's frustration. She was finding Bea a surprise in more ways than one.

Lady Jersey said much the same thing, and

Johanna had a hard time keeping her face straight as the garrulous woman known as 'Silence' to her own generation, lavished praise on Bea. 'One gets so tired of dealing with the caprices and fussations of the more dashing type of person. Your cousin is quite the easiest guest imaginable, with impeccable manners and an elegant simplicity in her dress that has taken very well with the other patronesses. You must be sure to bring her to Almack's.' She raised one eyebrow. 'Dowry?'

'I believe my mother has settled twenty thousand on her.'

'Indeed. Then it should not be hard to find her a suitable *parti*.'

Justin, arriving late, as usual, for a musical evening, found himself pausing in the doorway to listen to a pleasant contralto voice, nothing out of the ordinary, but the sort of thing it was a pleasure to listen to, especially as it was singing something in English instead of one of those incomprehensible German Lieder that always sounded like funeral dirges to him. He blinked in surprise when he saw that the singer was Miss Beatrice Dencey, for he would have thought her too shy to perform in public. He did not realise that the

Dowager had had both girls well taught and had insisted on them singing for her and her very occasional guests until it had become a commonplace.

When it was over, Beatrice, face slightly flushed at the applause, settled back at the piano to accompany first one, then another young lady, her skill being such that they were able to show off their vocal prowess to the very best advantage. Her popularity, he saw afterwards, was assured, even with her own sex, for all her quietness and her self-effacing manners.

Beatrice found that several of the very young ladies took to confiding in her, as they could not do to their own mamas. With them treating her like an elder sister or cousin, and eagerly awaiting her arrival at parties, she could not feel an outcast, even though she still found most entertainments rather shallow.

Lady Jersey let it be known that Miss Dencey had a very respectable dowry and was in the market for a husband, and this set the seal upon Beatrice's success. It was only necessary to whisper the size of the dowry to one or two known gossips for that information to be spread all over town. Beatrice would have been horrified, if she had known it, but Johanna took care that she did not find out. It was the way things were done in their world. Like her mother, Johanna believed that marriage was first and foremost a business contract. She would as soon have let her own daughters marry a penniless younger son as she would have shaven her head.

Brothers, younger sons and nephews were summoned up to London and displayed to Miss Dencey in all their masculine glory at a variety of functions. Beatrice studied them more for Eleanor's sake than her own and did not realise at first that some of the interest was in herself. The marks and notes against the names on the Dowager's list multiplied rapidly.

The first proposal shocked her to the core, coming from a gentleman whom she scarcely knew. When he swept her into an anteroom after a dance, she protested. 'Mr Tarrow, I don't think we should...' then fell silent in horror as he fell to his knees before her. 'My dear Miss Dencey,' he began, seizing her hand and covering it with wet kisses.

'Oh, please. Mr Tarrow, please do not!' She was scarlet with embarrassment by now.

'Miss Dencey, I must! I cannot wait any longer. Since the moment I first saw you I have longed to call you my own. Only say that you will marry me and I shall be the happiest man in town!' He tried to kiss her again and in desperation, she pushed at his chest with both hands. Since he was kneeling on one knee at the time, this made him lose his balance and by the time he had scrambled to his feet, he was as red-faced as she was.

'My dear Miss Dencey...'

'No!'

For a moment, his expression was anything but conciliatory. 'Dash it all,' he began, 'what else are you here for but to find a husband? The word's out all over town about your dowry.'

'What!' She took a deep breath, rage kindling her eyes into brilliance, then repeated firmly, 'I have no desire to marry you, or anyone else, for that matter.' She retreated strategically behind a pot plant. 'And I shall not change my mind. Please go, Mr Tarrow!'

He opened his mouth, saw the expression on her face and bowed stiffly, his movements constrained by the size and height of his now rather crumpled neckcloth, before striding out of the room.

She stayed where she was for a moment, hands pressed to her burning cheeks, then said aloud, 'How did he find out about that dreadful dowry?' As she was waiting for the flush to subside, she caught sight of two feet behind a potted palm tree and gasped. 'Oh, no! Who's there?'

Justin sighed and moved forward. He would have preferred to remain unnoticed. 'I cry pardon, Miss Dencey! I had no wish to eavesdrop, believe me, but the gentleman was so eager that I had no time to reveal my presence before he had launched into his speech.' He took her fan from her trembling fingers and began to waft it gently to and fro in front of her flushed face.

'He was only eager to gain access to my fortune!' she said bitterly. 'As if I'd sell myself to a creature like him!' She looked at him shyly. 'He's – he's what I accused you of, Lord Serle, and I'm more sorry than ever for my error. It was because you always look so elegant that I, well, I mistook matters.'

He smiled, a genuine smile. 'Mr Tarrow is indeed one of the dandy set,' he murmured. 'All the crack, but to me he looks more like a fowl stuffed for the oven.'

'Yes. And that ridiculous neckcloth! It must be at least a foot high! He can't even turn his head, but must move his whole body to look sideways!' She laughed suddenly. 'If some of our older villagers could see him, they'd be convulsed and he'd hear a few home truths!'

'Can we not arrange it? I have a few old tenants who have a similar frankness of speech.'

'Oh, don't tempt me!' Her colour had faded to near normal and her expression still showed genuine amusement.

He returned the fan and offered her his arm. 'Perhaps we should return to Lady Ostdene now? Are you feeling better?'

'Yes. And I do thank you for being so understanding.'

Johanna was merely amused when Beatrice confessed about the offer she had received.

'Oh, Tarrow won't do!' she said, dismissing the man with a wave of her hand.

'But it was so humiliating!' Beatrice protested. 'How can you talk so casually? He wasn't offering for me, but for my dowry! How did he know of it?'

'Oh, these things get around. I may have mentioned it to one or two of my friends.' She saw the anger in Beatrice's eyes and shrugged. 'That's the way of the world, my dear, and you won't change it. And you *are* here to find a husband, are you not? I must say I thought that even Tarrow would have had more address, than to rush things. He must be badly dipped. He's a known gamester.'

Such frank talk disgusted Beatrice, but she could hardly complain to her kind hostess, who was going to inordinate trouble to take her around and introduce her to people.

The attentiveness of the gentlemen continued to increase, to her great embarrassment, and several times, Justin Serle rescued her in the nick of time from what she considered to be an unpleasant situation. She began to feel more comfortable with him and to treat him like a cousin or a brother.

Her blatant lack of interest in him as a man began to pique him. He was not at all sure he enjoyed the role of safe relative. It was one he had never played before.

Fortunately, not all the gentlemen were as blatant in their pursuit as Mr Tarrow, and Beatrice managed to enjoy herself some of the time, especially when they could go to the theatre or the opera, or when they could attend a salon where the guests were expected to talk of literature or poetry in a more intelligent way. Johanna pulled a face sometimes at the nature of the entertainments Beatrice preferred, but realised that she would not be able to keep her cousin happy if they only attended the frivolous functions she and her daughter enjoyed.

Justin Serle, whether he approached Beatrice himself or not, had taken to watching the attention she received with a frown on his handsome face. The frown became a scowl when he saw her several times talking to the same gentleman, a person whom, it appeared, she did consider worth her time.

Justin did not yet, Johanna thought, watching them both with growing amusement, realise the implications of his own interest. It was diverting to watch him and she threatened to murder Jennice if she dropped so much as a hint to anyone else about the possibility of any serious interest between Bea and Serle. If she did that, Beatrice would freeze and Justin retreat. For once, Jennice held her tongue. She was quite fond of Justin herself, and would be glad to see him married into the family.

Beatrice, more intent upon working through the Dowager's list of eligible suitors for Eleanor, treated all gentlemen who did not displease her with a distant kindness.

Johanna watched this in puzzlement and decided after a while that it was not going to be as easy as she had expected to find a husband who would be acceptable both to a stickler like her mother and to a serious-minded woman who declined to flirt, who rarely recognised it when a gentleman was paying her court and who was not really committed to settling her own future. Johanna could only be thankful that neither of *her* daughters had been so hard to marry off. They had both worked enthusiastically with her to find themselves husbands.

One day, she discussed the matter with Jennice. 'I really can't understand Bea. She makes no push to fix anyone's interest upon herself.'

Jennice chose another sugar plum and grimaced before the popped it in her mouth. 'Perhaps,' she began, her mouth full and her words almost inaudible, 'a clergyman would be more the thing for Bea? I mean, she's always so serious.'

'Yes.' Johanna looked thoughtful. 'If, that is, nothing comes of her acquaintance with Justin. I have not given up hope in that quarter, though they're both hopelessly slow. I could swear he likes her. He certainly seeks her company often enough.'

'And she seeks his,' agreed Jennice, licking the sugar from her fingers. 'I thought when they were waltzing the other night how well they looked together. She never looks as relaxed in anyone else's arms. And did you see her face when he was flirting with Gwendoline Firsby?'

'No! Did she look upset?'

'Yes. For a minute or two, anyway. Then she turned away and didn't look across at him again.'

'Hmm. That sounds a bit more promising, but I'd better not say anything to my mother yet. You know what she's like if she gets an idea into her head. I wouldn't put it past her to summon him down to Satherby and ask him his intentions.'

They both chuckled at the thought.

So although Johanna duly reported in her letters to her mother on the one or two gentlemen who were making a little progress with Bea, she did not mention Serle. She did describe one Henry Patcham, a widower of thirty or so, with two small daughters and modest estates in Dorset, who seemed to be quite a favourite. She herself found Mr Patcham as dull as ditchwater, but Bea smiled warmly when she met him at parties, and the two of them had long, involved conversations about the woes of cottagers, a subject which made Johanna and her daughter yawn openly.

Beatrice also seemed very interested to hear from Mr Patcham about his little daughters, to whom he was obviously devoted and she swopped tales with him about Eleanor's childhood escapades. But she never raised his name in conversation afterwards, as she did Justin's, and if he were not present at a party, she did not seem to miss him.

If Justin were not there, Jennice noted gleefully, Bea's eyes would scan the guests regularly and a slight frown would appear on her brow. Why didn't she *show* him she was interested? Really, Jennice could have spanked her sometimes.

Johanna also reported to her mother on the Reverend Paul Netherton, who was in town quite blatantly to find himself a wife. He was a little younger than Bea, to be sure, but she seemed to enjoy conversing with him. And he was quite eligible, since he had a good living and private means, not to mention coming from an impeccable, if minor, county family. The two of them were forever discussing how best to help the poor, as well as books and poetry and sketching. He was, for a time, the one who always turned her music at parties, and he accompanied her in the occasional duet. Then, very abruptly, he stopped seeking her company and Beatrice admitted, though only when taxed, that he had proposed marriage and that she had refused him.

'But why? You seemed to enjoy his company!'

Beatrice shrugged. 'I don't know. I just – couldn't imagine spending the rest of my life with him. He's very earnest. I think I would grow bored with his company.'

'Bored? What does that matter in a husband? You don't think we all go around doting on our spouses, do you? Why, my Harry and I never exchanged two words most days unless we were going to the same party in the evening. For goodness' sake, Bea!' She broke off, for she could see the look of distress in her cousin's gentle eyes. 'Oh, well, if you couldn't stomach him, you couldn't. However, I must warn you that you'll get a reputation as a blue-stocking if you don't take care.'

Bea laughed. 'What does that matter, when I don't intend to spend my life living idly in London? Perhaps I *am* a blue-stocking, Johanna.'

Her cousin shuddered. 'Don't even joke about it! Tell me instead what you think of Mr Patcham as husband material.'

Beatrice's expression grew chill. 'I don't care to discuss such things. I have little desire to marry.' Which was a lie, because she knew that she would love to marry and have a family. She could not imagine anything nicer, though not with Mr Patcham or Mr Netherton. The man she married must have other qualities. What, she was not sure, but something more than anyone who had sought her out so far. Besides, she had no time to think of herself? The Season was passing by and she had got nowhere with her real quest. All her attention from now on must be focused on providing a husband for Eleanor.

Lady Marguerite was becoming more and more querulous in her letters to her daughter, complaining bitterly about the delays in settling matters. Mama, Johanna told her daughter, always did expect people to obey her orders in an unreasonably short time. In her response she suggested that her mother consider extending the list of eligibles. She could think of several gentlemen who might very well be worth consideration for Eleanor. She mentioned one or two names as examples and received a stinging reply commanding her to do as she had promised and not to interfere with Beatrice's instructions. The Dowager was only interested in persons of rank!

After another two unproductive weeks, Lady Marguerite wrote a very sharp letter to Beatrice that had her drooping all day. By evening, Johanna could stand it no longer. 'You mustn't let Mama bully you, Bea. She means well, but you know what she's like.'

'She's right to complain,' said Bea, wringing her hands. 'I've been neglecting my duty quite shamefully and looking only to enjoy myself. I must stop going to so many concerts and, and...' Her voice faltered.

'You can't do much more than you are doing,' Johanna pointed out reasonably.

'I must!' She went up to her room and wrote an extremely detailed report on those gentlemen she had met so far. She would have been horrified if she had known that her report only made the Dowager thump her stick on the floor in rage and demand of heaven why she was saddled with such feeble-witted descendants.

'Is something wrong with Miss Dencey?' Lippings ventured to ask.

'Yes. She's turned into a timid romantic

nincompoop! Look at that!' She waved the letter in the air. 'She don't think any of them are suitable for Eleanor, and on the most ridiculous of grounds. Too stupid. Too reckless. Not kind enough. *Not kind enough!* What does she think we're looking for – a saint? They're men of breeding, ain't they? Some of them must be presentable!'

After a sleepless night, Lady Marguerite decided not to take issue with Bea about her failure to nominate some suitable candidates for Eleanor's hand. However, she told her maid grimly, if things did not improve within the next month, she would take matters into her own hands. She was not yet too old or too decrepit to manage her family's affairs, and so they would all find out.

FIVE

Other things were also upsetting the Dowager. Crispin Herforth, the heir to the estates, had declined her summons to visit the Abbey and had written to say that he would not be available to visit her until later in the year, as he was busy supervising some building projects on his home farm. That provoked a temper tantrum and a diatribe about ignorant clodpates who placed farming and such menial occupations before the well-being of estates which had belonged to The Family for centuries and which it was their bounden duty to preserve and protect. Such ill-bred upstarts did not know good fortune when it hit them in the eye and would soon find themselves ostracised by the county if they did not mend their manners and learn to behave in a way which was consonant with their new and totally undeserved consequence.

After this expenditure of nervous energy, The Dowager felt quite washed out for a few days and had to rest and recruit her strength while she decided on what tack to take next with the elusive heir.

Her fretting and fuming would have made Eleanor's life quite intolerable had that young lady not had several other things to divert her. She had lately found another supplier of romantic novels in the nearby town and walked around Satherby with her head stuffed full of the adventures of a series of dashing heroines so reckless that they regularly landed themselves in the direst straits just as the dinner bell rang and then poor Eleanor had to endure an evening's suspense before she found out how their problems were solved. In addition, there was Snowy. Beatrice had made her a parting gift of a fluffy white puppy, and its training and exercising occupied a considerable amount of Eleanor's time. A dog which was allowed inside the Dowager's residence needed impeccable manners.

Best of all, however, she had made a new acquaintance, unknown to her grand-mother, and one which added considerable interest to her days. The Dowager's inter-minable monologues and acidic strictures on the behaviour of the unworthy heir in refusing her olive branch passed mainly over her grand-daughter's head, so that Eleanor was then accused of not listening or not caring about matters of importance. There was no pleasing her ladyship at the moment.

Only Eleanor's groom, Anders, knew about her new acquaintance, and although he objected strongly at first, she persuaded him to suspend judgement. Anders had been her father's head groom and had brought Eleanor to the Abbey himself after the carriage accident that had killed her parents. Her governess, who had broken her ankle a week previously, had declined absolutely to subject herself to the jolting of a journey across country, and the rest of the staff, who lived in dire terror of the Dowager's rare visits, were glad to abnegate the responsibility.

Once at Satherby, Anders had been offered the job of being Miss Eleanor's personal groom, for the Dowager, grim-faced in flowing black, did not neglect her duty to look after her favourite son's faithful servants, however much she might be grieving over his death. Anders had jumped at the chance and from that day onwards had supervised Lady Eleanor and her riding with the utmost care. He now boasted that she was the best woman rider in the county and he took considerable pride in her prowess.

As the sole link with her past, he had been better able than anyone else to cheer up the solitary child mourning the loss of her parents. He had chosen her first proper horse for her, guided he through the mysteries of jumping and accompanied her to her first hunt. He was generally reckoned by the other servants to be willing to kill for her, if necessary. And he would have done.

Eleanor met the exciting stranger quite by chance when she was walking in the woods, disobeying the Dowager by doing so un-escorted by either maid or groom. It had been a trying week, with the Dowager's temper fluctuating between rage and scorn, and even Eleanor's sunny temperament had been dimmed.

The puppy strayed from the narrow path to follow a quite irresistible scent and re-fused to obey a command from his mistress to come to heel. Eleanor, terrified of losing Snowy, ran after him and it took her quite a while to catch up with the naughty creature. When she did, she found that he had got himself stuck down a rabbit hole and was cowering there, whimpering with fear, with only his shiny amber eyes showing in the shadows beyond the opening.

With no thought for her own appearance, she fell to her knees and at once started to try to dig the puppy out, scolding him all the time in a tender voice. She did not hear anyone approach and started in shock when a twig snapped beside her and a voice asked, 'Is something the matter?'

'Oh!' She brushed her cheek with one dirty hand, unaware that she had deposited a smear of dirt on it. 'Oh, you quite startled me, sir!' It did not occur to her to be afraid of the stranger, for it was not in her nature to be suspicious of others, and besides, he had a very warm smile.

'I'm sorry about that. I thought you must have heard me coming.'

She sat back on her heels and smiled. 'No I was too busy trying to help poor Snowy.'

'Yes, so I see. May I assist you?' He was staring at her in undisguised admiration and she found herself blushing slightly, while her breath caught in her throat.

'Well,' she managed, after a moment's hesitation, 'I'm having difficulty digging Snowy out, for the earth will keep falling back in again. I can't think how he got in there and I'm afraid that my poor little darling will be smothered if I'm not careful. And I daren't go for help, because he may bring the earth in on himself! Or I might not find him again.'

'Let me see if I can help.' He was undoubtedly a gentleman, neatly, though not fashionably dressed, and he did not seem to care that he too was dirtying his clothes. They knelt side by side, holding back the earth and enlarging the hole. With his help, the puppy was soon released. When it tried to walk, it yelped and sat down again, nuzzling at its back leg. The stranger picked it up and examined it, seeming to know what he was doing. 'I don't believe the leg is broken, but he must have twisted the joint when he fell down the hole so it'll be sore for a day or two.'

'Oh, thank you, sir!' Still on her knees, she kissed the puppy's face, but desisted when its effort to lick her nose in return made it yelp again. 'Be still, Snowy!' she commanded.

When they stood up, Eleanor found that the gentleman was only slightly taller than she was, for the Graceovers were a tall family, but she decided that in spite of that defect – for all the heroes in her novels were at least six feet tall – he was rather handsome. Not as handsome as the Duke of Hanmouth in *Cressida's Revenge*, of course, but he was quite the best-looking gentleman she had ever met in real life – in a quiet, comfortable sort of way.

Not that she had met many young gentlemen, she thought ruefully, for they lived so quietly at Satherby. She had not even been allowed to become well acquainted with the few she did encounter from time to time at the hunt or at the houses of neighbours. They were, the Dowager invariably said, not of sufficient consequence to be seriously considered as future conjugal partners for a Graceover. It never seemed to occur to her that one might just enjoy their company without marrying them.

'I don't think I've met you before,' she said, in her forthright way. 'Are you new to the district?'

'Yes. I'm visiting my friends at Treevers Hall. My name's – er – Lanby – Christopher Lanby.'

She did not notice his hesitation, but held out her hand with her usual sunny smile, 'And I'm Eleanor Graceover. I live at Satherby Abbey.'

He took the hand in his and she could not help noticing that he held it for a moment or two longer than was necessary, but she did not mind that. Unlike Beatrice, Eleanor was quite prepared to flirt with eligible gentlemen and her only impediment so far had been the unavailability of suitable gentlemen upon whom to practice that art.

'Yes, I've heard of you,' he said after a minute. 'The Dowager Lady Graceover's grand-daughter, are you not?'

'Yes.' She removed her hand from his. Of course, it was not quite the thing to talk to strange gentlemen in the woods, but he *had* saved poor little Snowy and in fact was still carrying him. 'Oh, do give Snowy back to me! He's dirtying your waistcoat.'

'It'll come clean. And if it doesn't, I'll buy another.'

She rather liked his indifference to his appearance. She was an unceremonious creature herself, for all the Dowager's love of formality. She patted Snowy's head, well aware that this brought her own head nearer to Mr Lanby's. 'He's been a very naughty boy, but he's sorry now. Are you not, young sir?'

The dog wriggled with delight, then yelped again.

'Oh, you poor little darling!'

'He'll need carrying, I think. Let me do that for you, Lady Eleanor.' He was holding the little animal as if he were quite used to dealing with such creatures and Snowy was now trying to lick his fingers, so Eleanor knew that he must be a nice person, in spite of them not having been introduced properly. Anders said that dogs could always tell.

She was still standing very close to him and wondered why she should suddenly feel rather breathless. Perhaps it was just the after-effects of the shock. She moved back a step or two. 'Well, all right, then. And, thank you, Mr Lanby. We're not far from the Abbey if we go in this direction.'

As they walked through the woods together, they began to talk and found that they had one or two acquaintances in common, though she had not heard of him before. She soon grew very comfortable with him and chatted gaily about her life at Satherby, telling him about her grand-mamma and poor Bea, who had been forced to undergo a London Season when it was the last thing someone like her would enjoy.

'Not that you're to think Bea is a boring sort of person. She isn't! It's just that she has little interest in fashion and gossip. I can't imagine how she's coping with everything.'

'I thought all ladies were addicted to both.'

She wrinkled her nose at him. 'There *are* other things in life, sir.' Then she spoiled the effect of that by adding, 'Not that I wouldn't like to visit London myself. I'd love to go to a few ton parties!'

'Why did you not go with her, then?'

She made a further moue, that made him want to kiss those soft pouting lips. He stopped walking for a minute, to stare at her in shock, then realised that she was looking at him in puzzlement and asked hastily, 'Why did your – Bea, that is, go to London, then, if she doesn't like fashionable parties?'

'When Grandmama decides on something, it's hard to refuse to do it. I think there was another reason for her going, but Grandmama didn't confide in me.' She didn't add that it seemed to concern her, for that might have sounded conceited.

'So Bea is not enjoying herself.'

'Not completely. She is enjoying the theatre and the opera, of course, but not so much the parties. As I could have predicted, if anyone had bothered to ask me!'

Mr Lanby had a lovely smile and he was listening to what she said with flattering attention. Several times, she found herself responding to that smile in kind. Once they had discovered that they shared a passionate love of riding, they spent the rest of the walk exchanging tales of their favourite horses.

When they got to the edge of the woods, however, Mr Lanby hesitated.

She paused beside him. 'Please come in and meet my grandmother.'

He looked ruefully at his clothes, which were covered in black smears from the digging, as well as dribble from the puppy, which was now chewing happily away at the remains of one of his coat buttons. 'I think I'd better not. I'm not fit to meet anyone, least of all your grandmother.'

'Oh, Grandmama won't mind that! And she'll wish to thank you for helping me.'

He shook his head, looking embarrassed, 'I – look, I'm afraid there's no way of hiding it, Lady Eleanor. I don't think I'd better come in at all. Lady Graceover was not on the best of terms with my parents and I rather think I would not be welcome in her house.'

'Oh bother, if that's not just like her!' said Eleanor. 'She has the strangest ideas of our family consequence and is forever snubbing perfectly nice people!' Now she would not be able to pursue his acquaintance. And she liked him, as well as feeling herself under an obligation to him. 'Perhaps when she hears how you've helped me, she'll change her mind?' she ventured hopefully.

He shook his head. 'I doubt it. The – er – disagreement is of long standing. I have not, of course, met the lady myself, but from what I hear of her...' Delicately he left the sentence unfinished, but shook his head again.

Eleanor's face fell. 'I'm afraid you're right. If she really takes a dislike to someone, Grandmama rarely changes her mind. And that includes their family as well.' She sought desperately for a reason to detain him. 'But how am I to let you know about Snowy? You'll wish to know how he goes on, won't you, since you saved his life?'

He looked down at her with an even warmer smile than before, for she was as transparent in her intentions as any schoolgirl. In fact, she was one of the most delightful girls he had ever met, fresh, un-spoiled and pretty as a picture. 'Yes, I would rather like to know how he goes on,' he agreed with a straight face.

She started fiddling with the puppy's ears, wondering what to suggest.

He was more experienced. 'Do you often go for walks in that part of the woods, Lady Eleanor?'

She dimpled at him, quick to seize on this opportunity. 'Oh yes, most afternoons, sir, for Grandmama likes me to get some exercise and she takes her nap then.' She did not notice that she was standing close enough for the puppy to chew on one of the ribbons of her dress. In fact, they had both quite forgotten the little creature.

He repressed a sudden urge to kiss the dirt-smudged bloom of her cheek. 'Exercise is very good for one,' he agreed. 'I'm fond of it myself.' He decided that her eyes were

143

hazel shot with gold and that her hair was the most beautiful shade of russet brown that he had ever seen.

She looked down, a little afraid of the sensations rising within her. What the Dowager had actually said to her was, 'Get out and use up some of that dratted energy, child, for I can't abide people who fidget in their chairs! Got for a walk or a ride or whatever you young people like to do nowadays! And take that silly creature with you!' Lady Marguerite only tolerated the puppy's presence because she realised how much Eleanor was missing Beatrice. She assumed, quite wrongly that her grand-daughter would take a servant with her as well on these outings.

'The strange thing is,' Mr Lanby said, his eyes dancing, 'that I'm rather fond of walking myself, and my hosts also like to rest in the afternoons. An amazing set of coincidences, is it not?' In fact, his hosts had been friends of his parents, not of himself, and were nearer to the Dowager's age than his own.

'Then I shall see you tomorrow, perhaps?' she said, toe tracing patterns on the ground as she avoided his eyes.

'I very much hope so. It's much more

pleasant to have someone to talk to. I have no acquaintances in the immediate district as yet, apart from my host and hostess. Perhaps you could tell me what there is to see, the best rides and so on? I don't know this part of the world at all and I shall be here for a week or two.'

She beamed at him, with no attempt to conceal her pleasure at the prospect of his company. 'Oh yes, I'd be happy to. It's a good time of the year for walks and we have some very beautiful rides in the district – if you don't mind a few fences, that is?'

'One can always dismount and find a gate,' he said, keeping his face straight.

She gave the most delicious gurgle of laughter. 'Now you're teasing me. A man who knows as much about horses as you do can have no fear of jumps!'

What a beautiful child she was! 'We must pray, then, that it doesn't rain.'

She examined the sky anxiously. 'N-no. I don't think it will. I shall ask my groom when I get back. Anders always knows about the weather.'

Her realised that he must take his leave before anyone from the house saw them together, reluctant as he was to part from her. Don't get in too deep, you fool, he said to himself. You've only just met her. And they may already have plans for her, plans which don't include someone like you. Aloud he said, 'Take your dog then, Lady Eleanor. There! Will you be all right now?'

'Oh, yes. It's not far.' It was really strange, she thought as she watched him walk away, the sensation she had felt when his hands touched hers. As if something was making them tingle. She stayed at the edge of the lawns, watching him until he was out of sight, her head on one side, her thoughts in turmoil and the puppy's wrigglings completely ignored.

Anders would in no way hear of Eleanor going off on her own to meet a strange gentleman the following afternoon, and he scolded her at length for having gone for a walk without an escort. 'I thought you'd grown out of such tricks, miss!'

She tilted her head at him. 'Really, Anders, you can be as stuffy as Grandmama sometimes! She explained carefully the delicate situation between Mr Lanby's parents and the Dowager, but Anders was not to be moved.

'That's as may be, Lady Eleanor, but it still doesn't make it right for a young lady like you to go out for walks on her own and well you know it! Downright disobedient, you were today, and what her ladyship would say if she knew about it, I dread to think! And as for talking to strange gentlemen and arranging to meet them again! What's the world coming to when a young lady in your position does such things? Her ladyship would have a fit if she knew about it.'

She laid her hand on his arm, coaxingly, afraid that he would tell her grandmother. 'We only talked a little, Anders. Mr Lanby is a very well-mannered gentleman. No one, absolutely no one, could have faulted his behaviour. And if he's staying at Treevers Hall, well, he must be respectable, because they're as ancient and as fussy as Grandmama!'

He folded his arms and shook his head in a way he had when he was displeased with her, but his words showed that he was softening. 'Well, you can do your talking in my company next time, or you'll not do it at all!'

She looked at him pleadingly, but could see no sign of him relenting further. 'Oh, very well!' she said crossly, then hesitated, before adding. 'Please don't tell Grandmama about Mr Lanby! You won't, *dear*

Anders, will you? You know how unreason-able she can be when she takes a dislike to someone's family!'

'I'll meet the gentleman first, Lady Eleanor, and then we'll see. If he seems res-pectable, and if you promise me faithful that you'll always take someone with you when you go to meet him, then perhaps, just per-haps, we need not inform her ladyship. But I'm making no promises, mind!'

She flung her arms round his neck and hugged him ruthlessly, in spite of his protests. 'You're a dear and I don't know what I'd do without you, Ander-Panders!' It had been her childhood name for him.

'Give over, do, Lady Eleanor!' he said, quite failing to conceal his pleasure. 'What would her ladyship say if she saw you a-hugging of me like that?'

'She'd say I was being over-familiar with menials and give me a scolding about what's due to my rank,' said Eleanor, pulling a face. 'But I don't care for such nonsense! Why, I've known you for longer than absolutely anyone else, even Bea, and if I can't hug you, who can I hug? And anyway, Grand-mama never comes down to the stables, does she, so we're quite safe?' She grinned at him cheekily and he shook his head at her again. A minx she was, a proper minx, he thought fondly.

He stood and watched her run back to the house, leaving the dirty, yawning puppy sprawled across his boots, chewing at their laces. When she had disappeared, he bent down to pick the little animal up, sighing. Not for him to question her ladyship's ways, but it was a shame to keep a lively lass like Lady Eleanor shut up away from other folk of her own age, a proper shame, it was! He would not allow his young lady to make any unsuitable acquaintances, but well, it would not hurt to look this fellow over. If he was visiting the local gentry, he must be a gentleman himself, and Lady Eleanor had been moping about since Miss Beatrice went up to London, in spite of that dratted puppy.

He would also make enquiries among the other grooms in the district about this fellow, just to check up on him a little. The servants' grapevine could yield a lot of information that would have surprised the gentry. He picked the puppy up, looked it in the eyes and shook it slightly. 'See what you've done now, little fellow! You'd better watch your step in future, you had, or I shall give you a proper scolding!'

It yelped softly and tried to nick his nose.

He cradled it against his chest. 'Well, let's go and take a look at that leg of yours, shall we? And I daresay a bowl of bread and milk wouldn't come amiss, either, eh?'

One rough fingertip trickled it gently under the chin, but a frown remained on his face as he ministered to the puppy. He wished very much that Miss Beatrice were here to take charge of the situation. She'd know what was right, would Miss Beatrice. He had a great deal of respect for her judgement. The idea of this strange gentleman taking advantage of Lady Eleanor was a worry nibbling away at his dreams that night.

SIX

Johanna continued to puzzle over Bea's future while the pair of them worked their way through the rest of the eligible families on the list. It was not hard for Johanna to ensure that Bea got to meet and inspect all the unattached scions of those particular lines who were presently in town. Some of them were quite young gentlemen, some of them not so young. The Dowager's instructions specified that all unmarried males up to the age of forty were to be considered.

'Does Mama honestly expect,' Johanna asked in frustration, 'that a girl as young as Eleanor would consider marrying men of thirty or older?'

Beatrice gave it as her opinion that the Dowager expected everyone in her household to do exactly as she told them, whether it was reasonable or not. 'But I don't think Eleanor will obey meekly in something as important as this,' she added thoughtfully. 'She tries to avoid clashes with my aunt, but they're very alike and she has a will of her own.'

The two ladies sat down after each meeting with a new gentleman and compared notes in a way which would have horrified most of the young bloods concerned. Beatrice, unwilling to discuss her own suitors, was happy to discuss at length those who were under consideration for Eleanor. She set ridiculously high standards, though, in Johanna's opinion, and she was more concerned with the gentlemen's personal qualities than with their station in life and their fortunes.

Johanna was absolutely certain that her

mother would not approve of that. She herself did not quite approve, either, for although she would never have wished any young woman to be coerced into an unhappy union, she had been brought up to regard marriage as too important a business to be entered into on a whim or for mere affection. One needed to look for security and breeding in a potential spouse, both for oneself and for one's children. But nothing she said could make Beatrice change her mind.

'What about young Lord Haroldby?' she asked one day, feeling that the latest candidate had been better than most.

'Young Lord Haroldby,' declared Beatrice, lips curling scornfully, 'is far too daredevil in his ways and will undoubtedly kill himself within the year. Did you see that horse he was riding in the park yesterday?'

'Well...'

'And someone told me that he is ready to accept any wager, *any wager,* and even makes it a point of honour to do so, however ridiculous.'

'Well, most young gentlemen are like that. He'll settle down, once he's married.'

'I have no wish to see my dear Elenaor widowed young. He won't do.'

Johanna rolled her eyes towards the ceiling.

One afternoon a few days later, they were chatting over a cup of tea. 'What about the Barrowdene heir?' Johanna asked, reaching for an apple tartlet. 'He's rather handsome, don't you think?'

'If you like that sort of pale good looks. He's just aping Lord Byron, of course. No originality. And he's far too moody. That would never do for dear Eleanor. She's the most affectionate, sunny-natured person in all creation, and his moods would drive her to distraction in a fortnight.' She saw Johanna begin to open her mouth and said savagely, 'And if you're going to ask about the Honourable Fergus Kitsby, I have to tell you that I've never been so disappointed in anyone in all my life.'

Johanna could only sigh. The Honourable in question was making more than one young debutante act in a foolish way and dampen her pillow with fruitless yearning. 'He's thought to be very stylish,' she ventured.

'When seen at a distance on the dance floor or at the theatre, perhaps.'

'And his smile is...'

'Is pleasant enough, I will admit, but that

makes it all the worse when you find out that he has shockingly bad breath. He must eat nothing but onions! *And,*' she paused before revealing the most dreadful tidings of all, 'he not only wears padded shoulders, but also a padded chestpiece to his coats.'

'It's all the crack for gentlemen to have a broad silhouette!'

Beatrice was not to be moved. 'Falsity is a thing which I've always abhorred.' The padded chestpiece had been the final straw in a long list of disappointments. She could just imagine what her aunt would say about that!

'You know, you're far too demanding, my dear. You really can't condemn a man because he wears padding! He's only following fashion, after all.'

'Well, I find I don't care for that particular fashion. I think that *that* amount of padding reflects a deviousness of spirit. And I care too much about Eleanor's happiness to entrust her to a man who presents a false appearance to the world. Who knows what lies and deceits he would practise upon *her* after they were married!'

Beatrice was looking so worried that Johanna was moved to hug her. 'Look, love, forget about Eleanor for a while! Let's turn our thoughts to your own future. You really should be trying to find a husband for yourself. You'll never have a better opportunity.'

Beatrice shook her head, lips tightly pursed. 'I don't matter half as much. There's plenty of time for me to find myself a husband later if I so choose. And I do keep it in mind, I assure you. I've already come to the conclusion that I'd prefer to marry someone who lives mainly in the country. That's enough progress for now.'

She fiddled with a fold of her skirt. 'I know you think I'm being over-fussy, but your mother is very concerned about Eleanor's future, and it's not good for her to worry so. I just can't settle to thinking of myself until I have something sorted out about Eleanor. I promised Aunt Marguerite faithfully that I wouldn't fail her in this.' She had still not confided in Johanna that the Dowager's health was deteriorating fast, and this omission was preying on her conscience, for it never seemed to occur to Johanna that anything *could* happen to her mother. Or to most people. Satherby without her ladyship was unthinkable.

A spirit of mischief made Johanna say, 'Then it must be Justin Serle, after all, Bea! His cousin is his heir now that his brother's dead, and Luke Serle is a gambler and a reprobate. I never thought to see Serle brought to the altar, but Luke's doing it.'

Beatrice shrugged and opened her mouth to introduce some other subject of conversation.

'I wonder whom he'll choose,' Johanna continued quickly, giving her no chance.

'Choose?' exclaimed Beatrice, in tones of great disgust *'Choose!* You speak as though he had only to signal and any woman would come running!'

'Well, he is very eligible, you know, not to mention handsome. He's been much sought after for years.'

'Handsome is not everything!' declared Beatrice, nose in the air. 'Lord Serle is not as arrogant or trivial-minded as I had thought at first, I will admit, but although he may not be a dandy, he *does* spend a lot of time on his appearance and his conversation is frequently very frivolous. I cannot approve of that.'

'My dear, what do you expect him to talk about at social gatherings? Riots and mayhem?' Johanna was watching her closely. 'I like Justin. I'm not sure he'd make an excellent husband for Eleanor. He's always very pleasant company and you must admit that he's an exquisite dancer.'

Beatrice could not disagree with that. She had had the pleasure of dancing with Lord Serle at many functions recently and found him the perfect partner. Their steps matched so well that they did not have to think what they were doing, but could float away on the music. She did not, however, intend to admit that to Johanna. 'Well, I think a man of his station and wealth ought to set a better example than he does! Fancy being famous for the way you tie your cravat! Or for the horses you drive! A man should stand on his own merit, not that of his animals! And him a great landowner, too! He should spend more time thinking about his tenants and about – about agriculture!'

'Oh, pooh! Agriculture! Who cares about things like that when one is in London? Agriculture is a topic only suitable for the country, and then in very small doses. The land he owns may be what makes Justin so eligible, but to be prosing on about turnips would make him the greatest bore in town!'

Beatrice resolutely held her tongue, wondering now if she was being deliberately provoked.

'Anyway,' Johanna continued airily, 'Boris tells me that Justin *is* seriously looking for a wife, so I can't help being interested in whom he'll choose. He's been impervious to a whole series of beauties who've set their caps at him over the years.' She looked sideways at Beatrice and asked casually, 'What do you say to the Metterleigh heiress? She might do for him, don't you think?'

'*Her!* I never met such an empty-headed featherbrain in all my life! She hasn't got an idea in her head, apart from clothes and dancing. Even Lord Serle wouldn't choose someone like her!' Eleanor sighed and added half to herself, 'Though I dare say he'll choose someone just as frivolous and they'll spend their time discussing clothes and the latest gossip and how to tie cravats!'

'You're very scathing. Don't you like Justin?'

'Oh, he's very pleasant, I agree,' Beatrice was avoiding Johanna's laughing, knowing eyes, 'and my aunt thinks a great deal of the family, but well,' her fingers were fiddling with a ribbon now, 'there's not enough substance to him. Though I do owe him a debt of gratitude, for he did save me from those men, and I try not to forget it. But I couldn't think a man like him right for Eleanor, whatever you say. And I couldn't marry a man like him myself!'

She tossed her head at the mere idea, which no one had raised but herself, then changed the subject hurriedly. 'Did I tell you how well poor Tom is doing? He's found himself respectable lodgings and his cough's completely gone.'

Johanna raised here eyes to heaven and let the question of matrimony drop. She had come to the conclusion that her cousin Beatrice, for all her sweet biddable ways, was as stubborn as the Dowager underneath. Beatrice would do anything Johanna wished, go anywhere, meet anyone, sing to them, smile at them all sweetly, but afterwards, she found fault with every gentleman to whom she had been introduced on her own behalf and she refused to consider seriously any of those listed for Eleanor.

After a few fruitless weeks, they had to take Jennice, who was still staying with her mother in town, into their full confidence. She entered into the search with real enthusiasm, for it was just the sort of thing she enjoyed. She was in blooming health, but was beginning to show her condition, so she was making the most of what she called her last weeks of freedom to indulge in a frenetic round of social engagements and shopping, her only concession to Boris's worries about the baby being to take a nap every afternoon. And that, she confided in her mother with a grimace, was only because she really did feel sleepy.

Jennice studied the Dowager's list carefully, for she naturally knew all the families on it. 'Hmm,' she said after a while, 'Grandmama is very choosy, isn't she? I can think of a dozen other gentlemen I'd have considered eligible – and several of them have nice juicy fortunes – yet they're not on her list. And why on earth have you crossed Justin's name off, Bea? You can't accuse *him* of being too fat or of having a sniff, and he certainly doesn't pad his coats! Why, he's easily the most eligible bachelor in town! I did consider him for myself at one time, you know, but I decided that he'd be just too hard to manage. My dear Boris suits me much better – though even he's getting a bit troublesome since we started having the baby!' She shook her head and repeated in puzzlement, 'Why *did* you cross Justin's name off, Bea?'

'Beatrice thinks he's not serious-minded enough,' explained her mother, eyes twinkling.

'Justin?' Jennice screamed with laughter. 'Oh dear, I must tell him! Such criticism has never been offered to him in all his life before! Most people simply *fawn* over him, whatever he says to them!'

'Don't you dare say a word to him!' commanded her mother. 'You'll only embarrass poor Beatrice and you'll put him in a fit of temper. In fact, if you breathe a word of any of this, we won't let you help us at all.'

Jennice pulled a face. 'Well, I wouldn't really tell him, of course I wouldn't – I'm not rag-mannered – but I can't help wishing I could tease him just a little about it.' She sighed with regret at the delicate prospect of giving Justin Serle an unanswerable set-down, for he was always teasing her and usually won their verbal bouts. After a few minutes' more perusal, she handed the dog-eared sheet of paper back to Beatrice. 'What are you going to do if you can't find anyone suitable?'

'I don't know. You've no idea how I worry about that! I've met everyone on the list who's in town. I can hardly go round the countryside knocking at the doors of the rest of them, can I?'

Jennice's eyes narrowed and she began to chew her fingertip. After a moment she took back the list abruptly. 'Let me see this again, Bea.' She studied it with a frown, counting something on her fingers, then she looked up at them with a triumphant smile. 'I have an idea! A *brilliant* idea! Mama, you can't say that Beatrice is enjoying her Season, can you? Even though she's setting a new fashion in her own quiet way, I never saw anyone so uninterested in parties and balls. She might just as well not be on the market.'

'Don't be vulgar, dear!'

Beatrice flushed. 'Oh, surely my feelings don't show so clearly! I thought that I'd...'

Jennice grinned. 'They may not show to others, but *we* know you a little better, my dear and *we* hear what you say *after* the parties.'

Beatrice turned to her kind hostess. 'Johanna, it's got nothing to do with you or your hospitality, really it hasn't! You couldn't have been kinder to me! I'm just– I'm not cut out for this sort of life. I prefer life in the country and – real things.'

Johanna nodded gloomily, but reached across to pat her hand reassuringly. Bea's feelings about life among the ton were more than obvious to her! I know, love.'

'Well, then,' said Jennice, positively beaming at them, 'no less than three of the families listed here live near us, well, near enough to visit occasionally, and I know half a dozen other eligibles in our district alone who might suit Bea, even if Grandmama would not consider them good enough for the Last of the Graceovers. And Boris is growing so impatient for me to return home,' she sighed, 'that I suppose I'll have to go soon – but – well, it might not be so bad if I had some company. Why don't you and Bea come back to Lymbsy with us, Mama? Stay for a while. I'll engage to introduce Bea to *dozens* of eligible gentlemen!'

Johanna looked at her thoughtfully, then eyed Beatrice sideways. What Jennice had not mentioned was that Melborough Park, the Serle demesne, was the next estate to Lymbsy. It would be very interesting to see whether Justin followed them there. And how Beatrice reacted to that. 'Why not?' she asked lightly. 'What do you think, Bea? You keep saying that you're not fond of town life. We could go and spend a week or two with Jennice if you like.'

'Oh, I'd love it!' Anything to avoid returning to the Dowager as a failure. The last letter from Satherby had contained a very sharp query as to why none of the gentlemen on the list had yet been invited to the Abbey, not to mention why Beatrice had done nothing about herself, when Johanna reported a considerable interest being shown in her.

'We'll do it, then!' said Johanna, who intensely disliked country life, but who intended to see how this comedy played itself out. They set out within the week, an impressive cavalcade consisting of a carriage large enough to carry four persons in extreme comfort, followed by the servants in another vehicle (including an excited Lizzie, who had to be told twice by Johanna's Sarah to sit still and behave like a proper lady's maid before she would stop jiggling around). Their baggage followed in two more vehicles.

Lord Newthorpe chose at the last minute to ride, with his groom in attendance, which Jennice said was a blessing, as he was the most fidgety traveller in the world and never stopped criticising the way the vehicle was being driven.

The journey into Hertfordshire was neither long nor onerous. Jennice sometimes talked as if she lived in a remote country, but actually, she was within three hours of the metropolis, and a pleasant drive at that, thought Beatrice. And how pretty Hertfordshire was! She settled back to enjoy the scenery and allowed the others to gossip as they wished.

Lymbsy Hall was a modern Georgian residence, built by Boris's grandfather, who had indeed made his fortune in tea, to the Dowager's everlasting disgust, but who had also been the younger son of a perfectly respectable old country family. Boris's parents were now dead, but he had inherited their love of Lymsby and was a passionate landscape gardener when he was not hunting or shooting or fishing. Luckily for marital harmony, the neighbourhood was not short of families with whom the young couple might enjoy a varied social life and there were some very reasonable assembly balls held in a nearby town – if, Jennice said scathingly, one took one's own party and kept away from the local shopkeepers. In fact, young Lady Newthorpe was not nearly as short of entertainments as she would have had them believe, but she seemed to Beatrice to be quite terrified of her own company.

Beatrice, shown up to an elegant suite on the first floor, looked out over the beautiful parklands that surrounded Lymsby and drew in a deep breath of pleasure. Surely no one could object to her going for long walks here? She could take Lizzie with her, if necessary. She had by now grown quite fond of the girl and had to admit that it did make life easier to have a maid looking after one's clothes. In fact, it was an absolute necessity when one was involved in as many social events as she had been over the past few weeks. She had already decided to ask Lizzie to stay on with her after her return to Satherby. The Dowager would not object, for she had been telling Beatrice for years to get herself a proper lady's maid.

From what Jennice had been planning on the journey, there would seem to be no shortage of company at Lymbsy. This had caused several squabbles with her husband before their departure, for he seemed to think she should take to her bed immediately upon arrival and stay there until after the baby was born. Not until Johanna assured him that it was better for pregnant ladies' health if they took regular exercise, did he desist from his plans to immure Jennice in an overheated chamber, with several attendants at hand to prevent her from lifting even a fingertip.

No, Johanna had agreed patiently, when he went on to discuss what kind of exercise would be safe, riding would not at all suitable, but regular walks in the grounds would be just the thing for a lady in a delicate condition. And definitely, regular outings in the carriage to visit their friends and neighbours, for this would prevent the expectant mother from moping. Moping was the worst possible thing for ladies in Jennice's condition.

Beatrice was obliged to hide her smiles as Boris was manipulated into agreeing to everything Jennice wished to do, while Jennice happily promised not to do anything she disliked, such as tramping through the woods.

Jennice in the country was far more to Beatrice's taste than Jennice in the town. They found interests in common in the running of a country mansion and the vagaries of servants, though Jennice's staff seemed to give her far more trouble than the servants at Satherby had ever given Beatrice. But then, Jennice seemed to thrive on crises, and if one were lacking, she was quite capable of creating some drama or other to add interest to the day.

The first week they were a little short of company, Jennice said, and she sulked until Boris coaxed her out of her mood with the gift of a pretty new bracelet. Their social life developed rapidly after that, however, and soon there was a dinner party somewhere most evenings, or an impromptu hop, or an al fresco luncheon, or some other outing to enliven the day. These casual country affairs were much more to Beatrice's taste than the London events had been, but even so, she would have welcomed fewer of them and ventured to say so.

Jennice looked at her reproachfully. 'Have you forgotten that one of the reasons we came here was so that you could meet some of the gentlemen on your list?'

Beatrice blushed and admitted that she had.

'Don't you want to find yourself a husband?'

'Not – not someone only interested in my dowry.'

'Well, what do you think of the Vicar as a potential husband? For you, of course, not for Eleanor. He'd be too old for her.'

Beatrice realised guiltily that she had nearly forgotten her mission for a few days in her enjoyment of the beautiful country-side around Lymbsy. Her heart sank and she felt suffused with guilt. She was letting her aunt down once more. 'I'm sorry, Jennice. I was just enjoying being in the country again.'

'And the Vicar?'

'No. I think he's too old for me as well, and besides, I've never liked men with red hair.'

'No. It makes their complexions seem so washed-out, doesn't it? Well, it does if they're as pale as he is.'

It was several days before Beatrice found out that Serle was their closest neighbour.

'Be good to have old Justin back,' said Boris one day over breakfast. He beamed at them all impartially, in the best of humours because one of his mares had just foaled.

Beatrice's fork froze in mid-air and Jennice nudged her mother. 'Lord Serle? I was not aware – does he live nearby, then?'

'Next estate, if you don't count the Thatchburies,' said Boris indistinctly, his mouth full of kidneys. 'And we don't.'

'I – hadn't realised.'

'How did you find out he was expected, Boris dear?' asked Jennice, all sweet innocence. She had already known about it, but had kept quiet, wishing to see Beatrice's reaction when surprised by the news. She would have preferred Justin to have just walked in on them. The shock of that would surely have caused Beatrice to betray her feelings. 'I had heard nothing.'

'Oh, my groom heard it from one of his friends yesterday evening in the village alehouse. Justin will probably be here today or tomorrow.'

'Is he – has he brought anyone down with him?' asked Johanna, since Beatrice was re-arranging the contents of her plate very carefully and showing no sign that she wished to participate in the conversation.

'Don't think so. He doesn't usually. But I daresay he'll hold a dinner or two while he's here. He'll probably ask you to act as his hostess, as he usually does, Jen, but *you* could do it instead, Mother-in-law. Jen'd better not tire herself.' Jennice pulled a face at him behind his back. 'We can get some shooting in,' he went on, still full of enthusiasm. 'Justin's woods are overrun by pigeons and he'll have to do something about them or they'll be moving into my coverts next!'

Beatrice grimaced, thus betraying the fact that she had been listening. She could never bear to see birds slaughtered, though the Dowager always gloated over the size of the bag and allowed favoured persons to shoot at Satherby during the hunting season, as long as they stayed elsewhere. She detested holding house-parties.

Boris turned to his guests. 'You ladies may care to take a gun out with us one day, eh?'

Jennice looked pained. 'Not in my condition.'

'I wasn't considering you,' her spouse told her. 'It's obvious *you* couldn't do anything like that now.' His eyes rested gloatingly on her stomach.

'Yes, I'm far too big to go clambering through the woods, aren't I?' Jennice looked down at her increasingly pear-shaped figure with immense satisfaction. 'It's growing so quickly, I wouldn't be surprised if I didn't have twins.'

Boris paled. 'Twins! Have you asked Dr Sangler about that?'

'Good heavens, no! He's such a fussy old bore I don't mean to see him for ages yet.'

'What? Jennice, I gave strict orders that you were to consult him as soon as we returned!'

Jennice tilted her nose at him. 'Well, I haven't, my lord, so there! I feeling perfectly well, thank you, and I don't *need* to see a doctor!'

Boris stood up and thumped the table, shooting forgotten. 'In that case, I shall fetch him myself this very day and ensure that you *do* see him! If you think, madam, that I'm going to risk the life of my unborn son...'

'Or daughter,' put in Johanna, unable to resist the temptation.

'Daughter!' exclaimed Boris, scandalised. 'We Newthorpes *never* have daughters first, I'll have you know, or we haven't for generations! Though I wouldn't put it past *my* wife to do so, if only to spite me!'

Jennice tittered. 'Well you can't do anything about that, my lord! Even a Newthorpe can't dictate the sex of his offspring.'

'No, but I *can* see that you get proper attention while you're in this condition. And what's more, if you try to avoid seeing Dr Sangler, I shall bring him to your room and hold you down myself while he examines you.'

'You wouldn't *dare!*'

'Oh, wouldn't I?'

'I shall lock the door.'

'I'll break it down.'

Tears suddenly sparkled on Jennice's lashes. 'Oh, how can you be so cruel to me?' she asked, her voice breaking pathetically as she spoke. She sniffed delicately and applied a lace handkerchief to her eyes.

'Cruel? Is it cruel to care about your welfare?' demanded her outraged husband, not to be cajoled when such an important matter as his unborn son was at stake.

Johanna nudged Beatrice and they left the two lovers to continued their quarrel and reconciliation in peace and comfort. However, for once Boris had his way, and the afternoon saw the doctor's gig bowl up to the door and that gentleman shown straight up to my lady's bedchamber by Lord Newthorpe in person. Nor did the door prove to be locked.

'Well,' said Johanna, smiling broadly, 'I never would have believed it! She doesn't usually give in so easily.'

'I think I'll go for a ride,' said Beatrice, who had been pacing about restlessly for a while. After receiving yet another peremptory missive from Satherby, she was suffering from another wave of guilt at having failed to comply with her aunt's dying wishes. She had dutifully allowed Jennice to introduce her to several gentlemen from the district, whom Jennice described as eligible, and these had included two more from the Dowager's list.

But Lord Whinber's son and heir had proved to be a red-faced, hunting-mad country bumpkin, however elevated his breeding, and he was so lacking in sensible conversation that he would have driven Eleanor or herself insane within an hour. And as for Mr Standrey, well, he might look better when he had recovered from his cold, but she doubted it. A nose as large as that could not but intrude upon one's marital life.

A groom saddled a horse for Beatrice and would have accompanied her on her outing, but she waved him away. 'I'm only going for a gentle ride round the home park,' she said. 'You needn't come with me.'

'But his lordship said that...'

She stared at him frostily. 'I do not wish for company, thank you, Semsby. I've already stated that I shall be staying within the park. I can't possibly come to any harm there!' As Eleanor had suspected, Beatrice could be very determined when she really wanted something and what she desperately needed at the moment was some time alone to think through her predicament, for predicament it was undoubtedly becoming.

She rode slowly along the leafy alleys cut through the woods by Lord Newthorpe's father to enhance the pleasures of just such outings. Gradually the peace of the day seeped into her and made her relax. She was quite content to let the horse pick its way slowly over the soft earth so that her own thoughts could drift miles away.

After a while, she came to a quiet pool which she had not seen before. It was so beautiful there in the glade that she decided to dismount and sit for a while on a fallen tree trunk. But her cogitations led nowhere. She could make no sense of her own feelings or come to any conclusion about a suitable husband for Eleanor.

Suddenly she realised that the sun was appreciably lower in the sky than she would have expected and was startled, when she looked at the little fob watch pinned to her waist, to realise that she had been out for over two hours. They would be starting to worry about her and probably the groom would now be in trouble on her account, which was quite unfair, because he had tried to do his duty. Hastily she put on her gloves and picked up her riding switch.

The mare was contentedly munching the lush grass at the edge of the clearing. She strode over to the animal and set her foot in the stirrup, but just as she was starting to mount, two birds screeched out of the undergrowth, right under the mare's hooves and the animal reared in fright. Unprepared, Beatrice lost her grip on the reins and was thrown to the ground, for which Anders would have scolded her soundly. Always keep hold of the reins, Miss Beatrice, he had told her times without number. Whatever happens, don't let go of your horse's reins!

She tried to get to her feet and found that she had twisted her ankle and could not stand. She could only sit and watch the mare vanish from sight, still galloping and whinnying in protest at the birds' unprovoked attack. She tried to get up again, but finding that she could bear no weight on that foot, she had to sink back to the ground, grimacing in pain.

'How stupid of me!' she exclaimed aloud. 'Any idiot knows to keep hold of the reins!'

'Careless indeed,' a voice informed her. 'You seem to be remarkably prone to accidents, Miss Dencey. And it appears that I shall need to rescue you once again.'

She blushed scarlet in embarrassment. 'Oh no! Lord Serle!'

'None other,' he said lightly. 'And as I am myself on foot, I'm afraid I can't rush off to catch your horse for you. How came you to be riding alone? I'm sure Boris would not have sanctioned that. He is, if anything, overprotective of his womenfolk.'

She could feel that her colour was still high and she did know how to look him in the face. 'I – I wanted to think about something, so I dismissed the groom.' She moved incautiously and winced.

He came over and knelt beside her. 'Where are you hurt?'

'I think I've sprained my ankle.'

'Let me see it.'

She drew back. 'It's just a sprain. There's nothing you can do about it.' The thought of exposing her leg to his gaze made her feel suddenly shy.

'I hadn't expected *you* to be missish,' he said sarcastically. 'Let me see it. You may have broken something.'

'Of course I haven't! I'd know if it were broken. It's just a sprain, I tell you!'

'Nonetheless, I prefer to check for myself.' He held her hand aside and raised her skirt to remove her boot.

'I can remove the stocking myself, thank you.' She could feel herself blushing furiously.

He grinned and averted his gaze, then, when she said she was ready, he turned to examine her ankle. With gentle fingers he palpated the joint, which was swelling rapidly. 'No, you're right. It's not broken. But I think we should bathe it in cold water or it will continue to swell and become very painful. There's a rock by the pool that you can sit on while you dangle your foot in the water. Put your arms around my neck.'

For a second time, she found herself scooped up in his arms and pressed closely against his chest. She was again filled with an inexplicable urge to nestle against him, but she resisted it sternly. The pain of being set down made her draw in her breath and forget such fancies.

'It'll feel better when you've held it in the water, I promise you,' he said encouragingly. He helped her to immerse her ankle, noting that she was rather pale and seeing how she gritted her teeth as the coldness of the water began to penetrate. 'It's uncomfortable, I know, but there's nothing quite as good for a swelling. Bear with it for a while, if you please.'

She nodded, unable to speak, for the ankle had started throbbing and shock was now setting in. 'I'm all right,' she managed after a while.

'Of course you're not, woman! That ankle must be hurting abominably and will hurt more when we try to move you. What were you thinking of to ride so far on your own! You're in my grounds now, you know, not Boris's!'

'I'm sorry if I'm trespassing,' she flung back at him. 'I hadn't realised that this was *your* land. There aren't any signs, you know!'

'The people who live round here know the district and Boris's guests don't usually behave in such a bacon-brained manner.'

She burst into tears.

He was horrified. How could he have bullied her like that when she was in pain? Without thinking of the consequences, he took her in his arms. 'Ah, don't cry, Bea! I'm sorry! I didn't mean to rip up at you.' Neither of them noticed till afterwards that he had used her pet name.

'I don't – don't normally cry like this,' she gasped, leaning against him. 'I despise women who cry for nothing. It must be the – the shock.' She tried to stop, but the effort only made her sob the harder, her worries having left her feeling very low. And the embarrassment of having to be rescued a second time by Justin Serle made everything worse, somehow, for she had crossed his name off her list and he didn't deserve that insult.

When she had eventually hiccupped to a halt, still leaning against his chest and now clutching his sodden handkerchief, she tried to apologise for making such a fuss, but he

179

would not hear of it. 'It's my fault. I was far too sharp with you. I should have realised that you were in a state of shock. And that ankle must be hurting like the devil.'

'It is,' she said in a small voice. 'But it's my own fault, after all.' Getting myself into a scrape again! What an idiot he must think me! She scrubbed furiously at her eyes.

'Let me look at that ankle again.' He removed her foot gently from the water and held it in his warm hands. The swelling had gone down, but the leg was blue with cold and the swollen ankle was now showing signs of bruising. He could hear her teeth chattering as well.

'How on earth are we to get you back to Lymsby?' he worried, putting his arm round her.

She laid her head on his shoulder, giving in to temptation just for a moment. 'I – I can perhaps limp along – if you will help on one side and if you can find me a piece of wood to lean on.'

'Impossible! That ankle will start throbbing once you begin moving around. We'll have to get you back to Melborough, but it's too far for me to carry you, so I must seek help. Mrs Powis will be delighted to have someone to fuss over.'

'Mrs Powis?'

'My old nurse. She's a tartar, but she's excellent with all manner of hurts. I gave her plenty of practice when I was young, as she never lets me forget. Now, let me help you away from the water. Your ankle's quite blue.'

The rock was small and he was already balancing on its edge where water had dropped from her foot. As he helped her to rise, his foot started to slip and before either of them could do anything to prevent it, they had both fallen into the water. Luckily, it was only a couple of feet deep at that point, but as they both surfaced, Justin was betrayed into a curse and Beatrice started spluttering and splashing.

He caught hold of her and held her head above the water. 'Are you all right? My God, I'm so sorry! Of all the clumsy things!'

She was shaking in his arms.

'Beatrice! Miss Dencey! Please – it's all my fault – but I'll soon get help and...' He broke off as he realised that she was laughing, not crying.

'Look at us!' she spluttered. 'Did you ever see anything as ridiculous? Your hair, my lord, is covered in green weeds.'

The humour of the situation began to

dawn on him. 'And you, Miss Dencey, are also wearing a coronet of weed.' Chuckling, he knelt in the water beside her and helped her move the worst of the clinging green strands.

When he offered to pull her up, she burst out laughing again. 'I hardly dare! We'll probably wind up under the water again! Oh, oh, my stomach hurts from laughing!'

Very gingerly, he helped her to stand, then assisted her out of the water and back to the rock. It was at that moment that he was astonished to realise that he loved her. How splendid she was! What other woman would have seen the humour in this situation! What other woman was so brave! Unlike the rest of London society, he had sincerely admired the way she had chased the thief, though he had not known how to tell her that, and had scolded her from sheer relief that she was not injured. Now he realised that one could enjoy sharing one's life with a sensible woman like this. That one's life would, in fact, be blighted beyond redemption if one did not spend the rest of it with her.

When she was safety on the rock, their laughter tailed off as they both began to shiver. 'I think it'll be best if I run back to the house for help, rather than trying to assist you to limp along,' he said anxiously. 'You mustn't jolt that ankle. Will you be all right on your own for a few minutes?'

'Yes, of course.' The ankle was throbbing again, she was freezing cold and her urge to laugh had completely faded, but she saw no use in complaining. She watched him run off through the woods, her expression bemused. Why had she crossed him off the list? He would make an excellent husband. Strong, intelligent, possessor of a good sense of humour, well-born. No wonder the Dowager had put him near the top of her list!

The memory of his laughing face as they sat spluttering in the water made her smile briefly, then the smile vanished as she realised that she herself found him extremely attractive. That he was the one man she had met whom... No! She mustn't think of that! She had no right to love him! He was Aunt Marguerite's first choice for Eleanor. He was the only one on the list whom she herself could think at all suitable as a husband for her niece. She had made a promise to the Dowager, a most sacred promise to a dying woman. She drew a deep breath and began to give herself a severe talking to. By the time he returned with help, she was able to face him with reasonable calm, glad that her shivering hid any personal feelings she might betray.

SEVEN

The day following Snowy's adventure produced a sunny sky over Satherby and, since the Dowager was still a little lethargic, no impediment arose to prevent Eleanor from keeping her rendezvous with Mr Lanby. She dressed in one of her prettier gowns and spent a long time fussing over her hair, till her maid, Betty, started to stare at her. There were not likely to be any callers. Why was Lady Eleanor dressing in her new things?

After lunching with her grandmother, Eleanor found the time passing very slowly, and it seemed ages until she could reasonably set off for a stroll, without appearing too eager for another meeting with *him*.

She went down to the stables to meet Anders, as arranged, not daring to disobey him, for she knew that he would keep his promise to inform the Dowager if she tried to leave him behind. Anders always kept his word. She spent a minute or two petting Snowy, who was still convalescing in one of the stalls, then suggested that they leave.

He shook his head, sighing. 'Aye, Miss Eleanor, I suppose we can. But I doubt I'm doing the right thing, letting you go.'

'You said you would!'

'Yes, well, that was yesterday. Today, I'm not so sure. Mind now, if I say we're to return, then you must do as you're told straight away. Promise me, now!'

'Well, I will promise, but only because I'm sure you will find nothing to object to in Mr Lanby.' She danced along the woodland path beside him, chattering happily about the progress of the latest foal and speculating as to how soon Snowy's leg would be better. 'Perhaps I can take him up to the house when we... Oh, Mr Lanby! You quite startled me!'

He had been waiting for her for over an hour, angry with himself at how afraid he was of missing her. When he saw that she had brought a guardian with her, he looked towards the man, who was obviously a servant, questioningly. Servant or not, the fellow looked disapproving.

Eleanor blushed and stopped dead, for some reason finding it difficult to breathe properly. After a minute, she found her voice again and said off-handedly, 'This is my groom, Anders, come to keep an eye on me.'

Anders was at his most wooden. 'You'll pardon me for coming along, sir, but Lady Eleanor's grandmother doesn't normally let her walk in the woods alone.'

Mr Lanby nodded, his bearing rather stiff. He had no right to feel so disappointed. It was only to be expected that she would have her guardians.

'I have to look after her,' Anders continued, 'for she's as trusting as a kitten.' His tone seemed to imply that he was not.

'Well!' exclaimed Eleanor. 'What an awful thing to say, Anders!'

'It's true, though, miss. Anyway, I'll just drop back a little and leave you two to choose the path. It's a pleasant day for a stroll, and no mistake.'

When Anders was out of hearing, Mr Lanby laughed softly. 'So you brought your guardian angel along to look me over!'

'I didn't bring him,' she said, a trifle sulkily. 'He insisted on coming. The trouble with servants who've known one all one's life is that they never recognise when one has grown up.'

'I have a butler who feels just the same about me.'

Her dimples returned. 'Well, then, Mr Lanby, you will understand my feelings precisely. Now, there's a very pleasant walk through the woods to the right here, which comes out at a bit of high ground. You get a lovely view of the village from there. It's one of my favourites.'

When they got back to the stables, she turned to Anders and demanded, 'Well, don't you think he's a proper enough gentleman?'

'He does seem pleasant enough. But proper is as proper does. You still can't go a-meeting him on your own.'

They met four times that week, with Anders accompanying them doggedly each time, in spite of all Eleanor's protests and pleading. The two of them were totally at ease together, as if they'd known each other all their lives and Anders could see the love growing between them as if it were something tangible, even if they themselves did not yet realise it. It kept him awake at night worrying, for he knew that her ladyship had had some disagreement with the gentleman's family. Yet they did seem made for each other. Even an old bachelor like him could sense that.

But how was he to find out the gentleman's circumstances? How to check up on his background? Mr Lanby was, as he had said, staying with the Treebys, and the groom there said he was as pleasant a gentleman as you'd ever wish to serve. But what about his home, his finances? How to check on those?

Anders half suspected that there was some sort of secret. Mr Lanby would talk about his home and his horses all afternoon, but every now and then he caught himself up in the middle of a sentence, and he seemed to avoid giving place names. Perhaps he was an adventurer. Perhaps he was setting a trap for Lady Eleanor, who had a fortune waiting for her. These suspicions faded when they were with Mr Lanby, for a more open-looking face you couldn't wish to find, but they came back to Anders in the dark hours of the night.

When Anders laid his fears before Eleanor, she sat frowning and pulling Snowy's ears. 'It can't be anything bad,' she said eventually. 'I just *know* it can't, Anders!'

'Miss, please be careful!'

'Yes. I will. I'll be very careful indeed, Anders.' Then she walked away, heedless of the little animal left whining behind her. Which was not like his Lady Eleanor at all.

On the tenth day of this idyll, Eleanor and her young gentleman went again to the look-out and sat there on the grassy knoll, staring across the valley. 'I think,' he told her, 'that I had better confess something to you, Lady Eleanor, before we – before this – goes any further.'

Her heart jumped in her breast, for he looked so serious, and a cold feeling crept up her spine. She knew she could not bear it if anything were to separate them now.

She said, more calmly than she felt, 'Go on.'

'I – I haven't been quite honest with you.'

She could only stare at him. 'About what?' she asked, her voice tight with tension.

He took a deep breath. 'My name isn't Christopher Lanby.' He seemed to be having trouble continuing.

'What is your name?' she prompted at last.

'It's – Crispin.'

She gasped aloud. It was such an unusual name that she asked immediately, 'Not Crispin Herforth?'

'Yes. I'm afraid so.'

'But – why did you not tell me that at once? Why do you need to go incognito?'

'I wanted to see my inheritance. A few weeks ago your grandmother invited me to stay, to get to know Satherby. A rather condescending letter. It made me angry. I refused. Then I was sorry. So I asked the General if I could come and stay with them – very quietly. I wanted to find out if I had sunk myself beyond reproach in your grandmother's eyes.'

'Grandmama was very angry that you didn't come.'

'Yes. I meant her to be. I grew up hearing how fearsome she was, so I didn't want to risk a snub, or worse, in a house which would be mine one day.'

'No. I can see that. She can be – well, difficult. Is that all you have to confess?'

'Isn't it enough?'

'Well, it doesn't seem so very terrible to me.' Her voice was gently teasing, but her expression became serious again as she added, 'I guessed that something was worrying you. You've been a bit quiet the last day or two.'

'Yes. And you've been very patient with me.'

'I was waiting for you to Reveal All,' she

said demurely, eyes glinting at him, 'as they do in novels.'

'Minx!'

She smiled. 'So now we know where we stand, do we not – Crispin?'

'Not quite. There's something else which needs settling.' He pulled her into his arms and kissed her soft lips, as he'd been longing to do since the first day they met. And she made no protest, only raising one hand shyly to stroke the blond curls on his temples.

'I think I've fallen in love with you, Lady Eleanor Graceover,' he said abruptly, holding her slightly away from him.

'I should hope so, Mr Herforth.' She smiled at him, not shyly, but showing her own feelings quite openly. 'I wouldn't like to think that you kiss all the young ladies you meet in the woods in that manner.'

For answer, he kissed her again and growled in her ear, 'Nor you all the gentlemen you meet!'

All thoughts of flirtation had left her mind days ago and she was more concerned to verify the exact moment when he had known that he loved her and to tell him how she had known it as early as the second day when she saw him waiting for her in the woods.

Neither of them remembered Anders, sitting on a fallen log some twenty paces behind them and he remained where he was and did nothing to stop them kissing one another. His mind was greatly relieved, for he had unashamedly eavesdropped upon their conversation, not moving away until he had heard who Mr Lanby really was. The heir to Satherby was not out to gain Lady Eleanor's fortune, for he would have a greater one himself. And Mr Herforth was a nice young gentleman, just right for Anders' young lady. The only thing that really worried Anders was what the Dowager's attitude would be to this whirlwind romance. Her ladyship had a lot of high-nosed notions about what was right and even Anders knew that she did not consider most gentlemen remotely worthy of her granddaughter.

Still, he thought to himself, chewing on the stem of his unlit pipe, it was Miss Eleanor's happiness that mattered most, not that of a bossy old woman nearing the end of her life. And so he would tell the old lady if she made trouble for these two – even if he lost his place because of it.

The lovers spent a precious half-hour telling each other exactly what had made them fall in love and stealing a kiss or two.

It was Eleanor, who was nothing if not practical, who said thoughtfully in the end, 'I don't know what Grandmama is going to say to this, Crispin. She's not all that fond of your family, you know, and she intends me to marry a Person of Rank.' She pulled a face at the thought. 'In fact, she's been discussing marriage settlements secretly with the lawyers for months and I'm sure that's why she's sent poor Bea up to town, to look over the eligible gentlemen.' She spoke rather hesitantly, for he had said nothing of marriage yet, but surely, she thought, she could not be mistaken.

The arm around her tightened. 'I must see her ladyship at once, then, and tell her how we feel. You will marry me, will you not, my dearest girl? I don't think I could bear it if you didn't.'

She smiled radiantly at him. 'Well, of course I will, silly, but,' the smile was replaced by a puckering of the brows, 'I don't think you should go and see her! Not just yet, anyway!'

'Why ever not? Surely, even your grandmother will see that it's a very good solution to the inheritance problem? It'll keep her precious Satherby Abbey in the family.'

'Well, Grandmama's not quite like other people. She may approve eventually, if things are put to her in just the right way, but there again, she may not. You can never tell. She rarely changes her mind about people. She's *very* set on me marrying someone of whose family she approves. And she most definitely does *not* approve of your family!'

'She'll have to be made to change her mind.'

'Oh, yes, I know that! But it's better to tread softly with Grandmama and let her think that something is her own idea. You could never *force* her to do anything. And besides, Crispin, I don't want to make her unhappy. She's very autocratic, but I love her dearly and I won't have her hurt.'

He sighed. 'What do you think we should do, then?'

She frowned and began tracing lines on the back of his hand. 'I think you should go home and write to her that you've been thinking things over. Say that you feel she was right about your coming to Satherby.'

'Will she still welcome me?'

'I don't think she'll welcome you at all, but she'll probably wish you to come. She thinks that you'll need showing how to run the estate.'

194

'As if I haven't been running my own for years!'

'Oh, how many years? I had thought you were only twenty-four.'

'I am, but my father was never much interested in it, so I've been more or less managing things since just before I was sixteen. Go on, my love. Once I get here, what must I do? Pretend to fall in love with you all over again?'

'Under no circumstances! Grandmama strongly disapproves of people who fall in love. She considers it vulgar. We must pretend to be completely indifferent to one another.'

'I don't think I can!' He gave in to the temptation to plant a kiss on the tip of her nose and that led them to a more lingering embrace.

When they had drawn apart again, she said severely, 'You *must* hide the fact that you love me, Crispin! Believe me, I know her! The important thing is to persuade Grandmama that you're worthy of inheriting and that you really will care for the estate. We can't confuse her by falling in love! She'd likely send you away again and tell you to wait until she's dead to claim the estate.'

'She sounds ferocious.'

'She is! Make no mistake about that, Crispin! She's had a hard life, lost nearly everyone she loved, and yet she's survived and not given in to her grief.'

'You're very fond of her, aren't you?'

She looked rather surprised. 'Yes. Yes, I am. I hadn't realised quite how much until now. I should hate to be at odds with her.' When she looked at him, she had tears in her eyes. 'And especially just now.'

'Why now, my precious one?'

'Because I think she's not got long to live. She seems so much weaker lately. She hasn't said anything to me, she never would! But you can tell by the way she moves and by how long she has to rest if she does anything. It would be nice to do everything in a way that would please her. Do you understand?'

'Of course I do, my darling. And it will be no trouble to show her how much I care about the estate. It's the loveliest place I've ever seen. I'm afraid you've agreed to marry a man who's a farmer at heart. I could only be happy in the country, dealing with the land. So if you hanker after the fashionable life…'

'Oh, no! I'm a country girl, too. Both Bea and I are. And I love Satherby.' She looked at him shyly. 'That's not why I want to marry you. I would want to, anyway, but it does make things quite perfect.'

'Then we're particularly well suited.'

She looked at him, her head on one side. 'You know, it may sound strange, but I understand now what Grandmama meant when she said that marriage was a business arrangement. I don't think I could easily contemplate marriage with a man who wished to live in a town, however handsome he was, or however engaging his ways. Does that sound mercenary?'

'No, for I feel the same. That's yet another reason why you're the perfect woman for me. But Eleanor, you're mine now and I mean to keep you. Whatever I have to do to achieve that, I shall! Even if your grandmother doesn't approve. Even if it means abducting you!'

She could see that he meant every word and a thrill went through her. 'Good,' she said, somewhat breathlessly. 'Because I don't think you'll really like what I'm going to say.' She was back to tracing patterns on his hand.

He raised her chin and kissed her very gently on the lips. 'Tell me, then, adorable one.'

'Well, while you're learning about the

estate, I think I must find an unsuitable gentleman to fall in love with, or at least, to flirt with.'

He stiffened. 'No! I couldn't bear that! Even in pretence.'

She sighed in exasperation. 'I told you you wouldn't like it. But it's the only way I can see, so you'll just *have* to bear it.'

'But why?'

She answered him obliquely. 'Crispin, I'm the only person in the world, I think, who can manage Grandmama, and even then, it doesn't always work. She's a very powerful person. Bea just does as she's told, well, most of the time, anyway. Even the lawyer is terrified of Grandmama! And the bailiff creeps in like a mouse to see her. So you absolutely *must* promise to do as I say, because it's our only hope. I won't go against her dearest wishes, not openly, anyway. And I won't make her final years unhappy. She's had too much unhappiness in her life already.'

'You have no doubts about marrying me, though?' he asked, surprised to see how resolute she could be when she wanted something. He began to wonder whether she did not, perhaps, resemble her grandmother more than anyone realised. But, he decided, she was not the only one with a stubborn streak. He was bred from Graceover stock, too. He would go along with what she said for now, even though he did not like it, because she really did know Lady Marguerite better than he did. But he would not follow along meekly forever. If he had to, he'd whisk her away and make a runaway match of it.

'Of course I don't have any doubts! I always know my own mind.' She beamed at him.

'I think I must be the most fortunate man on earth.'

She sighed in delight. 'That's the nicest thing anyone ever said to me! Say some more!'

He spent the next ten minutes telling her how beautiful she was and how he longed to make her his wife, and she sat with her head against him, chuckling with delight at his more outrageous compliments. This dalliance was much superior to the behaviour of the heroes in novels, who never seemed to have any sense of humour at all, just as her Crispin was superior to the various counts and marquises about whom the tales were built. He might not be tall or wonderfully handsome, but somehow he was just what she wanted.

EIGHT

By the time Justin's grooms had helped him to carry Beatrice back to the house, her teeth were chattering uncontrollably, in spite of the horse blankets he had snatched from the stables to wrap around her. Mrs Powis had been warned to prepare for them and the minute they entered the house, they were both swept away to their separate rooms, where hot baths and even hotter cups of chocolate awaited them.

Mrs Powis's curiosity about this mystery lady led her to tend the stranger herself and to abandon her nursling to the ministrations of his valet, who had a little more sense in his head than most men. She was determined to find out why her master was meeting unknown ladies in the woods. She hoped desperately that the lady would prove firstly to be a lady and not the other sort, though surely Master Justin would not bring such a creature back to a respectable household, and secondly, she hoped that the lady was indeed the object of his affections.

It was more than time Master Justin settled down, and so she had been telling him this age, but had he listened? No! He had always been a stubborn one, always. When his brother was alive, it hadn't mattered quite so much whether he married early or not, because there was an heir to the name, but since Waterloo and poor Master Peter's death – those French monsters had a lot to answer for! – the question of marriage had grown urgent, as even Master Justin had begun to admit at last.

A very little time with Beatrice served to convince Mrs Powis that this was no scheming harpy, but a sensible lady with whom it was a pleasure to chat, or it would have been had the lady not been shivering so violently. When the shivering continued, Mrs Powis decided to reinforce the cup of hot chocolate with a brandy toddy made to her own special recipe. This she insisted on Beatrice swallowing, in spite of the latter's protests.

'Never shall I forgive myself,' declared Mrs Powis, arms akimbo, 'if I let you catch a chill when it can be prevented! Nor will his lordship forgive me, either! We have a better regard than that for our guests at Melborough.' She spoiled this high moral tone by adding, 'Though how he came to be so clumsy as to tip you both into the water, I can't imagine! I thought he'd grown out of all that sort of thing years ago! I shall have a word or two to say to him later about it, I promise you!'

In vain did Beatrice protest that she was not given to taking chills and that she hated brandy.

'Nor should I think you're given to immersing yourself in cold water on a nasty chilly afternoon, miss! Middle of May and still as cold as February!' declared Mrs Powis, eyes alight with the fervour of one who has devoted her life to looking after the health and welfare of others. 'We'll not risk the chill, thank you, so I'd be grateful if you'd just swallow this down while it's hot.'

'I really don't need…' began Beatrice.

Mrs Powis swelled up to twice her normal size and asked, with awe-inspiring dignity, whether miss did not trust her to know her own business.

Quite cowed, Beatrice swallowed the toddy and allowed herself to be tucked into a bed which had just been thoroughly warmed by a bustling maidservant with a red-hot warming pan. She lay luxuriating in the warmth, and before long, she had fallen asleep.

'Ah,' said Mrs Powis to herself, as she prepared to leave the room a few minutes later. 'That's more like it, miss!' She turned to the maid who had been posted discreetly in a corner away from the bed and whispered, 'You just continue to keep an eye on Miss Dencey, if you please, Mary, while I check that his lordship is all right.'

Mary nodded and sat down, eyes glued to the recumbent figure in the four-poster. Satisfied that Miss Dencey was in safe hands, Mrs Powis strode along the corridor to find out from his lordship just what this lady was doing in his grounds and just what *he* had been doing to tumble them both into the water. Downright careless, that was! But Miss Dencey didn't seem to bear him a grudge for it, which was a good sign.

When Beatrice awoke, it was to find the room half in darkness and Johanna sitting by her bed. 'Oh! I didn't mean to fall asleep!' she gasped, still confused.

'If Mrs Powis meant you to sleep, then you had no choice, believe me! How are you feeling, my dear?'

'Embarrassed!'

Johanna chuckled. 'You do seem to make a habit of getting into scrapes and letting Serle rescue you from them, don't you?'

Beatrice was thankful that the room was dark enough to hide her blushes. 'It was an accident. And it was *his* fault we fell into the pond, not mine!' Honesty compelled her to admit, 'Though it was my stupidity which left me without a horse.'

Johanna just chuckled again.

'I'll get up at once,' Beatrice said, very much on her dignity. 'I'm sorry to have caused all this trouble. I don't know why they sent for you! I'm perfectly all right now, except for my foot.'

Johanna's hand pressed her back against the pillows. 'Don't you dare get up!'

Beatrice stared up at her in astonishment.

'If you set one foot out of that bed, you'll bring Mrs Powis's wrath down upon me and that's a fate I'd rather escape, thank you very much! I have strict instructions to send for her the minute you wake up and not to let you leave the bed under any circumstances until she's seen you, and, my dear, I dare do nothing but follow those instructions to the letter. No one who is at all acquainted with Mrs Powis would dare to defy her!'

'But Johanna, I'm perfectly all... Wait! No!'

But it was too late. The bell had been pulled and not long afterwards, Mrs Powis surged in. She immediately felt Beatrice's forehead and tutted to herself. 'Just as I thought! Feverish!'

'It's nothing! I'm perfectly all right, Mrs Powis! Really I am!'

'Ah, but will you be all right tomorrow and the day after if we let you get up so soon?' demanded the domestic tyrant. She turned to Johanna. 'It's a good thing you sent for your things, your ladyship, so that you can stay with us tonight. Miss Dencey will be sneezing by tomorrow and in no fit state to travel, if we don't look after her now.' She tucked the blankets firmly around Beatrice.

'The master's just the same,' she went on. 'Falling into a pond on a freezing spring day at his age! And pulling a lady with him. Did you ever hear of such a thing? Mind you he was even worse when he was a boy! If he couldn't find something to fall into, he'd find something to fall out of, with equally bad results. He'd only to see a tree to want to climb it! The number of times I've had to nurse him better, and Master Peter with him, it's a wonder I'm not in my grave already!'

'This time it was partly my fault,' ventured Beatrice, not wishing Lord Serle to bear the blame. 'I'd sprained my ankle and he said it would be better if it were soaked in cold water.'

'His lordship has already explained what happened, thank you, miss. And I'll say to you what I said to him: it's one thing to soak an ankle – which I'll allow is the sensible thing to do – but it's quite another to soak the whole person! Master Justin loses any sense he ever had when he gets near water. I couldn't count the number of times he's fallen into that very same pond and come home covered in nasty green weed. You should hear what the laundry-maid said about the state of his shirt today!'

'Yes, but it was only because he was trying to help me,' pursued Beatrice, still trying to protect her rescuer, 'so we can't blame him!'

'I personally would like to know why you were out riding without a groom in the first place,' said Johanna. 'What on earth got into you today, Bea?'

'I wanted to have a think. Somewhere quiet.'

'Well, Lymsby's anything but quiet today, I'll grant you that!' Johanna sighed.

Mrs Powis cleared her throat and when she had their full attention, she gave her instructions. 'I'll go and order a light meal now, Lady Ostdene, and then when she's eaten it, every scrap, if you please! Miss Dencey is to go to sleep again. There's nothing like a good long sleep for reducing the chances of a chill.' She marched majestically out of the room, tossing over her shoulder, 'By tomorrow, she'll be able to limp on that foot, if she does as she's told now, that is, and I'll see that a walking stick is found to help her.'

When she had left, Johanna put her hand over Beatrice's. 'My dear, I'd be *very* obliged if you did as you were told while we're here.'

'But Johanna...'

'Please! You see, Jennice is going to ask for Mrs Powis's help with the birth, so we want to keep her in a good mood. She may be expecting twins, you see. Jennice, I mean! The doctor thinks her very large, for this stage. And twins do run in the family.'

'Oh!'

Johanna looked at her pleadingly. 'Mrs Powis is the best midwife hereabouts, even if she does terrify everyone.'

Beatrice sighed. 'Very well, then.'

After a few minutes, there was a knock on the door and Lizzie appeared with a tray. 'Mrs Powis says you're to eat every scrap, miss, and not to get out of bed till the morning. She'll be along in a few minutes with a draught for you to take.' The maid had wasted no time in taking Mrs Powis's measure and had, like every other servant in the house, taken her orders literally.

Beatrice muttered to herself, but gave in and did as she was told. She was surrounded by well-wishers who were driving her mad and who were all in league against her. Besides, she did not wish to cause more trouble for his lordship, with Mrs Powis or with anyone else. Just as she was drifting off to sleep, she jerked upright and clutched at Johanna's arm. 'Johanna! You won't tell anyone about this, will you? Promise me! I couldn't bear people in town to know!'

'My dear girl, surely you've lived in the country for long enough to realise that we won't *need* to tell anyone anything. The news will already have wafted around the district and it'll creep across the county of its own accord.'

'Oh dear! You're right. It's just the same at Satherby.' She stared into the distance, then said firmly, 'That settles it, then! I'm *not* going back to London! I can't face what people will say after having *him* rescue me again! I just can't!'

'We'll think of something,' Johanna said

soothingly. 'There's no need to do anything drastic. Now, go to sleep, do!'

In the morning, Mrs Powis reluctantly conceded that the danger of chills had probably been averted and that Beatrice could leave Melborough, though not until after luncheon, when the day would have warmed up a little. In this, she was somewhat compromising her honesty as a nurse, for she wished to give his lordship time to speak to the lady in private, if that was in his mind, and from the tone of his voice when he spoke of Miss Dencey, she rather suspected that it was. And about time, too!

Beatrice found her ankle to be much better and, after a little practice, she learned to move around quite easily with the stick. When she limped downstairs, she was met by her host, with a rueful smile on his face. 'I hope you're all right now, my dear Miss Dencey? I'm so sorry for tipping you into the water! Terrible thing to have done. Can you ever forgive me?' His smile was particularly warm, begging her to share the joke.

Aware that both Johanna and Mrs Powis were watching them with great interest, Beatrice said stiffly. 'It was an accident. I'm perfectly all right, thank you, Lord Serle.'

Justin also became aware of the two pairs

of eyes observing them closely and said in a low voice, 'Look, I need to talk to you, Beatrice. Alone.' He raised his voice and added, 'Would you like to come and see my father's collection of oil paintings, Miss Dencey?'

After a moment's hesitation and a doubtful look at her cousin, Beatrice agreed, accepted his lordship's arm and allowed him to escort her along to the gallery. Now would be as good a time as any to cut short his attentions. She would then have the satisfaction of knowing that she was doing her duty to her aunt and it must be just the aftermath of the accident which was making her feel like bursting into tears.

When Mrs Powis came back a little later with a light snack, she found only Lady Ostdene sitting thoughtfully by the fire.

'They're still looking at the paintings,' Johanna said, yawning and stretching like a well-fed cat. 'I don't think we should disturb them just yet.'

'We'll leave them to come back of their own accord, then,' Mrs Powis agreed. 'If I might ask, your ladyship, has Master Justin known Miss Dencey for long?'

'For a month or two. They seem to get on well, most of the time, anyway, but don't get your hopes up, Mrs Powis, for there's been nothing lover-like about them so far. In fact, they very frequently quarrel.'

Mrs Powis's eyes brightened. 'That's a very good sign, if you don't mind me saying so, your ladyship. He would never be happy with a lady who didn't stand up to him. He's like his father there.'

'We'll see. My cousin's not really interested in finding a husband for herself, though it's what her aunt, my mother, you know, wishes.'

'Even better. Master Justin detests it when ladies chase after him.'

Johanna shook her head but did not try to explain the situation more fully. It was far too complicated and she wasn't even sure that she understood it all herself. She had begun to wonder whether Bea was hiding something from her.

With any other couple, she would be sitting here expecting an interesting announcement. With Bea and Serle, she had no idea what to expect. She looked at the clock, sighed and decided to take advantage of the moment. 'I shall be glad to return to Lymsby, for I don't mind telling *you*, Mrs Powis, that my daughter has just been informed by the doctor that it's possible she may be carrying twins.'

Mrs Powis beamed at her. 'Why, that's wonderful! Master Boris *will* be pleased!'

'Well, I'm not sure Jennice feels the same way! She's not the maternal type, you know.'

'That's because she's not had the chance yet. You make sure they put the babies into her arms the minute they're born. It never fails!'

'The trouble is,' Johanna confided, 'the doctor also said that Jennice has been racketing about too much and that she's to take things more easily from now on. Boris is determined to see that she does, and the two of them have done nothing but squabble ever since the doctor left. I think, between you and me, that poor Jennice is very upset about the prospect of twins. She doesn't wish to give up her parties and her socialising with her neighbours.'

'She needs a good talking to! The idea of it, and her probably carrying The Heir to Lymsby! Still, I daresay she'll grow accustomed. Women usually do. Do twins run in your family, then?' Mrs Powis had a hungry expression on her face.

'Oh yes! In both the Dencey and Graceover lines. My grandmother had twins.' Johanna's face clouded. 'Unfortunately, they both died, poor things. But I believe there have been several other cases with happier outcomes. We'd have to ask my mother for details. She knows everything about the family.'

'Twins do need careful rearing, that's for sure,' said Mrs Powis thoughtfully, convinced that no twins entrusted to *her* care would dare do anything but thrive. The knowledge that twins ran in the family made her even more inclined to favour Miss Dencey as a possible bride for Master Justin. She just hoped that he was seizing his opportunity and not messing things up. 'If I can be of any assistance to Miss Jennice…' she offered delicately, thinking that it might be useful to get in some practice.

'Oh, Mrs Powis, if only you would! I'm sure that with *you* to help her give birth and to look after them all afterwards, Jennice would cope very well. A stranger is never the same. The doctor is talking about bringing in a month-nurse from Watford, but how do we know what she'd be like?'

Mrs Powis nodded, seizing her opportunity. 'We don't know. And I shall be delighted to help, Lady Ostdene. Delighted!'

In the picture gallery, Justin was trying to

make the most of his opportunity. He looked at Beatrice, wondering how to start. Strange that he had thought her silly on first acquaintance! She was probably the most intelligent woman he had ever met. And the bravest. Not to mention being beautiful. And who else would have been able to laugh at their misfortunes yesterday? He wondered whether to press his suit immediately or whether he should try to lead up to the declaration with a few compliments. He felt horribly uncomfortable, nervous as he had not been since he was a callow young man. And Beatrice, who had a distant air, was not contributing much to the conversation, or even looking at him, which did not help matters.

When he suggested that it might be more pleasant to sit outside in the sunshine and offered her his arm again, she jumped back as if he were poisonous. 'Oh, no! Thank you, but I'd rather study the paintings.' She stopped in front of a landscape and perused it earnestly, though it might have been a page of algebraical equations, for all she noticed about it. 'Lovely,' she said in a faint voice and as he moved towards her, she passed hurriedly to the next.

'I'm glad you like them. We share several

interests, do we not?'

Her heart lurched at the warmth in his eyes. If only she did not – she would not allow herself to finish that thought. She stared at another blur of colour. She could hardly be so rude as to cut him short and flee to her cousin's protection, so she continued to move along the line of paintings, jerking on to the next every time he drew too near or took a deep breath, as if about to speak.

After a few minutes of this, a firm hand turned Beatrice round and she was forced to face him. 'I rather get the impression that you're trying to prevent me from speaking, Miss Dencey.'

Her face flamed. 'Oh, no, I – I just… I'm still feeling a trifle out of sorts. That's all. What did you wish to say to me?'

He tried to pull her towards him and she pushed him away quite roughly, letting her walking stick fall to the ground. 'Oh pray don't! We mustn't!'

He picked up the stick and handed it to her. 'Why must we not? I had thought that we were getting on well together. You've seemed to enjoy my company over the past few weeks. As I have yours. Even when I pushed you into the pool you didn't seem to hate me!'

'No! I mean, yes, but it's not right! We can't...!' She wrung her hands and turned towards him eyes so full of anguish, that he was startled into asking, 'have I offended you in some way, Miss Dencey?'

'No. Oh, no!' How could it offend her for a man like him to pay her attention? But she must not allow it! He was marked by the Dowager for Eleanor, he was the only one suitable on the whole list and if anyone deserved a good husband, Eleanor did. And she owed so much to her aunt, that she could not let her down out of sheer selfishness.

He looked at her earnestly. 'The last thing I wish to do is to distress you, Miss Dencey, but I thought this a suitable time to talk about ourselves. Perhaps, though, if you're still feeling a little under the weather, we should postpone our discussion until tomorrow?'

'Oh, yes! Yes, that's a very good idea!' She hardly knew how to stop herself from bursting into tears at the pain of having to prevent his proposal, and she found herself quite incapable of telling him to his face that she did not wish to marry him. She wished very much to marry him. 'I'm feeling a trifle dizzy. If I could just s-sit down and be quiet...'

'Certainly. There's a couch over here. Let me help you to...'

'No!' The violence of her rejection surprised them both. 'Actually, I'd – what I'd really like is to retire to my room, if you don't mind, your lordship. Mrs Powis was right. An immersion in cold water can lead to a chill. I must be a trifle – a trifle feverish.'

He knew that there was something wrong, but he did not feel he could press her just then, when she was looking so desperately unhappy. He could not forget the feel of her in his arms when they danced, the good sense of her conversation, the beauty of her eyes, a dozen things about her which had grown upon him gradually, so that he was now quite determined to make her his wife. He did not feel that she was indifferent to him, either. He had noticed the radiant smile when she first saw him across a room, and it revealed more about her true feelings than she realised.

Justin Serle had not expected to fall in love, not after all these years on the town, and he was feeling rather hesitant about it. Perhaps Beatrice was too. Perhaps that was it. She was older than most women looking at marriage and probably afraid of ridicule. Perhaps she had given up any thought of marriage and now needed time to grow used to the idea again.

For the moment, he could only escort her to her bedchamber and then go down to let Lady Ostdene know that her cousin was feeling unwell.

In her room, Beatrice threw herself upon the bed and burst into tears. A touch on her arm made her catch her breath on a sob and stare up at the worried face of her maid. 'Oh! Lizzie! I d-didn't see you.'

'Is there anything I can do, miss, anything at all?'

Beatrice shook her head. 'No. No one can help. Please, I can't talk about it. Will you just pack my things for me?'

'Are we leaving now, then, miss?'

'Yes. I – I can't stay here. He will... I must get away from him!'

Lizzie instantly determined to kill Lord Serle if he ever upset her mistress like this again.

'I think,' said Beatrice jerkily, 'I think it's time for me to return to Satherby. Lizzie, would you consider coming to work for me as my maid – permanently. I think we might deal very well together.'

Lizzie's face broke into a beaming smile. 'Oh, miss! Oh, I'd love to!'

'It'll mean moving away from London. I could never live in a city. I don't think I'll ever return.'

'Oh, I don't mind where I live, miss. It's the people as counts in life, isn't it?'

Beatrice's eyes filled again. 'Yes. The people.' And the main people in her life were, had to be, Eleanor, whom she had helped raise, and the Dowager, who had taken her in when she was destitute, and who had so little time left to live. Their wishes and their happiness were far more important than her own.

There was a knock on the door and Johanna poked her head inside. 'May I talk to you for a moment, my dear?'

Beatrice nodded dismissal to Lizzie and prepared for the first onslaught. She took the initiative by declaring her intention of returning to Satherby the very next day and refusing to give her reasons, or to explain why she had been weeping.

'But my dear, there must be something wrong. It must be Serle. How has he upset you?'

'Lord Serle? Upset me? Nonsense! Please don't think that! Don't ever think such a thing! He's been, he's been extremely kind to me. It's not him, it's me! I'm just home-sick. You know I don't like all this – this fuss and sociability. And I haven't really enjoyed London, either, though you've been quite wonderful to me!'

'But why rush off home like this? Why now?'

'I told you. I feel homesick. And as for now, well, now you have Jennice to look after. How proud you'll be to be the grandmother of twins!'

'Bea, dear...'

'Oh, Johanna, please don't try to stop me! I need to go home!' Tears welled in her eyes. 'Please, just let me go home!'

She sounded so agonised that Johanna stopped trying to argue. 'I don't know what's upsetting you, my love, and I'm not going to pry into your private affairs, but please believe me that if I can ever help you in any way, I shall be happy to do so.'

That started Beatrice's tears falling again and she threw her arms round her cousin and sobbed incoherently into her shoulder. But she still would not say what had happened between herself and Serle.

NINE

The carriage bowled smoothly along the highway in the early summer sunshine, but it might as well have been the middle of the night, for all that Beatrice noticed of the scenery.

Lizzie tried to make herself invisible in the corner so as to leave her mistress in peace with her thoughts. She did not know what Lord Serle had done to upset Miss Dencey, but whatever it was, he should not have done it, and the trouble must be his fault, because Miss Dencey was the kindest mistress as ever lived, and why she wasn't married, with a home of her own, Lizzie did not know, for she was as pretty as she was kind. All Lizzie did know was that she'd do her best to look after her mistress from now on, and heaven help anyone who tried to upset her!

When they arrived in Satherby village, Beatrice took a deep breath and turned resolutely to Lizzie. 'You cannot help but notice that I'm not very happy about things, and that it concerns Lord Serle. I'd be grateful, very grateful indeed, if you would not discuss my problems, not even to hint about things, with the other servants, Lizzie.'

'I hope I know how to behave better than that, miss.'

'Thank you.' Beatrice put her hands up to check her bonnet. 'Is it straight, Lizzie?'

'Just a minute, miss. Let me tie the ribbons again. There you are! And a proper treat you look, too.'

Beatrice nodded, totally indifferent to her appearance, as long as it was neat. She took another deep breath. From now onwards, she had to keep up a pretence of being glad to be home. No one must suspect that she had allowed her affections to stray where they should not. And whatever Justin Serle had thought about his feelings towards her, he would surely, once he met Eleanor, realize that she was a much more suitable wife for him. Beatrice did not try to smile, for she did not think she could manage that for long, but she tried for a pleasant expression and felt that she more or less succeeded. Watching her, Lizzie thought how strained and sad her mistress looked.

As the carriage turned into the driveway,

Beatrice put the conversation back on an impersonal level by explaining to Lizzie that Satherby had once been an abbey and that the ruins of the religious house were still there in the grounds.

'Ooh, miss, I hope there aren't any ghosts!'

Even Beatrice, with her broken heart, could raise a half smile at this. 'No, Lizzie. I don't think my aunt would allow them.'

When the carriage pulled up inside the front portico, she explained that Lizzie must follow her into the hallway and then wait there for Mrs Inchby, the housekeeper, to show her up to her mistress's room. Accommodation would be found for her later in the servants' quarters. 'I think you'll enjoy having a room of your own, won't you?'

Lizzie nodded. Not many mistresses would bother to explain what was expected like that or worry about whether you would be comfortable or not. She looked around, her eyes wide open to take in everything, determined to do credit to her new mistress. And she would die a thousand deaths before she'd say a word about how things stood. She suspected, as did Johanna, that Miss Dencey's heart was not untouched by Lord Serle, but for some reason her mistress considered it unsuitable to marry him, or perhaps he had not asked her. He had definitely upset her. Anyway, nothing was to come of it, so that was that. Lizzie's lips were sealed.

The front doors were so enormous that Lizzie could not help staring up at them in awe. Then Borrill, the butler, appeared, flanked by two footmen. Lady Marguerite preferred to live in an outmoded state and still employed several footmen, though the fashion for menservants was starting to pass. Lizzie clasped her hands in front of her, which Sarah said was the best thing to do with them if you had nothing to hold, and bobbed a quick curtsey when introduced to Mr Borrill. He was younger than Mr Moreton and looked a lot friendlier, but you could never tell.

Beatrice was just turning to go to her grandmother's suite, when there was a shriek of joy and a girl in pink almost tumbled down the stairs in her haste to fling herself into Beatrice's arms and pelt her with questions.

That would be Lady Eleanor, Lizzie guessed, the one Miss Dencey had brought up, the one she was so fond of. She watched with interest as the two ladies embraced, seeing a distinct resemblance between them: both tall they were, with lovely hair, a pleasure to dress, with those figures. When the younger woman gestured towards the stairs, Miss Dencey shook her head and they went off in the other direction. Didn't want to be alone with her yet, in Lizzie's opinion.

An older woman in rustling black, with a massive key chain at her waist came round the corner and made straight for the newcomer. Lizzie bobbed another curtsey, just to be safe, and waited to be instructed. The woman looked her up and down with a shrewd expression on her face. That one won't stand no nonsense, Lizzie decided.

'I'm Mrs Inchby, the housekeeper.'

'Yes, ma'am.'

'You're Miss Beatrice's new maid, I believe? Lizzie, isn't it?'

'Yes, ma'am. Lizzie Hulls. And I used to work for Lady Ostdene before Miss Dencey took me on, ma'am.' She knew that housekeepers preferred staff who had been with the family for a while. In some country houses, only relatives of staff or offspring of tenants on the estate could get jobs at all.

The housekeeper's expression relaxed slightly. 'Our Miss Johanna, we still think of her as. Is she well?'

'Oh, yes, Mrs Inchby, very well.'

'And how long did you work for her?'

'Since I was fourteen, ma'am. Eight years. I started off as a housemaid, but her ladyship's maid, Sarah, has been training me up for a lady's maid and now I'm to work for Miss Dencey.'

'We call her Miss Beatrice here.'

'Yes, ma'am. I'll try to remember that, ma'am.'

'Well, you seem to know your manners. Are you good at your trade, Lizzie?'

Lizzie hesitated, then decided that the truth would be safer with this woman. 'I'm still learning it, ma'am, to tell the truth, but Miss D – Miss Beatrice seems pleased with my work and I'll do my best not to let anyone down, I'm sure.'

Mrs Inchby nodded again. She had already guessed that the girl was not a properly-trained lady's maid. She was too cheerful and honest. Ladies' maids often had an exaggerated notion of their own worth, which was probably why Miss Beatrice had chosen this one, because likely she just wanted someone cheerful and pleasant to look after her clothes. 'Well, Lizzie, I'll take you up to your mistress's rooms now and you can unpack her things while I'm having a bedroom prepared for you. We're well housed here and well fed. The family looks after its own, so see you serve them well in return. And if you have any problems or questions, come to me with them.

'You'll take your meals at my table, of course, with the upper servants, not in the servants' hall. We dine at seven, just after the family. If you get hungry before then, someone in the kitchen will find you a snack. I'll send one of the housemaids up with a cup of tea for you now, and she can show you where everything is. Or perhaps Lady Eleanor's maid might be better, if she's free. Her name's Betty. I think you two will get on well. You're much of an age. She grew up on the estate, of course, as did most of us here.'

Lizzie followed Mrs Inchby upstairs sedately enough, but her heart was singing inside her narrow chest. To eat with the upper servants at the housekeeper's table! That was a step up in the world for her and no mistake! She was very impressed by the size of Satherby, but was amazed at how old its furnishings were. You'd think they could afford new curtains and some more modern furniture! As for the suits of armour, they fair gave her the creeps, for they looked ready to leap out at you. And it wasn't very nice to stick swords and spears all over the walls, was it? Plain unfriendly, if you asked her.

Downstairs, Beatrice was endeavouring to answer the questions her aunt threw at her. She thought she was doing quite well, but after a while, Lady Marguerite dismissed Eleanor and demanded to know why Beatrice had returned so unexpectedly.

'I was homesick, Aunt Marguerite, and I think I've completed your commission. And though I haven't found a husband for myself – well, I just wanted to come home. I'm not sure I'm the marrying kind.'

'Hmmph!' The Dowager's shrewd old eyes rested on her for a moment, but she did not press the point just then. 'What about the chit, then? Whom have you decided upon?'

'I thought Lord Serle. He is most superior in every way to the other gentlemen I met.'

'Aha! I thought he would be! Good stock, the Serles, except for that worthless cousin of his, and *he* must take after his mother's side! Pity young Peter Serle got himself killed at Waterloo. Why they didn't execute that murderer, Bonaparte, when he started all the fighting up again, instead of sending him to live in comfort on another of those islands, I'll never know. He'll find some way of escaping again, mark my words!' She sat back and looked smugly at her niece. 'That's why I've already invited him down for a visit.'

'Who?' Beatrice was still thinking of Bonaparte.

'Serle, of course!'

Beatrice's face turned chalk white, but her aunt's eyesight was not good and the old lady did not notice.

'I didn't want to wait any longer. You were shilly-shallying about. So I took matters into my own hands. He should receive the invitation today. I sent one of the grooms across country with it. I don't trust those mails. Never have. I knew Serle's grandmother quite well, you know, we came out together, but she didn't make old bones, poor Elizabeth. Knew her son, too, Serle's father. And his mother.'

Beatrice swallowed hard. 'Well, then, we shall have to see whether he accepts your invitation. He's a rather, well, an independent sort of person. It might have been better to have asked Johanna to sound him out first, so that he'd know why he was being invited.'

A smile flickered over the Dowager's face. 'Oh, I think he'll come! And I'll tell him why he's been invited once he's met Eleanor and I've had time to look him over myself. But what about you? Why have you not got yourself engaged? Wasn't the dowry enough?'

Beatrice blushed bright scarlet. 'It was *more* than enough! Far too much for me! They, some of the men were only interested in the money. I just didn't, I don't think, I...' She fumbled to a halt for a moment, then pulled herself together and said bluntly, 'Aunt, I tried, I really did, but you know I never liked the idea of your buying me a husband. It makes me feel very uncomfortable. And besides, I don't think I wish to marry. I think I'd prefer to remain single.'

'Hmm. We'll see about that. But not now. You look tired, girl. That's what London does to you. Too many late nights and too much racketing around. I must say you're well turned out, though. That colour suits you. Trust Johanna for that.' She studied her niece's face. 'We'll discuss your future another time, Beatrice. Oh, before I forget, how's that younger daughter of Johanna's? Breeding, ain't she?'

'Yes. And the doctor told them, just before I left, that she was probably expecting twins.'

'Twins, eh? Good girl! That's doing your duty with a vengeance.' She chuckled at the thought. 'Of course, they run in the Grace-over family. And in the Denceys, too.'

'Good heavens!' said Beatrice faintly. 'Both of them!'

'Oh, yes. Good stock on both sides. Mind, twins do give you a bit more trouble, so Johanna's right to take care of Jennice.'

'That's another reason I thought it best to leave. Jennice needs her mother just now. Her husband, Boris, gets quite dictatorial at times, and they argue, and well, I thought it best to leave them to themselves.'

'Hmm. The Newthorpes always were autocratic with their women. Handsome family, but I don't like the connection with trade. Jennice will have to put her foot down with him. I wouldn't allow a husband to treat *me* like that.'

'Jennice doesn't, that is, she manages him fairly well, but she's not quite herself just now.' She looked her aunt in the eyes and added, 'The main reason I came back, though, was my own – my homesickness.'

'Well, as it turns out, I'm not displeased

that you've come home. I should have known better than to expect you to manage things for me, though I'm sure you did your best. You're too gentle for your own good, Beatrice, and always have been. Like your father. Never could stand up for himself, Warren. And you're the same.' It did not seem to occur to her that she flew into tantrums with people who did try to stand up to her and was very scathing about their selfishness.

Beatrice bit her lip. She did not intend to get into arguments with her aunt, any more than she intended to marry a man whom she did not respect. Or love, a voice whispered in her head, but she refused to listen to that. Love was out of her reach now.

'I've got myself a maid at last,' she announced, to divert her aunt's attention from talk of husbands.

The Dowager allowed herself to be diverted and listened to the story of Lizzie's trial and appointment, approving the idea of a lady's maid in principle, but reserving judgement until she had met the girl. She then allowed Beatrice to guide the conversation towards clothes and listened with an appearance of interest to a description of the ravishing ensembles Odette had designed for her, not to mention the elaborate court dress and its accompanying feathers. '…though I'm afraid Odette was very expensive,' Beatrice wound up apologetically.

Lady Marguerite dismissed that with a wave of her hand. 'Persons of rank,' her favourite phrase made Beatrice smile still, in spite of her unhappiness, 'must dress to suit their station in life, and to set an example to others, not to please themselves.'

'I think,' said Beatrice, when she had run out of clothes and bonnets to describe, 'that I'd like to go and freshen myself up a little now, Aunt Marguerite. Travelling always makes one feel so grubby.'

'You do that, my dear girl!' The Dowager watched her go, still with that affable smile on her face. 'I should have known that she was too shy to look after her own interests,' she said aloud when she was alone. 'Well, I still have a few surprises up my sleeve, miss, as you'll shortly find out. Lippings, bring me my writing materials and tell them I need another groom to deliver a message.'

Beatrice found Eleanor in her room, getting acquainted with Lizzie and examining the new clothes. 'I hope you don't mind,

Bea. I couldn't wait to see your London things!'

'Of course I don't mind. Thank you, Lizzie. You may leave us for a while.'

Eleanor started fiddling with a pair of gloves. 'Was Grandmama pleased with what you did in London, Bea?'

'What do you know about that?' Her voice came out more sharply than she had intended.

Eleanor opened her eyes very wide. 'Nothing much, Bea, just that Grandmama wished you to undertake some commissions for her in London.'

Beatrice forced herself to stay calm. She was seeing problems where there were none, she told herself firmly. 'Well, I think I did what she wished, more or less, anyway. Though she really wanted me to find myself a husband.'

'I thought so. And was there no one you liked?'

'I doubt I'm the marrying kind.' Beatrice was pleased that she had managed to speak lightly. 'How do you like my new clothes?'

Like the Dowager, Eleanor allowed herself to be diverted from the dangerous topic, but she too had noticed how Bea avoided answering her question directly. She had also noticed how sad Bea was looking. 'I adore them! Before I'm very much older, I intend to go up to London myself and have some clothes made for me by a fashionable modiste. These are ravishing! I like this apricot one best. It's such a pretty colour.'

Beatrice fingered it wistfully. That's what I was wearing the first time I really talked to Serle, the day Boris came up to town, I've always liked it. She stiffened her spine, smiled brightly and said, 'Yes. It's my favourite too. Odette is very clever. And I see you've been making the acquaintance of Lizzie. What do you think of her?'

'She seems nice. I'm going to introduce her to my Betty when she gets back from the village. They're bound to become great friends, just like we are. Why, I daresay they'll tell each other all their secrets … just like we do.'

Beatrice looked at her with narrowed eyes and Eleanor smiled with such an innocent expression that Beatrice at once became suspicious. However, she did not wish to probe any subject deeply just now, so she continued to show off the new garments and bonnets, and talked about London parties until it was time to get changed for dinner. She did not allow herself to dwell on the thought of Justin Serle coming to Satherby. It was too much to face at the moment. Surely he would refuse?

Lizzie came back to help her dress, and was then swept off by an excited Betty, who was longing to make a friend of her own age in that household of elderly servants.

During dinner, Eleanor asked casually, 'What's Lord Serle like, Bea?'

Beatrice choked on her fish. 'Why do you ask?'

Eleanor was still wearing her guileless expression, which definitely meant that she was up to something. 'Well, you've invited him down to stay, haven't you, Grandmama?' she asked. 'I thought Bea might have met him in London.'

Beatrice had regained control of her emotions, if not of her colour. 'Yes, I did meet him once or twice. He's about thirty. Elegantly dressed, but not a dandy. Something of a Corinthian, very fond of sporting pursuits. Tall, dark, not handsome exactly, but very distinguished looking.' She paused, then added without thinking, 'And he's a marvellous dancer. The easiest person I ever danced with, I think.'

'Is he a man of sense, though?' demanded the Dowager. 'Does he know what's due to his position in society?'

'Oh, yes. He's very, very...' She wanted to say autocratic but thought this would not appeal to Eleanor. 'Yes, he does,' she finished lamely.

The Dowager nodded, only partly satisfied, but diverted by the reference to dancing. 'I like a man who can show a neat leg. Your grandfather was an excellent dancer, Eleanor, as I was myself in my younger days.' She looked down at her twisted hands and sighed briefly.

Beatrice's heart was wrung for her. Her aunt never complained, but was obviously in a lot of pain. She must not let her down!

Eleanor made no comment on the description of Lord Serle and kept her own counsel about certain suspicions that were beginning to form in her mind. She would see what she could get out of Lizzie. She rather prided herself on her ability to elicit information from people without their realising it.

She was missing Crispin quite dreadfully, though he had only been gone a few days, but she had already received a letter from him, sent via Anders, and that had cheered her up greatly. Her first love letter! She knew it by heart already. And it was much more satisfying than the flowery language used in novels, for it talked of real things and of their future together.

The next morning, the Dowager joined them for breakfast, which showed that she was in fine fettle, for she normally had it in her rooms. She uttered a crow of triumph as she opened her mail. 'I thought he'd come round!' she exclaimed gleefully.

Her two young relatives looked at her.

'That Herforth fellow. The one with the silly name. Crispin! The heir. *You* know the one I mean!'

'Yes, Grandmama.' Eleanor kept her eyes down and started to butter a piece of toast. 'I remember you mentioned him.'

'I wrote to him while you were away, Bea, inviting him to come here for a visit and learn about the estate, and do you know, the fellow had the impudence to turn the invitation down! Well, he's soon come to his senses. See!' "Conscious of the honour of your invitation, regret that I was unable to accept immediately, have now arranged matters to be taken care of in my absence, quite see the necessity for getting to know Satherby, be happy to be with you as soon as I receive word." That's a bit more like it!'

'And shall you send him word, Grandmama?'

'Of course! He might as well come next week. We'll make a house-party of it. Serle won't refuse, and the Smeathleys are coming to stay as well.'

Beatrice and Eleanor exchanged puzzled glances. Who were the Smeathleys? Lady Marguerite rarely invited people to stay. She had been declaring for years that she was too old for house-parties. Who wanted to face strangers over breakfast, she always said scornfully, let alone spend all day entertaining them when they'd be better off at home, keeping their own houses in order!

The Dowager was still crowing in triumph over the heir's capitulation. 'I thought he'd see sense eventually.'

'Who are the Smeathleys, Grandmama?' asked Eleanor.

'What? Oh, yes. Better tell you about 'em. Connections by marriage, they are, relatives of your Uncle Alfred – the one who died so young. Pity I ever allowed him to marry my poor Harriet, but there you are. How was I to know he'd get himself killed without producing an heir? No use crying over spilt milk. She didn't live very long, either. Nice girl, my Harriet, but she was never strong. A bit like you, Bea, not one to look after her own best interests. Good thing she had me to sort her life out. Good thing you've got me, too! I can still hold my team together and don't you think otherwise!'

She was obviously in the most excellent spirits and was just as obviously plotting something. 'The Smeathleys,' she added with a smug smile, 'are a church family. It was Johanna who put it into my mind that a cleric might be just the thing for Beatrice here. She likes looking after the poor, helping the sick, all that sort of thing. Might as well do it to some purpose. The Smeathleys have a son. He's gone thirty now. Good age for an ambitious cleric to marry. And this one's ambitious. They've got some hopes that he'll end up with a bishopric. He's apparently well regarded. So I told them to bring him down to meet Bea.'

Beatrice, who had been growing steadily paler, could keep quite no longer. 'Aunt! I told you I have no wish, none at all! to marry! I'm too set in my ways. And I'm happy here.'

'Well, you won't be able to stay on here after I'm gone, so you'd better make up your mind to give this fellow a serious looking over. I won't force you to marry him if he turns out to be a nick-ninny or a mealy-mouthed Bible-spouter, but you owe it to me to look him over, Bea.' She paused and added quietly, 'Don't you think?'

Recalling the way the Dowager had once begged for her help and how she had let her down, Beatrice could only swallow and nod miserably. 'I'll be happy to meet him,' she said in a low voice. 'But don't expect too much of me. Please.'

'We'll just look him over,' said her aunt soothingly.

Beatrice pushed her plate away. 'I don't seem to be very hungry this morning.'

Eleanor intervened, to keep the Dowager's attention away from poor Bea, who was looking terrible. She definitely had some guilty secret. 'Grandmama, if the Smeathleys are coming here so that Bea can look their son over, why is Lord Serle coming?' she asked, judging her time to a nicety.

Lady Marguerite choked over her coffee and had to have her back patted before she could speak. She fixed a stern gaze upon her grand-daughter. 'Hmm. I suppose you'll have to be told some time. Sit up straight and pay attention.' She chewed her lip for a moment, then said, 'Well, Eleanor, I'm thinking of finding you a husband as well. You're the right age for marriage. That's why Bea went up to London, to look over some of the eligibles. As I'd expected, she thought Serle the most promising. I'd also hoped she'd find a husband for herself while she was at it; I settled a decent dowry on her, least I could do, and Johanna says that there was some interest, but it seems no one caught *her* fancy.'

The last was said with heavy sarcasm and a look which made Beatrice feel as if her aunt were heaping coals of fire upon her head. She could only stare down at her plate and long for the meal to end.

Eleanor clapped her hands, still intent on diverting attention. 'What fun! You'll have to tell me everything you can remember about Lord Serle, Bea! Every little detail. I shouldn't at all object to being married, Grandmama, as long as he isn't ugly, or too old, or unkind, or anything like that.'

She sat back with the air of one willing to oblige and she remained in a highly cheerful mood until the meal ended. If her grandmother believed it was time she married, that was one hurdle got over. The fact that it was Crispin she intended to marry need not be mentioned as yet.

Both the Dowager and Beatrice were rather surprised at the ease with which Eleanor had accept the possibility of marriage, but Beatrice was too upset on her own account to pursue the matter, and the Dowager was too used to getting her own way to take time to question the chit's feelings.

Eleanor decided that poor Bea needed some time alone, so she talked about the beautiful display of lily-of-the-valley in the South Wood, not to mention the fritillaries along the water meadows, until Beatrice said she thought she would go for a stroll and look at them. 'And I hope you don't mind, Eleanor, but I'd like to be alone for a while. I did nothing but meet people while I was away, and quite frankly, I'd welcome the chance for a bit of peace and quiet.'

'Oh, you go, Bea. I don't mind at all. I've got a new piano piece to practice.' She turned to leave, then swung back again. 'But would you mind if Betty and I asked Lizzie to show us all your new clothes again first, so that we can study the latest fashions? If I'm to meet a prospective husband, I must look my best, mustn't I? And I have a few lengths of material put by. We can soon get the dressmaker in. I shall want to look my best for Lord Serle, shan't I?'

'Do what you like!' Beatrice fled for the woods.

TEN

The day after his abortive attempt to propose to Beatrice, Justin went to Lymsby to see how she was recovering. He had decided that if things did not go well with his attempt to propose this time, he would confide in Lady Ostdene and ask for her help. He did not come to this conclusion without considerable thought, for he disliked feeling vulnerable.

Beatrice was not indifferent to him! Surely he could not be mistaken in that? The way she reacted to him. The way she felt in his arms! The way their bodies moulded together when they were waltzing! But then, why had she become so agitated when he tried to press his suit? He remembered the way they had sat and laughed together in the icy water of the pond and his confidence rose. Then he recalled the way she had avoided his eyes the previous day, changing the subject and generally rendering it impossible for him to declare himself, and his confidence sank again.

Justin Serle, having been courted shamelessly for years, was now finding it extremely difficult to plead his case and win fair lady. Perhaps he could ask help from Boris. But no, Boris was obsessed by his wife's pregnancy at the moment and even the head groom could get no sense from him. It must be Lady Ostdene, then, but to talk to her about it, to confess to a weakness, would be hard for him, for he was not in the habit of confiding his feelings to others. He smiled wryly as he handed his horse to a groom and walked up the steps to the front door.

Inside, he was shown into a salon and left to wait. Several minutes dragged by and he began to prowl around the room. It was not like the Newthorpes to keep a guest waiting. Perhaps something was wrong? After a while, Lady Ostdene came in, frowning. Justin's heart lurched. 'Is Miss Dencey all right?' he asked, his voice coming out harshly.

Johanna looked surprised at the abruptness of this greeting. 'It's kind of you to call, Serle, but I'm afraid you find us at sixes and sevens today.'

'Miss Dencey?' he prompted. 'She hasn't taken a chill?'

'Bea? Oh, didn't she tell you? She left this morning. She's decided to go back to

Satherby. She said she was homesick.'

'What?'

Anger had made his voice over-loud, and Johanna blinked and stared at him. 'Is something wrong, Serle?'

'I came to see Miss Dencey,' he said stiffly. 'I expected ... she knew ... she made no mention yesterday of any plans to leave.'

'Her decision was rather sudden.'

'She's taken no hurt from her drenching?'

'Oh, no. Bea's never ill. She has the most robust health of anyone I know, and Eleanor's much the same. My mother ascribes it to the excellence of Satherby's air and general situation.'

'I'm glad to hear that.' He began to fiddle with the braid on the arm of the chair on which he was sitting.

Johanna's attention was now fully engaged. 'I think you'd better tell me about it,' she said softly. 'I've never seen you like this before, Serle.'

He smiled at her ruefully. 'I've never felt like this before, Lady Ostdene.'

'Like what?' She held her breath and watched indecision and worry flit across his face. She was glad to see that he had lost that cool detached look he had worn for so long. 'It often helps to talk to someone,' she coaxed, 'and you've known me long enough to trust me, surely? I'm almost like an honorary aunt by now.'

'I'm not – I don't know how to start.'

When he did not continue, she asked quietly, 'It's Beatrice, isn't it?'

'Yes.' He stood up and went to stare out of the window, tossing the words over his shoulder at her. 'I've come to love her. I thought she felt the same. But yesterday, when I tried to speak, to ask her to marry me, well, she prevented me. She looked so upset that I couldn't continue. And yet,' he fumbled in his pocket and threw down a crumpled piece of paper, 'that came this morning. I don't know what to think.'

Johanna read her mother's invitation to stay at Satherby. 'Aaah,' she murmured.

'What do you mean by "Aaah"?' he asked irritably. 'If Beatrice has no feeling for me, why am I being invited to stay at Satherby?'

'I doubt Beatrice knew about this. It's from my mother. She sometimes takes the bit between her teeth. She can be a very determined woman.'

'So can your Cousin Beatrice!'

'We're not a family of ditherers,' she agreed smugly. 'Well, not usually.'

She was trying to make up her mind as to

how frank she dared be with him when the door crashed open and Boris strode in. He did not notice Justin, and even if he had, would have paid him no attention. 'You'll have to come and talk to her, Mother-in-law! She's determined to get up and *I will not have it!*'

'Boris, dear, go away!'

'She has no right to... What did you say?'

'I told you to go away. Serle and I are discussing something important.'

A shriek of anger from upstairs made Boris growl under his breath and stalk out of the door. Johanna ran her fingers through her hair distractedly, quite ruining Sarah's expert handiwork, a thing she would never normally have dared do, then turned to Justin. 'Look, I can't talk now, everything is in chaos here today. Jennice is not herself. Could you possibly come back tomorrow? I'll have time by then for a long talk with you. I can't deal with anything else at the moment, not until I've sorted out Jennice and Boris.'

He gave a grunt of frustration and stood up to leave. Johanna went over and laid her hand on his shoulder. 'It's not as bad as it seems, Serle. I don't think Beatrice is indifferent to you.' There was a loud burst of sobbing from upstairs and she closed her eyes in despair. 'I don't know what's got into Jennice! She's done nothing but have hysterics today. Would you, could you possibly lend us Mrs Powis for a few days? I'm beginning to think she's the only one who can talk sense into those two idiots upstairs.'

'Of course. I'll ask her to come across immediately.' There was nothing for him to do, but bow gracefully and leave. He rode home slowly and thoughtfully, but as he approached the house, he could not resist the temptation to turn aside and visit the pond. There, he sat on the rocks for nearly an hour, thinking hard, before coming to some conclusions of his own.

'Ha!' said the Dowager triumphantly at another breakfast, for her spirits had continued high. 'He's coming! Told you he would!'

'Who's coming, Grandmama?' asked Eleanor, suspending her enthusiastic demolition of a juicy piece of ham.

'Serle.'

Beatrice, at the other side of the table, tried to continue eating as if nothing special had been said, but her cheeks turned first red, then white, and the stricken expression which passed fleetingly across her face betrayed her. Only Eleanor noticed, however, the Dowager being too selfish to concern herself with other people's feelings and wishes, especially at this hour of the morning.

Eleanor turned back to her grandmother. 'When is he coming, Grandmama?'

'In two days.'

Beatrice dropped her fork with a clatter.

The Dowager frowned at her. 'It ain't like you to be so clumsy, girl! Are you feeling all right? We can't have you going down with something when there are guests to be entertained.'

'I'm sorry, Aunt Marguerite. I was just, just thinking about something and didn't watch what I was doing.'

'Well, be careful what you're doing over the next few days! You won't be able to breathe without someone watching you! House-parties are the devil and I'm too old to manage things! It'll be up to you two to keep the guests entertained. I shall go back to breakfasting in my rooms while they're here, I think. I never could face people on an empty stomach.'

Eleanor saw that Bea was still struggling to

appear normal, so stepped in. 'Yes, Grand-mama. We'll look after the guests for you.'

'And you'd better arrange a few picnics and dinners and invite the neighbours. Those worth inviting, that is! I won't have curates and farmers at Satherby. You can start making your plans today. I've told Mrs Inchby to get the rooms ready and confer with cook, but you'd better keep an eye on what she's doing as well, Beatrice. She hasn't had a houseful of visitors to look after for years. Not that I don't trust her, she knows her job, but we don't want anything going wrong, do we?' With the help of a footman she levered herself out of her chair and consented to be assisted to the wheeled chair she was moved around in.

'Is something wrong, Bea?' Eleanor asked softly when the footmen had pushed her ladyship away. 'You look – upset.'

'Wrong? No, of course not.' Beatrice real-ised that she could not hope to keep up this pretence with someone who knew her as well as Eleanor did and added hastily. 'Well, I do have just a bit of a headache, but it's nothing.'

'Perhaps you're starting the influenza?' offered Eleanor helpfully.

'I wouldn't dare!' Beatrice said, with a wry

smile. 'Not now. No, I just, well, to tell you the truth, Eleanor, I don't wish to get married. And certainly not to a stranger who wouldn't look at me twice if I had no money. I wish Aunt Marguerite hadn't invited these Smeathleys to visit us.' She paused for a moment, then said brusquely, 'Did I tell you that she's settled twenty thousand pounds on me as a dowry.'

'Why, that's marvellous! And you've certainly earned it! Think of the way you've looked after her all these years. And after me, too.' She went over to hug poor Bea, who had been looking very down in the mouth since her return. 'Don't you think that a woman should bring something of her own to a marriage? I do.'

'But that's the whole point! I don't want to get married!'

'What made you change your mind? You always said you did when we talked about it. And you said you'd like to have lots of children too. We even used to think of names for them. I think you'd make a *splendid* mother, Bea. It'd be pure waste if you didn't have children of your own. Just see how well you've done with me!' There was no response to her little joke, not even the curve of a lip. Bea must be feeling really bad, she thought. Whatever had happened to her in London?

Beatrice spoke emphatically, articulating every word with the utmost care. 'I *don't* want to marry someone who's just interested in my money, Eleanor! That's all the gentlemen in London cared about and that's all this Smeathley person is coming for! If he's an ambitious cleric, he wouldn't even consider a wife who brought him nothing. And I won't be sold like that! I won't!' She stormed out of the room.

Left alone with the remains of her ham, Eleanor nodded thoughtfully. 'There's definitely someone she's interested in,' she murmured. 'She wouldn't get so upset if it were just a question of finding herself a husband. She's already found him, only something's stopping them getting married.' She waved the fork to and fro in time with her thoughts, the ham forgotten. 'I wonder! She gets very agitated whenever Grandmama talks of the house-party, yet she's never even met the Smeathleys, or my Crispin, so that only leaves... Mmmm. I must definitely speak to her Lizzie.'

While Beatrice was conferring with the housekeeper, Eleanor cleared her plate with a speed which would have horrified her grandmother and went to look for Lizzie. Under the pretence of studying one of the dresses again, she managed to elicit a considerable amount of information about Bea and Lord Serle, including the involuntary dunking in the pond, which Beatrice had somehow quite failed to mention. Without realising what she was doing, Lizzie also revealed the fact that Lord Serle had upset her mistress greatly just before they left.

Humming to herself, Eleanor then went to have a serious think about things. This was not going to be easy to resolve. Her grandmother had not even thought of Crispin as a possible husband for her, presumably because she did not approve of that branch of the family. It was Serle whom Eleanor was supposed to marry, while Mr Smeathley was destined for Bea. If she was to carry out her plan to make the Dowager glad for her to marry Crispin, she had to pretend to be attracted to someone unsuitable first. But who? There was only Mr Smeathley and how on earth was she to persuade her grandmother and aunt that she had fallen in love with a middle-aged cleric? They were not stupid enough to believe any such thing!

Eleanor did not, however, allow herself to become depressed about this dilemma.

Problems were there to be solved. There was always a way if you looked hard enough, and she knew herself to be a very enterprising person, not to mention being utterly determined to marry her Crispin.

Two days later, the household was on tenterhooks and the Dowager was alternating between extreme satisfaction at her own cleverness and querulousness at the thought of her privacy being invaded and her infirmities paraded before strangers. In the afternoon, she summoned her niece and grand-daughter to attend her and sat bolt upright in the wheeled chair in the Chinese Salon, waiting for the guests to arrive.

When Crispin Herforth was shown in, the Dowager said 'Hmph!' quite audibly and her expression as she studied him did not seem to augur well for the young lovers.

'How kind of you to invite me, your ladyship,' he said, bowing over her hand.

She allowed him to touch the hand briefly, then repeated, 'Hmph!' in a disapproving tone.

He remained where he was, a slight smile on his lips, quietly confident of himself. Eleanor, watching him, thought how attractive he was looking, with his neat country gentleman's clothes and his blue eyes set so steadily and fearlessly upon the Dowager. Her heart swelled with pride. He was not afraid of anyone, her Crispin! After a moment, she lowered her eyes, in case her expression betrayed her. You could not be too careful with Grandmama.

'You don't take after the Graceovers!' declared the Dowager, still eyeing the newcomer. 'One would think you'd show *some* sign of the blood. We *never* have blond hair!'

'I believe I take after my mother's family in looks, your ladyship.'

'Pity, that! Still, there's nothing we can do about it now.'

'No, your ladyship.'

The stick rapped the floor for emphasis. 'I can't have you saying "your ladyship" every other minute like that, because you're one of the family, whether we like it or not. So you'd better call me Aunt Marguerite, though I'm not your aunt, just some sort of second cousin. Still, Aunt's more respectful to a woman of my age.'

'I shall be honoured, Aunt Marguerite.'

'Hmph! That's as may be. This is my niece, Beatrice Dencey, my brother's daughter. And this is my grand-daughter, Eleanor. It'll be best if you address them both as cousins.'

He gravely shook the hands of the two younger ladies, one of whom gave him a roguish wink.

The stick was rapped again, but not in anger. 'Right, then, we need to plan what to do with you. You'd better sit down. I'm getting a crick in my neck looking up at you, for all you don't carry the Graceover inches. I don't think one of *my* menfolk was under six feet tall.' She shook her head sadly.

'I'm very sorry to disappoint you, Aunt Marguerite.'

'No use crying over spilt milk. You're the heir now, and that's that! So, the bailiff will explain to you how the estate is run. I've told him to expect you tomorrow in the estate office, it's in the stable block. Eleanor or Beatrice can show you round the house when they have time. We're expecting guests, so there are bound to be plenty of riding parties in the district. You might as well go out with them, to get to know the estate. You'll join the rest of us for meals and in the evenings, of course, but you'll be busy with the bailiff during the day, I daresay. At least, you will if you do your duty.' She sounded rather dubious about this.

He inclined his head. 'I shall be happy to

get to know Satherby, Aunt Marguerite. And it may comfort you to know that I'm quite used to managing an estate already, for I've been doing it since I was sixteen, though not one as big as Satherby, of course.'

'But your father only died last year!'

'He'd left the management of things to me for several years. He preferred his books. He was quite a noted medieval scholar, actually. Something of an authority on the Code of Chivalry.'

'Hmph. He was always burying his head in his books when he was a lad, too. I was surprised that he bothered to marry at all. And what good are Latin and Greek to a landowner? I'll tell you. None! Do you think Satherby would be in such good heart if my John had sat in the library reading old books? No, it wouldn't!' She spluttered to a halt and stared at him, sighing that he should look so healthy while her own sons were long dead. When she spoke again, it was more moderately. 'Well, your father's dead now, and you seem to have more idea of your duty than he did, so I'll not say any more.'

'It isn't duty,' he said simply, 'but love of the land.'

'Hmph.' But the look she cast him was not

unfriendly. 'I don't know about your character, young man, so we'll have to wait and see.' She remembered a further point of grievance and glowered at him. 'But with a name like Crispin, you never can tell. What on earth got into your father to call you that?'

He did not allow himself to smile. The old lady was just as rude as his father had always said, but he rather liked her spirit. Most women of her age did little but sit and gossip, or hug their fires. She was still doing her duty, even though she was confined to a wheeled chair and twisted with arthritis. Besides, she was the grandmother of his darling, so he owned her a great deal of respect, for Eleanor's sake. 'It was my mother's choice, I believe,' he said apologetically. 'I daresay you'll grow used to it.' He decided to change the subject and gazed around him with appreciation. 'This is a lovely room.'

The Dowager nodded, accepting this tribute as natural, rather than taking it for flattery. 'M'father-in-law did it. It was all the vogue in his day. I haven't cared to change it and hope you won't, either. People should treasure their inheritance.'

'I wouldn't think of changing it. That's the most beautiful Chinese carpet I've ever seen. Their colours and designs are always so restful, don't you think? And this is a superb example of lacquer work.' He moved over to a cabinet and began to stroke it with knowing fingers. 'My own great-grand-mother was rather taken by the Chinese vogue and I was able to preserve her things from my aunt, who wished to throw them out when my mother died. I have them carefully stored in the attic at home. There's a cabinet which is almost the twin of this one, but smaller. It would look well in that corner.'

The Dowager blinked. She had thought of training him to preserve Satherby and its treasures, but had never even considered the possibility that he might be able to add to them.

'I'd be very grateful if someone would spare the time to show me round the house, whenever it's convenient,' Crispin con-tinued, not looking at Eleanor. 'I've heard a lot about it. And I believe that the remains of the Priory are still standing.'

'Hmph! Piles of old stones! Should have been cleared away years ago. Watch your step if you go there. It's dangerous. How long are you staying?'

Another of his neat bows. 'I'm at your

disposal for as long as you wish, Aunt Marguerite.'

'We'll have to see, then.' She was slightly mollified by his remarks, but was not going to show any softening of her attitude towards him until she had got to know him better. She rang the silver bell by her side and a footman answered. 'Show Mr Herforth up to his room, if you please, Robert.'

She turned back to Crispin. 'I've had them prepare the master's suite for you.' That decision had cost her a wakeful night, but she had come to the conclusion that she could do no less than give him the respect due to the heir, even though he was not worthy. 'It's yours by right, after all. You can go for a walk in the gardens once you've unpacked.'

Eleanor watched him leave through lowered lashes, then turned to her grandmother, eager to see what she thought about him.

'Pity he's so short, I prefer tall men!' declared her ladyship. 'Still, he don't dress like a man-milliner, I'll give him that. And he looks you in the eye, as a gentleman should. I can't abide fellows with shifty eyes. But there's no hint of Graceover in him, none at all. I'm disappointed in that. Your grandfather would have been heartbroken to see the estate pass from the true line.'

'Yes, what a pity!' said Eleanor. 'Why!' she smiled as if the idea had only just occurred to her. 'I'm the only one of the true line left now, aren't I?'

The Dowager treated her to a puzzled stare, as if she had said something strange.

Satisfied that she had planted a seed, Eleanor asked innocently, 'What did *you* think of him, Bea?'

'He seemed pleasant enough. Good looking in a quiet way, I suppose.' She spoke only to fill the silence, but was surprised to be rewarded with a beaming smile from Eleanor.

'We'll have to see how he turns out,' declared the Dowager. 'Don't like to make hasty judgements. Still, the fellow shows some signs of sense. Better than I'd hoped for. Better than his father, that's for sure.' For her, that was tantamount to an admission that Mr Herforth had made a favourable first impression.

They continued to sit in state in the salon. Beatrice tried to occupy herself with her embroidery, but the stitches went sadly awry. Eleanor chatted to her grandmother, encouraging the old lady to tell them about her youth, which usually put her in a good humour, but though her ladyship obliged automatically, it was plain that her heart was not in her reminiscences.

They had not long to wait. Beatrice's heart lurched at the sound of wheels on the gravel, and she gripped her embroidery tightly. Was this him? She was both longing and dreading to see him again.

'Shall I go and peep through the window and see who it is, Grandmama?' asked Eleanor, winking at Beatrice.

'Certainly not! A lady never peeps through windows! A lady maintains a calm decorum at all times.' But it was to be seen that her own mouth was tense and her hand was fidgeting on the silver handle of her cane.

'Yes, Grandmama.'

After a while, the door opened and the butler appeared. 'Mr and Mrs Smeathley, your ladyship, and Mr Augustus Smeathley.'

The Dowager's face briefly registered disappointment, then it became calm again.

The trio who entered were rather a surprise to everyone. All three were very tall and stately, with dark hair and pale complexions, and they moved like a matched set of horses. The two older Smeathleys showed a certain embonpoint and the darkness of their hair was touched with silver, but this in no way detracted from their massive dignity or from their startling resemblance to each other. As for Mr Augustus Smeathley, he was not only tall, but handsome, in a restrained sort of way. His face had the clearly-etched profile and alabaster complexion of a Greek statue, his dark hair curled immaculately across his brow and his movements were graceful and studied. He looked like a man who expected life to serve him, and who had not yet been disappointed. Beatrice's heart sank at the sight of him.

Eleanor, on the other hand, brightened visibly as the full glory of Augustus Smeathley burst upon them. What a piece of luck! He was so handsome that she could pretend to have fallen in love with him on sight. She waited for the trio to salute the Dowager, which they did with the air of imperial ambassadors greeting a minor king, and continued to observe them carefully as they were presented to Beatrice. It seemed to her that Augustus Smeathley studied her Aunt Bea very shrewdly indeed as he took her hand. That man has come to see if he can get a bargain for himself, she thought. He wouldn't do for Bea, even if she didn't love someone else. I don't think I like him very much.

As Augustus Smeathley turned from Beatrice and took Eleanor's hand, she allowed her eyelids to flutter and gazed up at him with a dazed expression on her face, as if she were quite stunned by his magnificence. He bowed over her hand and for a few seconds the calculating expression showed itself again, to be quickly wiped away and replaced by a smile. 'My dear Lady Eleanor, how *very* delighted I am to meet you!' he said, in a caressing mellifluous voice.

You sir, are a calculating hypocrite, she thought to herself. I shall have no qualms about deceiving you. 'I'm delighted to meet you too, Mr Smeathley,' she whispered shyly. 'I've heard so much about you!' It was very hard to keep her face straight as she said this, but by dint of thinking of Crispin, she managed it.

He patted her hand, which he still retained in his own. 'And I've heard a lot about you, my dear Lady Eleanor.'

The Dowager hrumphed loudly.

Augustus relinquished the hand and turned to give their hostess his very best attention. He had made quite an art of charming elderly ladies and did not doubt his ability to bend this one to his wishes. Miss Dencey would be quite a good catch, but he had decided before he came that the younger one would have far more to offer, if he could catch her interest. In addition, she was more to his taste, fresh and pliant as older women never were. One could mould a young female to one's own liking so much more easily. And Augustus Smeathley had very strong views on how his wife was to behave, both in the home and in the ecclesiastical world. However, nothing could be done without Lady Marguerite's approval, so he turned at once and began to give her of his best. He soon had the satisfaction of seeing her smiling at him and nodding approval to his parents.

Even after the second set of visitors had been dispatched to their rooms, Eleanor managed, by means of picturing the time when she would be married to her Crispin, to maintain a dreamy expression on her face, which had both the Dowager and Beatrice staring at her and then exchanging puzzled glances.

'What do you think of 'em, Bea?' asked her ladyship. 'Good looking, ain't he, young Smeathley?'

'Yes, Aunt Marguerite.'

'We'll have to see what he's like to get along with. First impressions aren't everything, not where husbands are concerned. That voice will sound excellent in a church, but it might be hard to live with. He's born to be a bishop, with that voice and that face.'

'I'd just love to hear him preach!' sighed Eleanor.

The Dowager frowned at her and said pointedly, 'Bea, you'd better make sure *you* sit next to him at dinner. Start getting to know him. His parents haven't changed at all. Always were full of their own importance, but they won't give us much trouble as long as we feed 'em well and supply 'em with plenty of newspapers and journals. That side of Aldred's family always was a little dull. Surprised they even managed to produce someone like this Augustus.'

The parents might be dull, but the son is a sharp customer and the way he was toad-eating Grandmama made me feel sick! thought Eleanor. It's going to be hard to pretend to be in love with *him!* Especially with Crispin in the same house. I'll have to find a way to get Crispin alone and tell him what I'm doing.

'Did you hear me, Bea?' repeated the Dowager sharply.

'Yes, Aunt Marguerite.' Beatrice's voice was hesitant. She had taken a violent dislike to Mr Smeathley on first sight, but dared not say so yet. His ordered curls and well-manicured white hands filled her with revulsion. Besides, he had lingered over Eleanor's hand, as if she were the one he had been brought there to meet. Perhaps he had other game in view? And why had Eleanor been looking so soulfully at him? Surely she could not have been taken in by a stuffed shirt like him? But then, she had met so very few eligible gentlemen that anything was possible. They knew nothing of how susceptible she was to good-looking gentlemen. The nightmare of this house-party was growing worse by the hour!

It was not until just before the dressing gong rang that the third carriage arrived and by this time, the Dowager was twitching with annoyance and fatigue. When Justin Serle was shown into the Chinese Salon, Beatrice's heart started to thud. He was as handsome as ever, and even after a journey, he managed to look supremely elegant, but his expression when he looked at her was inscrutable. What did he think of this visit? Why had he come? She must make sure he realised that it was Eleanor he had come to meet, not her.

He was bowing over her aunt's hand. 'I must apologise, your ladyship, for coming to greet you without changing my clothes, but your butler insisted, since you dine early.'

The Dowager took his hand and stared up at him. 'You look like your grandmother,' she said in a shaken voice. 'I hadn't expected that. Same hair. Same eyes. Elizabeth's smile.'

It wasn't often the Dowager allowed her vulnerability to show. Beatrice's tender heart went out to her. How terrible it must be to be the last survivor of your generation and to see all your friends and relatives die before you! Well, Aunt Marguerite should not have her dying wishes thwarted, if Beatrice could help it. She watched Serle smile down at the twisted figure in the wheeled chair. How genuine his smile was compared to Smeathley's, Beatrice thought, not realising that her own expression had become as dreamy as Eleanor's!

Eleanor did not miss a thing. Fancy Bea feeling like Crispin and I do, she thought in awe. At her age! I hope Lord Serle feels the same way about her.

'I'm honoured that you think so, your ladyship.' His voice was gentle and sincere. 'I have no recollection of her, unfortunately,

269

but her portrait hangs in our picture gallery and it's always been one of my favourites. She looks as if she smiled a lot.'

'She did. She did indeed.' The Dowager took a deep breath and recollected herself. 'Hrmph. You know my niece already, I believe?'

'Yes, of course I do. Good day, Miss Dencey.' He strode over to clasp Bea's hand and felt it shaking in his. 'We're old acquaintances.' As he looked down into her eyes, his own softened involuntarily. 'Are we not, Beatrice?' he added softly, so that the Dowager did not catch the words, which were a caress in themselves.

For a moment, Beatrice forgot herself and smiled back at him, her eyes betraying the love she was trying to deny, as clearly as if they had spoken aloud. 'How do you do, Lord Serle.'

'I hope your ankle is better.'

'I'm quite recovered, thank you.'

Goodness! Just look at them! thought Eleanor. Well, I don't need to worry about what to do with Serle. He loves her too. Bea's being very noble, keeping him for me, so I must find out why, but I'll be better off with my Crispin. What fun this is all going to be!

Beatrice took a deep breath and stood back. 'I don't think you've met my niece, Lord Serle. This is Eleanor.' Her voice had become cool and impersonal again, as if he were a stranger or a distant acquaintance.

Eleanor decided that she would have to get to know Serle as soon as possible. He might make a very useful ally. After all, there was a lot to arrange and her only hope of success lay in making the Dowager believe that a rearrangement of partners was her own idea. 'I'm very pleased to meet you, Lord Serle,' she said cheerfully. 'I hope you had a comfortable journey here.'

'Delightful. This is quite the pleasantest time of year, don't you think, Lady Eleanor?'

'Oh yes, very pleasant. The gardens are so pretty that one cannot help but enjoy being out of doors.' There, she thought, his eyes had strayed back to Beatrice, who was deliberately looking the other way. What had got into her aunt? If she loved him, she should be doing all she could to get herself married to him, not throwing him at her niece. Eleanor intended to fight for Crispin tooth and nail. But no, Bea was just the sort to be noble and self-sacrificing about everything.

The Dowager rapped her cane on the

ground. 'Well, I bid you welcome to Satherby, Serle, but as it's late, we'll have to pursue our acquaintance over dinner. It's time we all changed. We don't keep town hours here. We dine at six sharp.'

'I shan't keep you waiting, your ladyship. My man will have unpacked my things by now.' He followed the footman out, tossing over his shoulder for Beatrice's benefit, 'I'm no dandy!'

Beatrice blushed scarlet and deliberately upset her embroidery silks onto the floor to cover her confusion. How dared he toss such a reminder at her!

'Good-looking fellow,' said the Dowager before he was out of hearing.

Beatrice saw him cast a laughing glance over his shoulder and again averted her eyes. Eleanor observed with approval that Lord Serle had a good sense of humour.

'He *is* very good-looking, Grandmama,' Eleanor agreed, 'but not as good-looking as Mr Smeathley, do you think?'

'Smeathley?' the Dowager blinked in surprise. 'I suppose the fellow's all right, but he can't compare with a Serle. Don't like the way Smeathley does his hair, either. If those curls are natural, I'll eat my walking stick.'

'Oh, I'm sure you're wrong!' declared Eleanor, clasping her hands at her bosom and sighing. She wondered for a moment if she were overdoing things and had great trouble holding the pose.

Both ladies stared at her, but neither could think what to say. As she and Beatrice walked up to their rooms, Eleanor managed to prattle only of Augustus Smeathley, though even she was hard put to keep the eulogies going all the way upstairs.

Dinner was not a comfortable meal, for several members of the party had too much at stake to allow themselves to relax. The Dowager sat at the head of the table, flanked by Lord Serle and the elder Mr Smeathley. Eleanor was set at Lord Serle's right hand, with Crispin next to her. Beatrice sat on the other side of the table, between the two Mr Smeathleys, which made it very difficult for her to avoid Serle's eyes entirely. Beyond Mr Augustus Smeathley was his mother.

They were served in state by all four footmen and the butler. Eleanor was the life and soul of the party, prattling on about this and that, and fluttering her eyes at Mr Smeathley in a way that soon had Crispin frowning. Beatrice sent her one or two warning glances, which were totally ignored.

The Dowager, whose hearing was not of the best, maintained a dignified silence most of the time, for she hated to mistake what someone had said and thus betray her own weakness, but she threw sharp questions at her guests every now and then to show them that she was aware of their presence.

Beatrice sat wishing the floor would open up and swallow her. She had always considered those words, when she read them in books, to be as stupid as they were trite, but they exactly expressed her wishes at the moment. She did not think she could maintain her composure over several days and wondered whether she dared pretend to develop the influenza.

The elder Smeathleys were, as the Dowager had prophesied, no trouble to entertain, for they maintained a dignified silence for most of the meal and concentrated on their food, doing full justice to every dish offered. Their son proved himself not only an accomplished trencherman, but also one who was capable of contributing more than his fair share to the conversation. His unctuous utterances formed a regular bass counterpoint to Eleanor's bright prattle.

The sound of his voice began to set Beatrice's teeth on edge. The man is a practised sycophant, she thought indignantly, and if this is the way he intends to make his way through the ecclesiastical hierarchies, then the church is welcome to him. It amazed her to see Eleanor hanging upon his every word and treating his threadbare utterances like parcels of wisdom. And Eleanor was making little effort to converse with her neighbour, Lord Serle, though he had addressed several extremely intelligent remarks to her. By the time the meal was over, Beatrice was in a fair way to detesting the hapless Augustus Smeathley and had endowed him with a multitude of faults which he had not yet demonstrated.

Crispin Herforth was very quiet during the meal, observing everything more closely than was perhaps apparent to the other guests. He was not enjoying the sight of Eleanor hanging upon that buffoon's words and meant to have some sharp words with her about it afterwards. Already he was deeply regretting that he had agreed to be guided by her in winning her grandmother's consent to their marriage. To his mind, deceit never paid. He believed that life should be faced honestly and if it were up to him, he would seek an interview with the

Dowager the very next morning and let her know how he felt about her grand-daughter.

Serle was also quiet, for his attention was focused on Beatrice, who was looking so strained that his heart ached for her. She had kept herself in the background and avoided meeting his eyes ever since his arrival. Why on earth had the old lady invited him, then? Surely she did not think to match him with her grand-daughter? Eleanor was a lovely young thing, but he was too old for her, even if his affections had not been engaged. He rather thought the chit was up to some sort of mischief and he meant, if he could, to find out what, in case it was something which might upset his poor love. He watched with some amusement the way the young minx was flattering Smeathley. The man was taken in by it, like the veriest greenhead, for all his massive clerical dignity.

When the ladies eventually rose to leave the gentlemen to their port, the Dowager announced firmly that she would expect to see them in the drawing room within the half hour. She did not, she declared, staring round, approve of immoderate drinking at mixed parties.

In fact, it was barely twenty minutes

before the gentlemen abandoned their port, because each of the three younger gentlemen was so careful to guard what he said that conversation in no way flourished, while the elder Smeathley's attention was solely on his wine glass.

That port, Justin thought regretfully, had been one of the best he had ever tasted and should have been treated more respectfully than being gulped down as it was by the elder Mr Smeathley and ignored by Mr Augustus Smeathley, who was visibly fretting to rejoin the ladies. Herforth seemed a decent enough fellow and, in different circumstances, Justin would have been pleased to pursue a closer acquaintance with him, but for the moment, until he had summed up exactly who was playing which game, he would keep himself to himself.

He complimented the butler as he left the room on the way the port had been cellared and decanted, and made himself a staunch ally, because if Borrill had one passion in life, it was the proper management of good wines.

The ladies, having ensconced themselves in the Blue Drawing Room, passed an uncomfortable twenty minutes waiting for the gentlemen. Beatrice saw her aunt settled, realising that the old lady was already displaying signs of fatigue, then she sat down next to her and pretended to embroider. The Dowager and Mrs Smeathley made desultory conversation about mutual acquaintances and the foibles of long-dead relatives. Eleanor, after twitching restlessly for a few minutes, went to the piano and began to play.

It was there that Crispin saw her as he entered, her hair aureoled by the candelabrum behind her and her firm little hands caressing a delicate melody from the keys. She seemed for the moment to have forgotten that there were other people around her and her eyes were half closed as she played. Without thinking, he went to stand behind her to turn the pages and with a start she realised that the gentlemen had returned.

Under cover of the music, she was able to instruct him to meet her on the terrace half an hour after everyone had retired and to stay away from her until then. Further confidences were prevented by Augustus Smeathley, who loomed up beside them and began to hum the melody in a rich fruity voice.

Eleanor kicked Crispin on the ankle, which he correctly interpreted as an order to remove himself. He did so reluctantly, his lips tight with annoyance.

'Do you sing much, Cousin Augustus?' Eleanor was cooing behind him.

'I delight in it, my dear young lady, delight in it.'

Within minutes they had found some suitable music and were entertaining the company with a duet that proved Smeathley's boasted love of music to be no lie.

The Dowager watched them for a while, tapping out the tune with a wrinkled, twisted hand, but did not allow the tête-à-tête to continue beyond three duets. 'Excellent!' she called. 'Now come and find me that sketch-book of Beatrice's, child. I want to show Crispin the perspectives of the house and grounds.' Old and half deaf she might be, but within minutes she had them organised into the pairs she wanted. Crispin with herself, Serle with Eleanor and Smeathley with a very silent Beatrice. The senior Smeathleys were allowed to entertain themselves by dozing in a corner.

ELEVEN

Crispin tiptoed down the dark staircase, wishing that he dared light a candle. It was all very well for Eleanor, who knew the house like the back of her hand, to suggest that they meet on the terrace, but he would have preferred to wait until early morning, when he could see where he was going. He fumbled his way to the bottom of the stairs, praying that everyone else was sound asleep, and with some trepidation made his way across what seemed a vast expanse of hallway. A door opened and a shaft of light stopped him dead in his tracks. He waited where he was, heart pounding, to see who had caught him.

'Did you wish for something, sir?'

Crispin sighed with relief. It was the butler.

'Yes. I wanted to go outside for a smoke. I like a cigarillo every now and then. Not the sort of thing Lady Marguerite would appreciate one doing indoors, I suspect, and I didn't want to disturb the rest of the house.

Now that you're here, perhaps you'd tell me which is the best place to go. The terrace, I thought.'

'Yes, sir. If you'd follow me. I suggest you go out through the library onto the terrace.'

Crispin followed him, hoping he wouldn't wait to see the fictitious cigarillo. Damn! He'd better get hold of some, just in case he needed to repeat the excuse. That's where deceit got you, into tangles! 'Thank you.'

'Would you like me to light you a candle, sir?' Borrill gestured with his own candlestick towards an unlit candelabrum.

'Yes. Thank you. I'll leave it inside, though, and just use it to light the cigarillo. The moon's rising now and it's near enough full to provide me with all the light I want outside. You needn't wait. I'll lock up when I come in again. You won't mention my little weakness to my hostess, will you?'

Borrill smiled. He had already decided that he approved of The Heir. 'No, sir, for it's one I share.'

Crispin waited until the door of the library had closed behind Borrill before going outside. He did not dare call out and could only wait for Eleanor to find him. A rustle of skirts and a low chuckle heralded her appearance, and before he could take another step, she had thrown herself into his arms.

'Oh, how I missed you!' she sighed, when at last they tore themselves apart and went to sit on a bench.

'And I you, my darling. But I want to know before we talk about anything else just what the devil you mean by playing up to that buffoon! I came very near to calling this whole sham off tonight, I can tell you!'

She giggled. 'He is rather a fool, isn't he? I've not had much experience of men, but he seems to me very gullible. Am I doing it well, the flirting, I mean?'

'Much too well!' he growled, and kissed the tip of her ear, which was temptingly close to his lips. 'If he continues to drool over you in that disgusting way, I shall wind up punching him in the face! Stupid old windbag!'

'Well, I have to encourage him a little, so that Grandmama will think I'm falling in love with him. I can't pretend to like Lord Serle, for he's the one she *wants* me to marry. He seems quite nice, too, don't you think?'

'Hang Serle! Look, love, let's be done with this play-acting and just tell your grandmother straight out that we've fallen in love and wish to get married.'

'I wish we could!' she sighed. 'But I know her and I promise you it wouldn't work. Firstly, she doesn't believe that persons of rank should allow themselves to fall in love. When she caught Bea and me reading a novel once, she threw it on the fire and read us a dreadful lecture about only common persons falling in love.' She smiled reminiscently. 'And I was just about to find out whether Melissa escaped from the evil count and managed to be reunited with her childhood sweetheart.'

'Dreadful. Tell me its name and I'll buy you another copy.'

'Oh, there's no need. I got one of the housemaids to get me another copy on her day off.'

He shook with laughter. 'I might have known. And secondly, my love?' he prompted, succumbing to the temptation to kiss her cheek again.

'Secondly, if we told her the truth, it would probably mean that she'd send you away. No, I've got to show disinterest in Lord Serle and a fascination with Smeathley, until she decides to do something about it. At the same time, you'll be glad to know, Mr Herforth, that you've made an excellent first impression on her, in spite of being

283

called Crispin, and you must continue to win her favour. And...' she pushed him away, 'Stop it! I can't think when you're kissing me! My master stroke is that I've planted an idea in her mind about me being the last of the true Graceovers and what a pity it is that you're not like them. I rather think she'll decide to let me marry you in the end to keep the family breeding true, even if we have lost the title.'

He sighed and growled in her ear that she was a devious little schemer.

She clasped his hand and gazed earnestly into his face. 'Believe me, Crispin, we have to do things this way! Please bear with me.'

'Well, it sticks in my gullet!' he exclaimed, his voice rising a little with the vehemence of his feelings.

'Shhh! Someone will hear us!'

Serle, whose bedroom window looked out onto the terrace, was lying awake trying to work out how to get Beatrice on her own, so that they could have a frank discussion. As Crispin's voice rose, he realised that the whisperings he had put down to night animals and rustling leaves were people talking outside and he got out of bed to see who they were. By the time he had opened the window without making a noise, the couple below him on the terrace were once again entwined. Looking down, he could only see the tops of their heads, half obscured by the creeper that grew in profusion upon the old walls and by the branches of a tree that ought, he thought angrily, to have been better trimmed.

As the couple drew apart, Eleanor brushed her hair back behind her ears. Justin sucked his breath in sharply. He had seen Beatrice tuck her hair out of the way in just that manner many times. He leaned forward and tried desperately to make out the features of the people below him, but the lady was now sitting with her head on the gentleman's shoulder. By leaning perilously far out of the window, he managed to confirm that the man was Crispin Herforth, but he could neither confirm nor deny his fear that the woman might be Beatrice. He remained there, feeling murderous, for what seemed like an eternity.

Eventually, the two people below stood up and went indoors, but that was no help to the watcher above, for as soon as they left the bench, they were hidden by the building itself. Justin sighed and went back to toss around until the small hours of the morning on a bed which seemed to be full of lumps.

If that had been Beatrice on the terrace, it would explain a lot. She might have been attracted to him in London, but she was presumably already promised to another. And it was clearly a secret attachment, for Crispin had shown no signs of paying her attention during the evening. In fact, Mr Herforth had been remarkably self-composed. It might pay, Justin decided grimly, to get to know that gentleman better. He was not going to give Beatrice up without a struggle.

The following morning, the younger members of the party decided to ride out to what Eleanor had told them, with a mischievous smile aimed at no one in particular, was her favourite look-out. Augustus Smeathley proved to ride very heavily and to have little skill at managing even the very sluggish mount he had brought with him, which made the other four members of the party look at him in disgust. Crispin, finding himself next to Serle, could not help commenting on this.

'A heavy gentleman in every way,' agreed Justin. 'Had you met him before? He's some sort of a connection of yours, isn't he?'

'Good heavens, no! And if he were, I would never admit it. No, as far as I can make out, he's a connection of Lady Marguerite's younger daughter's husband.' He looked with loathing at Mr Smeathley's broad shoulders. 'No,' he repeated, almost to himself, 'that fine gentleman will never be invited to put his legs under *my* table, I can promise you! Do you know, he recommended some verses from the Bible to me this morning, as being suitable for those whom the Lord had favoured with excessive worldly wealth! The impudence of the fellow!'

'Did he, now?' Justin grinned. 'What did you say to that?'

'I recommended him to read Proverbs Three, Verse Seven.'

Justin stared at him. 'Did you, by heavens? I was not aware that you were deeply religious, Mr Herforth.'

Crispin grinned. 'I'm not, but I was forced to learn verses of the Bible many times in my youth, as a punishment. Never thought they'd come in useful, which just goes to show.'

'Might one ask what that particular verse says?'

The grin broadened. 'Be not wise in thine own eyes: fear the Lord and depart from evil.'

Justin let out a great shout of laughter that made the others turn their heads to stare at them. He decided that he definitely liked Mr Herforth and realised ruefully that he would not blame Beatrice for having formed an attachment to him. 'Is that your own mare?' he asked after a few moments. 'She's a neat-built creature.'

'Yes.' Crispin leaned forward to pat her neck. 'But I shan't be riding her for much longer, shall I, old girl? It's about time I bred from her. Be a pity to waste this line, just because I'm fond of riding her.'

The two of them went on to discuss horses and found a common interest in the breeding of suitable mounts, which both held to be more reliable than chancing to one's luck at the sales. You never knew what sort of temperament a strange horse might have.

During the course of the conversation it became apparent that Crispin knew the countryside round Satherby rather better than a man should who had only arrived the previous night. Realising that he had betrayed himself, he coloured and grimaced. 'I'm no good as a conspirator, am I? I must beg you not to betray me to Lady Marguerite, your lordship. I've been staying with friends in the neighbourhood, spying out the land.'

'Did you meet any of the family while you were here? That was a little risky, surely?'

'Oh, *she*'ll not betray me!' Crispin broke off again. 'Oh hell and damnation!' He stared at his companion. Lord Serle was a great deal more dangerous than he appeared. Crispin decided that he had better terminate the conversation at once. 'I think someone had better go and rescue Miss Dencey from that bore,' he said and spurred his horse forward.

Justin watched him go, lips tight and a frown between his brows. Surely Beatrice was not in love with Herforth? A pleasant enough fellow, without guile or malice, but much too young for her. It was more likely to be Eleanor whom Herforth had met if he'd been staying near here recently, he realised with a lightening of the spirit, and yet that young minx had given no sign of any attachment to him, not even glancing his way when she thought no one was looking.

Beatrice looked up with transparent relief as Crispin joined her and Mr Smeathley. Her smile was so warm that Justin muttered something under his breath and began to doubt his own conclusions, in spite of their unassailable logic. He wished bitterly that she would smile at him like that, as she had done in London.

'They say it's the first sign of madness, you know,' said a laughing voice beside him.

He looked up to find that Eleanor had dropped back to join him. 'I beg your pardon. I didn't see you, Lady Eleanor.'

'How interesting Mr Smeathley's conversation is!' she said, sighing and rolling her eyes.

'Don't try your tricks on me!' he said, deciding on shock tactics. 'You're no more taken by him than I am!'

She stared at him, then grinned. 'How very perceptive of you, Lord Serle! Pray don't tell Grandmama!'

'May I know why you're doing it?'

'Oh, just funning,' she said lightly. 'Beatrice said I couldn't fool Augustus Smeathley into believing I was attracted to him and I wagered that I could. I think I've succeeded, don't you?'

'To what purpose?'

She looked at him sideways, debating with herself how much to reveal. 'Why, to show Grandmama that he's not a suitable husband for poor Bea, of course.' A spark of mischief made her add, 'Particularly now,' and observe him carefully in her turn. She was gratified to see that she had his very fullest attention.

'Why now?' His tone was harsh and the words came out more sharply than he had intended.

'Because her affections are engaged elsewhere, of course,' she answered lightly, then, as Beatrice turned to call some query about which route they should take, she left Lord Serle's side and cantered up to join the rest of the party, leaving him no alternative but to follow suit.

What Eleanor had meant merely as a hint that she had guessed his secret, worked instead to make Serle further doubt Beatrice's feelings for himself. For a moment, he felt despair surge through him, then, his expression became grim. Even if Beatrice did have an understanding with Herforth, he decided, he did not intend to give up.

Mrs Powis would have recognised that look. Once Master Justin set his mind on something, the good Lord himself would have had trouble making him change it. Stubborn, that's what he was, stubborn as a mule!

Once at the look-out, they all dismounted, tied up their horses and sat down to enjoy the view from the shade of some trees. Mr Smeathley, annoyed that he could not pursue his suit with Eleanor in the middle of a party which stuck so closely together, did not sit down, but began to wander to and fro. After a while, he called out, 'Lady Eleanor, I wonder if you could tell me what that landmark is?'

As the landmark in question was not visible from where the others were sitting, she was obliged to join him. 'You ought to look at this too, Cousin Crispin,' she called over her shoulder. 'Grandmama wishes you to get to know every bit of the estate. Why don't you join us?'

'Certainly, Cousin Eleanor.'

Beatrice started to rise and follow them, but by the simple expedient of setting his hand on her skirt, Justin managed to prevent her from moving. 'We need to talk, Beatrice,' he said quietly.

'Please, no! We can have nothing private to say to each other!'

'Can we not? I had thought that...'

'No!' She pulled futilely at the skirt.

'I think you'd better explain why you say that. I believed we had a great deal to say to each other. And I also believed that I was receiving some encouragement from you.'

His expression was serious, and he reached out and seized her hand.

'Let me go!' she said furiously, trying in vain to pull away. 'You have no right...' She cast an anxious look at the rest of the party, but their backs were turned and they were concentrating on the view.

'I think I have every right, Beatrice, to ask what has happened? Why did you run away from me at Lymsby? Why could you not explain things to me then?'

She hung her head, very conscious of the warmth of his hand on hers. 'I was cowardly. I should not have, not have let my interest be engaged. It conflicted with, with...'

'With your other interest,' he finished harshly. To hear it from her own lips seemed so final. 'You should have remembered him sooner, should you not?' He released both hand and skirt, and stood up. 'Don't be afraid that I'll pursue where I'm not wanted, Miss Dencey! I'll find an excuse to leave at the first opportunity.'

'Oh no! Please, you mustn't!'

'But you've just told me that my suit is hopeless!' he said, still speaking angrily. 'Why on earth should I stay here?'

She flushed and avoided his eyes. 'Because of Aunt Marguerite. Oh please, *please* stay for a while longer!'

'Why? I wish your aunt no harm, but why in heaven's name should I wish to please a woman whom I've only just met. She has no claim upon me. Give me a reason in plain words, if you please, Miss Dencey!'

She took a deep breath. 'She wishes you to marry Eleanor. That's why she invited you here.'

He stared at her, amazed. 'Do you think me so fickle as to change my affections overnight?'

'N-no, but, but she – Eleanor, I mean – she's superior in every way to me. Once you get to know her, you cannot fail to like her better.' She did not know how to look him in the face.

'And that would please you?'

'Above all else!' she said fervently and the obvious sincerity of her words made him even more puzzled. 'I beg you to be kind to my aunt. She's growing old and, and she wishes to see Eleanor established. And she has a great regard, a very great regard, for your family.'

'It's quite gothic!' he declared. 'I have no intention of marrying to please someone else, especially when my affections are engaged already. I think you're concealing something from me, Beatrice.'

She could only shake her head and avoid his eyes. If he looked too closely, he would see the tears in her eyes.

When she did not speak, he took a deep breath. 'Come, this is fruitless. I suggest we join the others!' He reached out and pulled her to her feet before she had time to move of her own accord and they stood for a moment, close together, with him still holding her arm, while she found her balance. He bent his head over her and his nearness made her sway towards him, in spite of herself. 'Beatrice, Beatrice, I don't understand you at all. And I wish you would tell me the truth,' he murmured, his lips close to her face.

How she found the strength to step backwards and say calmly 'I've said all I wish to, my lord,' she never knew. 'Please better your acquaintance with my niece.'

He let her hand fall and shook his head in bewilderment as they walked across the grassy hillside to join the others. Eleanor at once noticed the tears trembling in Beatrice's eyes and managed to shield her from the others for the next few minutes. She was quite exasperated by her aunt's noble behaviour and longed to give her a good shaking. But it was almost time for luncheon when they arrived back and there was no time to do anything but rush upstairs to change their clothes. She would have to speak to Serle later.

Lizzie also noticed how upset her mistress was, but it was not her place to comment, so she merely chatted brightly about the doings of the other servants. She said nothing that needed an answer and she noticed with relief that Miss Dencey relaxed a little as her hair was brushed and pinned up.

After the meal, the company went to sit in a pleasant room next to the library. Crispin left them, reluctantly, to go and meet with the bailiff. What he learned stunned him. He had not realised how vast the Graceover holdings were and he could not quite believe that everything would belong to him one day. However, he was somewhat distracted from what the bailiff was saying by his fears about what Eleanor would get up to while he was apart from her, so he cut short the meeting as soon as he could.

While the other Smeathleys related to Eleanor one or two items of interest from the newspapers they had been perusing during the morning, Augustus described their outing to the Dowager in glowing terms and Bea sat silently by her aunt's side, the maltreated embroidery lying untouched on her lap. She said yes and no at intervals, or nodded her head, which was all that Mr Smeathley seemed to expect of her.

The Dowager grew a little restless, for she did not like to be talked at for too long. However, she wished to appraise Mr Smeathley, so she pressed her lips firmly together and studied him as he talked. Yesterday he had seemed quite promising, but now she was finding that his interminable prosing made her head ache and she was having second thoughts about asking Beatrice to tie herself to such a windbag.

Very soon, Eleanor found an excuse to join them and started to encourage Augustus to describe Wells Cathedral, on the subject of which he had already bored her to tears. He talked about it uninterrupted for about ten minutes, then, as the Dowager was growing visibly restless, Eleanor offered to show him the flower gardens. He rose with an alacrity which left the Dowager frowning. She turned to Beatrice, 'Why didn't you go with them?'

'I'd rather not. And anyway, I wasn't asked, was I?'

'Haven't taken to Smeathley, have you?'

her aunt asked abruptly.

'N-no, I'm afraid not. I did try, but...'

'He's setting his cap for Eleanor, unless I'm much mistaken,' the Dowager said, showing that she had noticed more than they thought. 'The impertinence of it! Who does he think he is?'

'Yes. But I don't think, surely she wouldn't...' Beatrice's voice trailed away, as she remembered the rapt attention with which Eleanor had listened to Mr Smeathley's erudite but tedious monologue on church architecture.

The stick quivered as the twisted old hand tightened on it. 'The chit's not had any experience of men, that's the trouble. It's my fault. I've protected her too much. I'll have to speak to Serle about her before this gets out of hand. Perhaps...' She did not finish her sentence, just said curtly. 'Ask Serle to come and see me in my rooms in a quarter of an hour, Bea, will you? And then go outside and join those two. I'm not leaving Eleanor alone with Smeathley. He won't do for her, won't do at all. He's only interested in her fortune.'

'Or mine,' Beatrice said, with a wan smile.

'Hmph.' Well, as you don't like him, he'll not get that, either, will he?' She reached out to pat Beatrice's hand. 'I would never force you into marriage with someone you disliked, child. You should realise that. Now, ring for my footman.'

Beatrice did as she was bidden and then moved across to speak to Lord Serle and pass on the Dowager's request. Lippings would come to fetch him when Lady Marguerite was ready to receive him. Afterwards she went outside with her usual quiet grace.

Justin watched her go bleakly. Once he had spoken to the Dowager, explained that he could not accede to her wishes, he thought it would be best to leave Satherby as soon as he decently could. If Beatrice did not trust him enough to confide in him, he did not intend to torture himself any longer by watching her with another man.

No sooner had he made that decision than he changed his mind. Why should he not stay and fight for her? Why give in so tamely? His thoughts see-sawed from one decision to another, in a way which he would not have believed possible a month previously. Justin Serle, in love for the first time at thirty, was finding it a most frustrating experience, and his own reactions quite bewildered him.

A quarter of an hour later, he followed

Lippings along to the East Wing, where Lady Marguerite had her own suite on the ground floor. He found her sitting by the window, sunk in thought, and when he moved across to join her, he saw that she was staring at the three people walking up and down in the rose garden.

'Ah, here you are, Lord Serle.'

She must have been very beautiful once, he thought, rather like Eleanor. Her spirit still shone undaunted in her eyes, though her body was clearly failing. 'The gardens at Satherby are very beautiful at this time of year,' he said, thinking how tired she was looking.

'What do I care about gardens!' she snapped. 'Sit down, will you, Serle? I can't abide looking up at people. Now, what do you think of my grand-daughter?'

So it *was* the younger girl she had in mind! 'She's a nice child,' he said carefully.

'Child? She's nineteen.'

'She seems a child to me,' he reiterated, hoping to avoid a confrontation.

'I'd rather hoped you'd find her attractive,' she said. 'In fact, to be plain, I'd welcome a match between our houses, and that's why I invited you here.'

There was a moment's silence, then he

shook his head. 'I regret to disappoint you, your ladyship, but it's not possible.'

'Not spoken for, are you? Beatrice said nothing about any other attachments.'

'It's not generally known. She won't look at me, anyway.'

'She's a fool, then!' The Dowager sighed and they both remained silent for a few minutes.

'You look very tired, ma'am,' he ventured after a while, for she was white as a sheet and her hand was trembling visibly on the arm of her chair. 'Allow me to send for your maid.'

She sighed again and crumpled forward suddenly. He caught the frail body before she could fall to the floor, then managed, without letting her go, to ring the hand bell that stood on the table beside her. She was as light as an autumn leaf in his arms and her skin had something of the same texture. Her body seemed a dried-out husk with its life juices nearly gone and that made him feel sad and protective.

Lippings rushed in and called out, 'Oh no!' before examining her mistress with the air of one who knew her business. 'Can you carry her through into the bedroom for me, my lord?' she asked. 'I think she's just fained. I thought for a moment – she has a bad heart, you see – but it's just a faint, I think.'

They got the Dowager onto her bed, then Lippings asked him not to tell the other guests, just to send Miss Beatrice in. 'She's the only one who knows how bad her ladyship is,' she said, without thinking to whom she was speaking. 'That's why her ladyship sent her to London. She was relying on her to…' She broke off, realising that shock had made her indiscreet. 'I beg your pardon, my lord.'

'Please don't stop there. Why exactly did Miss Dencey go to London?'

'To find a husband for Lady Eleanor, I believe. And for herself as well, if she could, but mainly for Lady Eleanor. Her ladyship gave her a list of suitable families.'

Hope began to dawn again in Justin. 'Did she, now?'

'I shouldn't be telling you this, sir. It was the shock. Please don't tell her ladyship. The slightest upset could kill her. The doctor said she hasn't long to live now. That's why she begged Miss Beatrice not to let her down.'

'No, I won't tell her.' He left the room without seeing anything around him and once he had fetched Beatrice, he made his way instinctively to the peace of his bed-room to think things through. Beatrice knew that her aunt had not long to live, knew that she had set her heart on him marrying Eleanor in order to keep her precious grand-daughter safe when she was dead! He tried to remember his exact conversations with Eleanor and Crispin. No one had actually said that Beatrice was in love with Crispin, or he with her. And the figure he had seen from the bedroom could just as easily have been, must have been, Eleanor. *That* was what the minx was concealing, though goodness only knew why! If the Dowager wished to see her married, surely the Heir to Satherby was a good match for anyone.

His face brightened and his heart began to thud as he realised that very possibly he had mistaken the whole affair, very possibly, Beatrice did love him. He moved towards the door, intending to confront her with this at once, then realised that she would still be with her aunt, so he went out for a walk, unable to sit quietly until he had got to the bottom of things.

TWELVE

The doctor was summoned and pro-
nounced Lady Marguerite to be suffering
from exhaustion. As he had compelled her
to take a draught that sent her to sleep,
Beatrice was not able to discuss with her
aunt what she wished done about the
guests. When she told them that their
hostess was simply overtired and must rest,
only Justin asked whether she wished them
to leave.

Beatrice stared at him, unable to think
clearly. If she said yes, then she would get
rid of the Smeathleys, but he would go too,
and he might still be able to do what her
aunt wished. And there was Crispin to think
of. He should remain here at this dangerous
time, in case ... her thoughts faltered.
Somehow, she could not imagine a world
without her aunt.

She realised dimly that someone was
supporting her and making her sit down.
'Put your head on your knees for a moment,
Miss Dencey!' commanded a firm, but

gentle voice. 'I think you're feeling a little faint yourself. It's probably delayed shock.' She obeyed because it was easier to do that than to argue.

The same voice told someone to fetch a glass of brandy and then its owner helped her to sit up and sip it. She found that she was once again leaning against Serle's chest and gasped aloud, but had not the strength to pull away.

'Take another sip, if you please, Miss Dencey, and don't try to speak for a minute or two. Smeathley, perhaps you and your parents would retire to another room and leave Miss Dencey to recover in peace. Herforth, could you go and find Lady Eleanor?'

They were alone in the room for a few precious minutes. When she ventured to look up at him, he planted a very fleeting kiss on her brow. 'You've been making a mountain out of a molehill, my dear. We'll find a way through this without upsetting your aunt, I promise you. I'm not giving you up.'

She stared at him for a moment, then gave in to temptation and leaned against his chest. 'You keep coming to my rescue,' she said, with a ghost of a chuckle. She was too tired to struggle anymore.

'You obviously need me around, then, or

who knows what trouble you will fall into.' He could see her lips curving gently into a smile and put a finger under her chin to make her look up at him. 'We shall be married as soon as possible,' he said in a voice that brooked no argument. 'You can't possibly manage everything here on your own and,' he put the same finger on her lips to prevent her from speaking, 'I find I do not wish to live without you, my dear.'

Tears overflowed from her eyes. 'Oh, Justin, how can I be so selfish?' she said. 'Especially now.'

'Blame it all on me. I need you, too.'

Her hand stole up to touch his crisp black hair. 'Do you, do you really think we can do this without upsetting my aunt?' Hope was growing in her.

'I'm sure of it. Will you marry me, Beatrice? You haven't replied to my proposal and I'm feeling rejected.'

'Oh, Justin! I...' she could not seem to breathe properly.

His grip tightened. 'No more prevarication. Yes or no?'

The hand stroked his cheek, then she looked up at him in wonderment. 'Yes. Yes, of course I will.' She was surprised that she had even considered any other course of action. A weight seemed to fall from her shoulders.

A cough from the doorway made them both turn round. Eleanor came in, shutting the door behind her, and said with mock severity, 'Dear me, Beatrice, a lady should never show her feelings in public! Or allow herself to be alone with a gentleman to whom she is not related.'

Justin would not allow Beatrice to move from the shelter of his arms. 'You may be the first to congratulate us, Miss Impertinence,' he said.

Eleanor squealed and rushed to plant a kiss on Beatrice's face, hesitated, then hugged Serle as well. 'Oh, I'm so glad! I was at my wit's end as to how to bring you two together!'

Two faces gaped at her and she said airily, 'Well, I couldn't help but see how you felt. I know Bea too well and your feelings showed sometimes when you looked at her, Serle – Lord Serle, I should say.'

'Impertinence is not a strong enough word for you, young lady!' Justin said with mock severity. 'And my friends and relatives usually call me Justin.'

She pulled a face at him. 'Justin, then.'

'Eleanor, you won't say anything until we

can tell Aunt Marguerite, will you?' Beatrice begged. 'Not to anyone. Promise me! The slightest shock could kill her.'

The laughter left Eleanor's face. 'Is that why you were being so noble about Serle and me? Is she – really bad?'

Beatrice nodded. The two of them clasped hands, for the thought of losing the old termagant who had looked after them both for the past ten years caused a pain too deep for words.

The door started to open and Justin moved away from Beatrice as Mrs Smeathley sailed in. 'I came to see how you were, Beatrice. We were worried about you, and it's not seemly to leave you alone with a gentleman. Surely your maid should have been summoned by now? And I think you should go and lie down for a while.'

Eleanor cleared her throat. 'You don't seem to have noticed, Mrs Smeathley, but Beatrice is *not* alone with a gentleman! I'm here.'

'It's very kind of you to worry about Miss Dencey,' Justin said, frowning at Eleanor to keep quiet, 'but I think we can leave her to Lady Eleanor's tender care. Allow me to escort you back to the drawing room.' He held out his arm in so imperative a manner that Mrs Smeathley found herself doing as she was bidden, though her son had instructed her to remain with Miss Dencey so that he could speak to Lady Eleanor alone. At the door Justin turned to smile briefly across the room at his love, his heart lifting at the answering softening of her eyes, then he led the older lady inexorably out.

Beatrice, who was still looking pale, agreed to go and rest for a while, so Eleanor left her in Lizzie's devoted hands and then went to look for Crispin. She could not tell him Bea's glorious news yet, but she would appreciate his company for a while until she had grown accustomed to the thought of losing her grandmama in the near future. Instead she met Augustus Smeathley, parading majestically to and fro on the terrace. He hastened towards her. 'My dear Lady Eleanor, how is your grandmother?'

'Sleeping. The doctor gave her a draught and told us to stop her from doing so much. It's exhaustion, he thinks.'

'She wishes to see you safely established before the Lord calls her to Him,' he said. 'One can see that she knows the end to be near.' He said this perfectly calmly, with no hint of regret or sorrow in his voice.

Eleanor found that by digging her nails

into the palms of her hands she could prevent herself speaking sharply to him. She took a deep breath and managed to say just as calmly, 'Do you think so? She's said nothing to me about it.'

'A clergyman has some experience of the type of things which cause concern to those whose days are numbered,' he intoned, as loudly as if they were in church.

A passing footman stared at them in surprise.

'Pray come for a walk among the roses,' she said hastily. 'I want to pick a bunch for Grandmama's room. Flowers always cheer one up, don't you think?'

'Indeed, yes. Flowers are one of our Lord's most beautiful gifts to mankind.' He escorted her with measured steps to the rose garden and as soon as they were of sight of the house, he fell upon one knee before her. 'Lady Eleanor, words cannot express how I feel,' he began. 'Suffice it to say that one glance was enough to show me that you were destined to become my wife.'

'It was Beatrice you came here to meet,' she could not resist pointing out.

'I believe that was mentioned as a possibility. But as soon as I saw you, I knew that the Lord had destined us for one another. And I could see that you felt the same.'

She stared at him in amazement. Did he really think this was the way to propose to someone?

'Although our fortunes are not equal, I can offer you a high status in the world, for I have every expectation of being offered a bishopric eventually.'

'Oh,' she exclaimed, clasping her hands and giving way to her sense of the ridiculous, 'I am not worthy of such an honour!'

He rose from his knee and carefully dusted his trousers. 'Have no fear on that score, my dear girl. You may be young and inexperienced, but under my guidance, you will learn all you need to know to support me in life as a wife should.' He seemed to take it for granted that she had accepted him and went on to describe the house he currently occupied, a most superior type of residence, though smaller than he liked, and then he began to detail the glories to be expected of a bishop's palace. He made no attempt to take her into his arms or even to kiss her cheek, but expounded enthusiastically upon the topic of his own dazzling future in the ecclesiastical hierarchies.

She decided that she could not keep up

the pretence any longer and said abruptly, 'I must retire to my room. I am quite overset by your offer, Mr Smeathley.'

'The female mind is easily thrown into turmoil,' he said in a kindly tone, nodding at her. 'Fear not! Once we are married, I shall guard you from all problems and guide you carefully through the mazes of life.'

'I haven't accepted you yet.'

'I beg your pardon?'

'I said I haven't accepted you yet.'

He stared at her through narrowed eyes, and blinked, as if seeing her for the first time.

She stared aback at him and shook her head decisively. 'Nor shall I accept you!'

'What did you say?'

'Nor shall I accept you,' she repeated, slowly and clearly. 'You're too old for me and far too mercenary. And,' she added, carried away by the pleasure of giving him a well-deserved set-down, 'I shall tell Bea about your proposal and beg her not to marry you, either. She wouldn't marry anyone I disliked and besides, I don't think she's taken to you herself.'

When she saw his expression, she realised that she had gone a bit too far and wished that she had just offered him a simple rejection. She took a step backwards, feeling suddenly afraid of him, for he was looming over her in a menacing way.

'Why, you little...'

To her relief, she saw Crispin at the other side of the rose garden and fled to his side. 'Cousin Crispin! You're just in time to escort me to my aunt.' She laid her hand on his and nipped his arm imperatively. He took the hint, inclined his head to Smeathley and led her away.

'What was all that about, might I ask? What has that fellow been saying to you?'

'I, well, he was just proposing,' she said, trying to sound airy, but only managing to sound upset.

'I see. Well, you've certainly been encouraging him to think you might favour his suit, so it was only to be expected!'

'Well, I've told him now that I wouldn't dream of marrying him.' She was biting her lip. 'Only after I did, well, I felt a bit afraid of him. He's so very – large.'

'It never pays to tamper with someone's affections, Eleanor. Even those of a fellow like him. And I've been thinking things over. I've decided that as soon as the Dowager has recovered, I shall seek an interview with her. And the earlier, the better. I categorically refuse to continue with this deceit any longer!'

She had never seen him in this mood before. All she could think of to say was, 'Yes, Crispin.'

'And mind you don't start flirting with anyone else!' he said, spoiling the masterful effect by adding, 'Until we're married, you're only allowed to flirt with me. And after that, I shall expect you to be a dutiful wife.'

'Oh, yes, Crispin,' she said enthusiastically and they both broke into laughter.

Mr Augustus Smeathley, left standing among the roses, watching the two of them walk away, was furious with both her and himself. He had allowed himself to be seduced by a pretty face and the prospect of a huge fortune, when the older woman and a very comfortable fortune could have been his for the taking. He hoped fervently that the Dowager would not recover too soon, for he realised that he would have little chance of her support in winning Beatrice after his pursuit of Eleanor.

He picked up a piece of fallen branch and swished viciously at the roses, sending a shower of blood-red petals fluttering across the path. Well, there were other ways of killing a cat than choking it on cream. Swish!

Given a little time and effort, it should be possible to facilitate matters with Beatrice. A man of determination could achieve much by the judicious application of force at crucial moments. Swish! And he was very determined. With a grim air that quite changed the noble cast of his countenance and rendered it far less handsome, he set off to explore the grounds. Only an hour later, he found exactly what he wanted and began to smile tightly and to weave his plans.

Dinner that evening was a brief meal, with little conversation. Beatrice begged Crispin to take the head of table, to Mrs Smeathley's ill-concealed annoyance, for she felt that, as the oldest lady present, she should have been awarded this honour. Consequently, she sat in majestic sulks for the whole meal. As no one noticed, she was even angrier with Miss Dencey by the time the meal ended and she was quite prepared to assist her son when he asked her for help.

Beatrice begged to be excused immediately after dinner, for she wished to see how her aunt was feeling and to check arrangements for her care during the night. Eleanor, who was hoping to have a chat with Crispin, went into the drawing-room and began to play softly upon the piano, but

Augustus stuck firmly in the room with them, as if determined to prevent a tête-à-tête. He was insistently affable, as if the incident in the rose garden had never occurred, but he still made her shiver and she had begun to wonder what really lay behind that mask of determined affability.

Serle, who had followed Beatrice from the room, managed to have a word alone with her before she retired, by dint of simply pulling her into the library and sweeping her into his arms. 'I'm sure I shouldn't,' she sighed, leaning her head against his shoulder.

'I'm sure you should,' he countered. 'You must be worn to a frazzle with the worry about your aunt on top of the strain of finding something to say to those fools.'

'You don't like the Smeathleys, either, do you?' she said, smiling in spite of herself.

'Can't stand them. Know the type well. He'll get on in the church, though not, perhaps, as high as he expects. Got an inflated opinion of his own worth. An imposing appearance isn't all it takes to become a bishop.'

She shuddered. 'I sometimes wonder if he isn't quite ruthless beneath that affability.'

He stared at her in amazement. 'I doubt it. He's shown no signs of it, anyway. But what can he do to you, even if he is the most ruthless man on earth? You're safe in your own home.'

'Not to me, to Eleanor. She has, well, she's led him on rather. I noticed at dinner that she appeared to have completely lost interest in him, didn't you?'

'I never thought she did have any interest in him. She told me she'd wagered with you that she could make him believe she was enamoured of him.'

'Wagered with me?' Her amazement was so patent that he frowned. 'Wagered!' she repeated, in a disgusted tone. 'Do you really think I'd encourage her to behave in such a vulgar way?'

'Then what was she up to with him?'

'I intend to find out, I promise you!'

In the morning, the Dowager was a little better, but the doctor, who had called upon her very early, refused to let her receive any visitors and only Beatrice was allowed to go ion and ask her how she was feeling.

'Tired,' sighed the old lady. 'I thought I could manage it one last time, but I can't, Bea, I can't. What are we going to do about them all?'

'Nothing at the moment,' said Beatrice firmly. 'You're not well enough to think clearly. And as the guests are no trouble to me, we'll just leave things as they are until you're a little better, shall we?'

Lady Marguerite nodded, her eyelids already drooping towards sleep.

Beatrice watched her for a moment, nodded to Lippings and tiptoed out, feeling as if the world were topsy-turvy. She had never seen her aunt quiescent like this.

During breakfast, Smeathley was so attentive to Beatrice that she could not fail to realise that he was now courting her again. When he requested that she walk with him in the gardens, she made an excuse of having a lot to do. Although she felt that Eleanor had treated him unfairly, she knew his heart had not been involved, only his greed. Her mild concern about his intentions would have turned to serious apprehension had she seen the expression on his face as she turned to leave the room.

Later in the morning, Augustus took himself off into the woods with a gun, but he made no attempt to shoot anything. Some intensive thought during his walk confirmed him in his decision to force the issue and he continued to make his plans accordingly. This involved him in a long discussion with his groom, a well-built man with a battered face, whom the rest of the stable staff left severely alone, because of his foul temper.

If he ever got a chance, Augustus thought afterwards with anger glinting in his eyes, he would teach Lady Eleanor Graceover a lesson she would not forget in a hurry. In the meantime, there was still the other one to make sure of. He was so assiduous in his attentions to Beatrice for the rest of the day that she begged Justin to stay near her and not to allow Smeathley a chance to be alone with her. Like Eleanor, she was beginning to find him a little frightening.

The following day, the Dowager was so much better that she started demanding to know when they would let her up again. As the weather had turned showery and the whole house felt damp, Beatrice and the doctor both decided she would be better keeping to her well-heated rooms. However, they did allow Crispin and Lord Serle to visit her briefly. Crispin took one look at the sunken face and knew this was not the time to press his suit. It was Justin who left her looking the happiest, for he chatted quietly of his home and of his closest neighbour, her grand-daughter, Jennice. He even made her splutter with laughter several times.

'How did you do it?' Beatrice asked him afterwards, awed at his skilful address.

'The secret is to treat old ladies as if they were still young,' he told her with a smile. 'Did you think that age rendered them impervious to a little attention?'

'My Aunt Marguerite?'

'Even your aunt. She's very proud of having outlived her generation, you know, and of still being in full possession of her faculties.' He smoothed the frown from her brow with a gentle fingertip. 'Don't worry. She's on the mend now and will last a while longer. Long enough to watch us marry.'

'If we can keep her from shocks and annoyances.'

'We'll do that.'

She stared at his eyes, still astonished that he should care for her so deeply, and then rested her head against his shoulder. 'I hope so, Justin.'

Somehow the rest of the day crawled past. The weather worsened, with grey skies and more showers, quite in tune, Beatrice thought, with her mood. However was she to bring her aunt round to the idea of Justin as a husband for herself instead of for Eleanor?

Shortly after Beatrice had retired to her

room that evening, there was a knock on the door. She gestured to Lizzie to answer it and continued to brush her hair, an activity which always helped her to think clearly.

'It's a note from Mrs Smeathley, miss.' Lizzie held out a screw of paper.

'Oh, bother, what does she want?' Beatrice opened the note and read it with a frown. 'She wishes to see me immediately upon a matter of extreme importance. Well, you can tell her maid that I've gone to bed and can't see anyone until the morning.'

'The maid told me Mrs Smeathley was already waiting for you in the library, miss. She didn't wait for an answer.'

Beatrice scowled into the mirror, then sighed. 'I suppose I'll have to go down, then. She *is* a guest, after all, though why she had to wait until now to see me, I don't know!' She pulled her hair back and tied it with a ribbon, examining the result in the mirror. 'That'll have to do. Don't wait up for me, Lizzie. I can easily manage this dress and I know you're tired.'

She whisked out of the room without waiting for an answer, so did not see Lizzie set her hands on her hips or hear her ask the mirror whether she looked like the sort of person who'd neglect a good mistress by selfishly going off to bed like that before her day's duties were finished.

No one was waiting in the library, and Beatrice looked round in puzzlement. She heard a sound outside and realised that the French window was open. It seemed a strange time to take the air, but then, she found the Smeathleys a strange family. She shook her head irritably and went to investigate.

Before she had realised what was happening, some thick material was thrown over her head and a heavy hand muffled her mouth. The whole operation was conducted so rapidly and skilfully that she had no time to scream before her mouth was filled with choking layers of cloth and she was dragged forward, away from the house. Amazement as much as fear prevented her from struggling at first, but then she realised the danger she was in and tried to free her arms from the encumbrance. When she could not, she bit the hand that held her mouth. A voice cursed and someone cuffed the side of her head, making it spin for a moment or two. Her attacker continued to drag her along the terrace.

Beatrice struggled, but the man holding her was immensely strong and her efforts were in vain. After a minute or two, she was thrown face down upon the ground. Someone pressed her head against the damp earth while her hands were tied firmly behind her back. It seemed obvious then that there was more than one assailant, but the cloth blanketed out sound as well as sight. Something was tied over the material across her mouth, which effectively prevented her from making anything but the most muffled of noises. At one time, she felt her foot make contact with something soft and a yelp issued from her mystery kidnapper, which gave her a brief feeling of satisfaction, but apart from that, he was very much in control of the situation. She felt panic rise in her. What did this person want of her?

Once her hands were tied, she was picked up and carried face down over someone's shoulder. After a few minutes of intense discomfort, she was dumped on the ground again, she heard a door opening and then she was dragged unceremoniously into what felt like some sort of building. The door closed and she was left alone with her fears.

For a while, she could only lie on the cold floor and wait for something dreadful to happen. Throughout the attack, her kidnapper had not said a word and that seemed to make it all so much more sinister.

After a time, when nothing further happened, she began to recover a little from her fright and to grow angry again. The darkness seemed suffocating beneath the thick folds of material, but she told herself firmly that she had managed to breathe so far inside it, so she was not likely to choke to death now. She forced herself to take deep even breaths and gradually her heart stopped fluttering.

Her mind was darting from one thing to another in the most disoriented way. A heroine in a novel, or even her dear Eleanor, would not have been caught out like this, though a heroine would probably have fainted first before doing something ingenious and making her escape against improbable odds. Only now did Beatrice realise how helpless one really was when one's hands were firmly tied behind one's back, and how much the novelists had lied about such situations.

She heard the door open again and at once froze where she lay, making a quick decision to pretend to be unconscious. But no one touched her. She strained her ears and thought she heard the sound of a scuffle and grunts as if two men were struggling close at hand. A cry, the sound of a falling body, then the door slammed again and she distinctly heard a bolt being shot.

If she had been able to, she would have shrieked with terror when she heard someone moving on the ground beside her, but the gag prevented this. Hands groped across her body, but she forced herself to lie still. The hands reached her head and to her relief began to unfasten the gag. When the stifling material was removed, a voice asked in the darkness, 'Who are you?'

To her astonishment it was Augustus Smeathley's voice. That did not make sense, so she continued her pretence of being unconscious. The way his hands roved across her body increased her fear, for this was not the way a clergyman should behave with an unknown and unconscious female. When the hands lingered and began to caress her breasts, she decided it was time to wake up.

'Uhhh. Where am I?' she asked, annoyed that she could think of nothing more dramatic to say.

'Miss Dencey! Is that really you?'

'Mr Smeathley!'

'It is indeed I, dear lady.'

'Where are we?'

'In a garden shed. We appear to be prisoners here. Are you all right? They haven't hurt you?'

'I'm not hurt, but my hands are tied behind my back. Can you not unfasten them?'

He fumbled with the ropes for a moment. 'No. The knots are too tight.'

Her intuition told her that his presence was no coincidence and the feeling persisted that he must have been involved in the kidnapping. It made a sort of sense, if he were now intending to marry her instead of Eleanor, she supposed. He was unsure of her and wished to compromise her. Well, whatever happened, she would *not* marry him! She would as soon marry a toad! Sooner! 'How did you come to be here?' she asked, judging it safer to behave as though she believed what he told her.

'I saw a stranger, an uncouth-looking man, behaving in a suspicious manner near the house, so I followed him. I must have made a noise, because he was waiting for me behind this shed. I fear he overpowered me and cast me inside. I am a man of God, not a pugilist!'

'But why should anyone lock me up here in the first place!' she demanded. 'What could he want with me?'

There was a silence, then he suggested dubiously, 'Ransom, perhaps?'

'I have no money!'

'But your aunt is an extremely rich woman.'

She sucked in her breath. 'And ill. This could kill her! Mr Smeathley, I've got to escape!'

'We must pray for guidance.'

She gave an angry snort. 'We'll, I'd find it easier to pray if my hands weren't tied behind my back!'

'The knots are too tight for me to...' he began.

'Then why don't you see whether you can find something to cut the ropes with?' she asked tartly. 'Even a man of God should be able to do that!'

'It's very dark in here.'

'Your hands aren't tied, are they? You can surely feel your way around. There must be something sharp.' She dared not let him see that she suspected him, or that she was afraid of him. She waited impatiently as she listened to him fumbling in the darkness.

'I've found something sharp,' he said at last. 'It's some sort of garden implement, I think.'

And you've no doubt realised how suspicious it would look if you didn't release me, she thought to herself. 'Thank goodness!' she said aloud. 'My arms are hurting.'

As he sat her up, his hands again strayed briefly across her body. She said nothing and he began to saw at her bonds. When they fell away and she tried to move, she cried out involuntarily.

'Pray allow me to massage your arms, Miss Dencey.'

'No! Keep away! I mean, thank you, Mr Smeathley, but there's no need.' She was only too conscious of the size of the body supporting her and was sure he could easily overpower her. 'Thank you for your help,' she said after a while, 'but I can sit on my own now.'

The arm round her shoulders did not move. 'However brave you're trying to be, my dear Miss Dencey, a female in your circumstances must be terrified. Allow me to comfort you until you are yourself again.'

'Oh, I always recover quickly when I've been kidnapped,' she said as lightly as she could. She pushed away from him and managed to stand up, but he did the same, and to her mingled fear and frustration, she found herself trapped in the corner by his body.

'I'm afraid you may faint, Miss Dencey.

Too sudden a movement could be danger-ous. Or you might trip over something in the darkness.'

'Pray move back! Such close contact with your body is unseemly, Mr Smeathley,' she snapped, losing patience.

'My name is Augustus.'

'I prefer to call you Mr Smeathley. We aren't related.'

He still did not move. 'Whatever we say or do,' he pointed out, 'this whole situation is highly unseemly, and I'm glad you've realised that. A young unmarried woman alone at night with a man to whom she is not related is a shocking thing, even when the man happens to be a clergyman with the purest of intentions. However, you need not worry. I shall, of course, marry you after-wards. I can do no less. Your good name is quite safe with me, my dear Beatrice.'

She pushed past him. 'I need to move around, sir, to restore my circulation.' She did not dare tell him what she thought of his offer. As long as she kept up the pretence of believing his tale, she might be safe. She bumped into a shelf and cried out involun-tarily. A large hand groped for her and she was firmly seized again.

'Are you all right, my dear Beatrice?' The

arm was again round her shoulders and his hand lingered quite openly on her breast. 'Ah,' breathed a voice in her ear, a voice husky with passion, 'you are a very womanly creature.' The hand continued to caress her.

She tried to pull away from him, but he was far stronger than she was.

THIRTEEN

When an hour had passed and Miss Dencey had not returned to her room, Lizzie began to get worried. Surely Mrs Smeathley could not be keeping her mistress for so long at this hour of the night? She went cautiously out into the dark corridor from which the main bedrooms opened and crept along, listening at doors. There was a light in the suite occupied by Mr and Mrs Smeathley and a murmur of voices from inside. The light went out. A short time listening at the door confirmed that husband and wife were both there, making ready for sleep.

Lizzie returned to her mistress's bedroom, lit a candle and made her way downstairs by its flickering light. The suits of armour made her shiver as she passed, because the moving shadows made them look as if they were waiting to pounce, but she pressed on. The house was silent, the front door was bolted and there was no sign of anyone. Where was Miss Beatrice? Even more worried than before, she went back up the stairs, again checked her mistress's room and then went to listen outside Miss Eleanor's. But that room too was dark and there was not even a hint of movement from inside.

As she turned to go back once again to her mistress's room, a hand covered her mouth and she jumped like a startled cat. She sagged in relief when a voice whispered in her ear, 'Be quiet! It's only me!'

'Oh, your lordship!'

'Shhh. What are you doing creeping round the corridors at this hour of the night?'

'I was looking for Miss Beatrice. She hasn't come back!'

'What! Where is she?'

'That's what I was trying to find out, your lordship.'

'We can't talk here. Let's go back to her room.'

Once there, Lizzie explained the message and how Miss Beatrice had not returned. 'And I'm ever so worried, sir, for it's all dark and locked up downstairs, even near her ladyship's rooms, and where else can Miss Beatrice have got to?'

'I don't know, but I promise you I'll find out. I…'

'Where's Bea?' Eleanor was standing in the doorway, in her nightgown, with a cloak clutched around her.

'Shh! That's what we're trying to work out.'

'Where is she, then?'

'We don't know.'

Eleanor stared at him in amazement. 'But she came up to bed ages ago!'

Another form appeared in the doorway.

'Oh Crispin, Bea's disappeared!' Eleanor threw herself into his arms and he clasped her to him.

In terse phrases, Justin explained the situation, as far as they knew it.

'We'd better go and look outside, then, on the terrace, perhaps,' said Crispin in a calm, matter-of-fact tone. 'She could have got locked out. Come along, Eleanor. You know the house and grounds better than we do.'

She refrained from pointing out that if Bea had been locked out, she would only have needed to knock on the door to gain admittance.

By the time they had started exploring the terrace, the butler had woken up and joined them. Serle had difficulty hiding his frustration as they were delayed for yet another explanation. Who knew what danger Beatrice was in? However, Borrill's appearance proved to be an advantage, for he produced three storm lanterns, whose light was an improvement on the flickering candles. They spread out along the terrace and started to search.

Crispin was the one who discovered broken twigs and leaves next to one of the bushes, and an overturned potted plant. Justin went further along that side of the house and found marks in the soft earth near a flowerbed, as if something had been dragged along. Careful scrutiny revealed large footprints leading away from the house, with slide marks alongside the first dozen or so, then a jumble of marks, then nothing but the large footprints.

'Someone's been dragged along here, I reckon,' said Borrill, who was proving an intelligent companion. 'Look at those slide marks, Mr Herforth. And they stop here. I reckon they picked Miss Dencey up and carried her after this.'

His unspoken assumption was that

Beatrice had been kidnapped, an assumption with which no one disagreed.

'Yes,' agreed Crispin. 'I'd say you were right.'

'Where does this path lead to, Eleanor?' demanded Serle, his voice sharp with anxiety.

'Well, nowhere, really. Just to some sheds.'

'Show me!'

Clutching her cloak around her, Eleanor led the way through the shrubbery, with Crispin holding a lantern to light her way. They were followed by Serle, whose face was grim and whose free hand clenched every now and then into a fist. Lizzie and Borrill came last, she determined not to be left out, he worrying about the protocol he should employ in this situation.

The sheds proved a disappointment, for they were empty of anything but garden implements and flowerpots. Serle prowled round the bushes behind the huts and then returned, frowning.

'Where can she be?' asked Eleanor loudly, without thinking.

'Shh!' Serle's whisper was so ferocious that everyone fell silent. He looked at Crispin. 'Did you hear something?'

'I'm not sure. Over there?'

'Yes.' They listened in silence, then, 'I definitely heard something that time,' Justin declared.

They pushed their way along an overgrown path, with Serle leading now. It led to another hut, but this one had its door firmly bolted from outside.

From inside, a voice called, 'Is anyone there?' The voice had a distinct quaver and at the sound of it, Serle thrust his lantern into Eleanor's hand and threw himself at the door, tearing back the bolt and nearly ripping it off its hinges. He snatched the lantern back and thrust his way through the narrow doorway. 'Oh, thank God! She's here!' When he came out a moment later, he was supporting Beatrice, who was leaning against his shoulder and clinging to him in a way that made Borrill and Lizzie exchange meaningful glances.

Eleanor threw herself at them and embraced her cousin and Serle indiscriminately. 'What happened? Oh, Bea, we were so worried about you! Oh, thank goodness you're safe!'

Beatrice shivered and pressed against Justin. 'I was abducted.'

Eleanor stared at her for a moment, then gasped, 'Like in *Cressida's Revenge?*'

'It wasn't at all like those stupid novels!' snapped Beatrice. 'I'll have you know, Eleanor, that when one's hands are tied behind one, it's just not possible to wriggle free. Nor can one spirit oneself through a heavy door that's bolted on the other side!'

'Oh!' Eleanor's tone was faintly disappointed.

'And what's more, one can't scream for help, with a mouth full of gag. In fact, adventures are not at all pleasant in real life and I hope I never have another one!'

Eleanor looked so disappointed that Crispin burst out laughing. 'There you are, then, my love. You'll just have to be content with a more mundane life.'

Lizzie exchanged another knowing glance with Borrill.

There was a groan from inside the hut.

'What's that?' Crispin demanded, amusement vanishing.

'Oh, I forgot to mention that Smeathley is in there, unconscious,' drawled Justin, not turning round. 'How did that happen, Bea?'

Beatrice began to fidget with his coat buttons. 'I'm afraid I hit him over the head with a flower pot. I seem to have hit him harder than I intended.'

'I daresay he has a thick skull. It certainly

looks thick.'

Crispin peered into the hut. 'His hands appear to be tied behind his back as well.'

Beatrice grew indignant. 'Well, he was trying to force his attentions on me, and telling me that we'd have to get married! As if I'd marry *him!* So I hit him on the head with the first thing that came to hand and then I tied him up with a strip of my petticoat.'

'That sounds as good as any heroine in a novel,' said Eleanor approvingly. 'How brave of you, Bea!'

'It wasn't bravery, it was desperation,' declared Beatrice, shuddering at the memory of Smeathley's hands on her body.

'As if I'd let you marry anyone else, whatever happened.' Justin drew her closer and kissed her cheek.

Lizzie beamed at her mistress and decided that Serle couldn't be so bad, after all.

'How did you get in there in the first place?' Justin asked, staring at the hut. 'Since the door was locked from the outside, I gather there must have been some other player in the game.'

'I didn't see anyone else, not even the one who kidnapped me. Smeathley pretended he had been following an intruder, but

Justin, I'm sure *he* was the one responsible for me being kidnapped.'

Justin's eyes took on a fierce gleam. 'Was he, now?' He took a step towards the hut.

Beatrice grabbed his coat. 'Please don't hit him any more! I think he'll have a very sore head in the morning and that's enough.'

'A sore head, my love, is not nearly enough punishment for trying to compel you to marry him. Or for forcing himself upon you. You must have been terrified!'

She nodded, swallowing hard. 'I was at first. Later, I grew angry.'

He smiled at that. 'Like the time you chased that pickpocket?'

Her answering smile shut out the rest of the group. 'A little like that.' Then her smile faded. 'But Justin, think for a moment! If we do anything to bring him to book, Aunt Marguerite will get to hear of it. And she'll be furious! And – and that wouldn't be good for her. Justin, please! Let the matter drop! For her sake!'

Crispin had come out of the hut as she was speaking. 'She's right, you know. We don't want the old lady upset, especially not now. But,' he grinned round at them, 'there's no reason why we shouldn't leave Smeathley in there to cool down. I've taken his bonds off and we can lock the door again. I daresay one of the gardeners will find him in the morning if he shouts loudly enough.'

Eleanor broke their startled silence by gurgling with laughter. 'That's not a mundane sort of thing to do, Crispin! That's a *wonderful* idea!' She gazed at him adoringly. 'How very clever you are!'

Borrilll coughed. 'I could ensure, sir, that Mr Smeathley would be found by someone who would not pay much attention to what he said. We have a gardener, Old Henry, who is very deaf and bad-tempered.' He gazed blandly at Crispin.

'An excellent idea!' said Crispin. 'We'd be very grateful for your help there, Borrill. In fact, you've been of great help to us tonight. I shan't forget that.'

'It's been a pleasure, sir. We servants are, if I may say so, very fond of Miss Beatrice. And you may be sure that no word of this will get out from myself or Miss Hulls.'

'No,' said Lizzie, drawing herself up straighter, 'But I think we ought to get Miss Beatrice back to her room now, your lordship. She's shivering.'

Serle nodded. 'You're perfectly right. And she doesn't even know yet that she owes her rescue to you, Lizzie.'

Lizzie went bright scarlet and didn't know where to look.

Serle pulled Beatrice gently towards the house. 'Come along, everyone. Bed!'

The next morning, Borrill reported regretfully that Old Henry, who had been told only that an intruder had been locked in the hut, had discovered the place to be quite empty at seven o'clock in the morning. He was, however, incensed to find that some unknown person had been smashing his plant pots. 'I made further enquiries, your lordship and discovered that Mr Smeathley's horse is missing from the stables and that a message had been left by him for her ladyship. It was delivered to her rooms before I could intercept it, I'm afraid.'

They looked at one another anxiously, but could only guess at what the note had contained. A conference of war was therefore held as to how the two couples could best approach the Dowager. The doctor had forbidden her, if she valued her life, to receive visitors before eleven o'clock in the morning, so they had more than enough time to discuss matters thoroughly. Crispin was all for being completely honest with her ladyship, Justin thought they might temper the truth slightly and their two fiancées were mainly concerned to spare their elderly relative any worry or upset.

Before a decision had been reached, Borrill brought a summons from her ladyship. Lord Serle and Mr Herforth were to present themselves at her private sitting room immediately.

'How did she look, Borrill?' asked Beatrice.

'Somewhat better, miss.'

'I'm coming with you, Crispin!' declared Eleanor.

'No. Let's see what she wants first.'

'But I'm the best one at getting round her! I'm the *only* one who can make her do anything.'

'Not this time, my love. This time, we shall do things my way.'

Beatrice intervened. 'He's right, Eleanor! You know how she hates it if anyone disobeys her or upsets her arrangements. She must have a reason for wanting to see Crispin and Justin. We'll have to leave her to do things her own way now, or we'll only make things worse.'

Eleanor scowled at them both, but could not maintain her bad humour for long. 'Oh, very well! But *do* hurry back as soon as you can, Crispin, for I'm *dying* to know what she wants!'

The two ladies fidgeted around for the next twenty minutes or so, speculating as to what could be happening in the East Wing, then at last Borrill came to summon them.

'Is my grandmother all right, Borrill?' demanded Eleanor. 'Does she look angry or upset?'

'Her ladyship seems to be in an excellent humour, miss.'

They entered the Dowager's rooms, to find Serle standing by the window and Crispin sitting on a couch beside her ladyship. Serle shook his head at them, which they took as a warning to say nothing.

'How are you, Grandmama?' said Eleanor brightly, bending to kiss her cheek. 'You look much better today.'

'I'll be better still when the other two Smeathleys have left. That young upstart of theirs wrote me a most impudent letter, not to mention departing without taking his leave of his hostess! Well, he'll not be invited *here* again! None of them will! I shall cut the connection. They're only related by marriage, anyway. There must be bad blood there somewhere. And I've a good mind to write to the Bishop to tell him not to do anything for that fellow!'

'What did Mr Smeathley say in his letter?' asked Beatrice.

'He had the impudence to tell me that he did not wish to offer for either of the two young ladies – as if I'd have let him marry you, once I'd met him – because he did not feel they would make suitable wives for a clergyman. The impertinence of it!'

When she started rapping the cane on the ground to emphasise her point, Beatrice realised that her aunt must be much better, and that, far from damaging her health, Smeathley's letter had quite invigorated her.

'*And* he added that he had taken his leave this way in order to spare the young ladies any embarrassment,' added her ladyship. 'As if *we* could have anything to be embarrassed about!'

'Spare us embarrassment!' exclaimed Eleanor, highly indignant. 'Why, that…'

'I must say that I didn't care for him myself,' Beatrice interrupted, afraid of what Eleanor might say, 'I found him a great bore.'

'Hmm! And what about you, miss?' demanded the Dowager, turning to Eleanor. 'It seemed to me at one stage that you were rather taken with him!'

'Oh, that was just a game.'

'Game, eh? And I suppose you told him so.'

'Well, when he proposed to me, I had to refuse him. I might have spoken a little bit frankly.'

The Dowager nodded in satisfaction. 'That'll be what upset him, then! Canting hypocrite! And what do *you* mean by flirting with anyone, miss? And you a Graceover!'

'I was just practising, Grandmama,' Eleanor said, with wide-eyed innocence. 'It didn't mean anything.'

'Practising flirting! Practising!' spluttered the Dowager. 'Persons of rank and breeding do not even consider indulging in such tasteless behaviour! If I ever catch you doing something so ill-bred again, miss, I'll teach you how to flirt, I will indeed!'

Eleanor cast her eyes down, but this did not prevent her from looking out of the corner of her eye at Crispin. She got no help from that quarter, for he looked displeased with her as well.

'Anyway, that's all over and done with!' Lady Marguerite said, changing tone and addressing the two young women. 'What I've decided upon isn't what I'd first planned,' she glared around the room, 'but it'll do, yes, it'll do tolerably well, given the circumstances, and I'll thank you two chits to do as you're told, for once.'

'What have you arranged, Grandmama?'

'I have decided, miss, that *you* had better marry your cousin Crispin. If you must flirt in future, you will kindly do so with your own husband. Though I personally had rather you behaved in a manner more in keeping with your station in life.'

Eleanor put her head on one side, as if she were thinking the proposal over.

The Dowager, never famous for her patience, waited only a minute, then snapped, 'Well, what do you have to say to that, hey?'

Crispin cocked an eyebrow at his beloved, grinning openly.

'Mmmm,' said Eleanor thoughtfully, 'I suppose it might just answer.'

'Might just answer! It's a perfect solution! It'll keep the Graceover blood at Satherby, even if the name has to change. You're to marry him at once and no more arguments, miss. Might just answer, indeed!'

Eleanor pouted. 'Well, I don't think that's fair at all, Grandmama!'

'Not fair! What's not fair? You just said it might answer. Make up your mind, young lady! Make up your mind! I won't force you into anything you dislike, but he seems fairly presentable to me, and you don't seem to object to his company. *He*'s willing, that's for sure.' She stared at Crispin, and cackled with laughter as he blushed slightly under her scrutiny.

'It's not that, Grandmama; it's the way you're doing it that isn't fair. You've stopped him proposing to me. How do you think it feels when one's grandmother does the proposing? Can't he speak for himself? I don't think it's fair at all if I'm not to have a proper proposal, on bended knee and everything!'

Crispin had difficulty keeping his face straight and Justin chuckled aloud.

Even the Dowager's lips twitched. 'And is that your only objection, miss?'

Eleanor looked at Crispin, pretending to consider him as her grandmother had, and he shook his head at her. 'Well,' she allowed, 'he's not bad looking, really, and I *should* rather like to stay at Satherby. But I do insist on a proper proposal. I'd feel cheated, otherwise, I really would.'

The Dowager gave a rusty spurt of laughter. 'Then you'd better take her away and propose properly, young Herforth! And see that you make a good job of it, too. Bended knee and all.'

'Yes, Aunt Marguerite.' He held out his hand to Eleanor and with a quick sideways glance at him, she placed her hand in his and allowed him to lead her from the room.

The Dowager watched them leave, then turned to Beatrice. 'I gather,' she said dryly, 'that you and Serle have already come to an understanding of sorts.'

Beatrice blushed. 'I'm afraid so. I, I hope you don't mind too much, Aunt Marguerite. I didn't mean to become attached to him. It just – happened.'

'I should have known you'd do something like this when I sent you to London without me. If Johanna couldn't keep her own daughters in order, why should she manage with you? Still, you've done quite well for yourself, I must say.'

Justin made a flourishing bow.

'Yes.' The Dowager's eyes were bright with amusement. 'Better than your father did, that's for sure. Serle is a man of breeding and has enough money, I gather, to make comfortable settlements upon you and your children. I wouldn't agree to a marriage, else! If things are not done properly, the next generation suffers for it.'

Beatrice's face was now bright scarlet. 'Aunt Marguerite!' she protested, embarrassed by this business-like attitude.

'It's true, miss, as you well know. No use denying the facts.'

Serle came across to take Beatrice's hand, smiling at her in a way that made her breath catch in her throat. 'I think you can rely upon me to keep matters on a proper footing, your ladyship. Beatrice is, alas, incurably romantic, but at least she has had the good taste to settle her affections on me and not on some low-born fellow.'

'True, true! I brought her up to know what she owes to the family.' The old lady waved her cane at them. 'I suppose she'll complain as well if I say any more. You'd better take her away and make her a proper proposal, Serle. We'll sort out the business arrangements later.'

'An excellent idea, your ladyship.'

Neither of them noticed the Dowager's lips twitching or heard the hoarse little chuckle that escaped her control as she watched them leave. 'Who do they all think they're fooling?' she asked the air around her as she rang for her maid. 'I'm not in my dotage yet, thank you!'

When Lippings came in, she found Lady

Marguerite still chuckling, and this developed into such a hearty bout of laughter that her ladyship fell into a choking fit and had to have her back pounded as if she were a common sort of person and not a member of the nobility.

Serle shepherded Beatrice from the room with the greatest celerity and pulled her into the library. The minute they were alone, he gathered her in his arms.

She held him off for a moment, in mock anger. 'How on earth did you persuade her to agree?' she demanded. 'Yes, and how dare you speak about me like that! Good taste to settle my affections on *you*, indeed!'

But before she could take him further to task, he had clasped her to him and had silenced her with a kiss which left her feeling so breathless that she could only cling to him and demand weakly, 'Well, aren't you going to propose to me properly, my lord?'

'I rather thought I had already done so, my dear. But if you insist...' he paused, smiling down at her in a way that made her heart lurch. 'Will you,' he punctuated each phrase with a gentle kiss on alternate cheeks, 'marry me, next week, if not sooner?'

'Oh, I'd think I'd better!' she gasped, clinging to him in a very unladylike manner, 'and as soon as possible, if you please, for I'm developing a tendency to embrace you whenever I'm alone with you, and that sort of behaviour will never do!'

He brushed a strand of hair from her forehead and looked down at her very seriously, clasping her lightly around the waist. 'Dearest Beatrice, are you sure?'

Being Beatrice, she did not try to avoid his glance, but looked him straight in the eyes and said softly, 'I'm very sure, Justin.' Then her smile returned, for she had never felt so gloriously happy in all her life. 'Mind, I'll only marry you if you promise not to throw me into any more pools.'

He threw back his head and roared with laughter, then pulled her into his arms again. 'I promise nothing,' he said in a husky voice, 'except to love you forever. And I demand the same from you.'

In fact, considering that they were all persons of rank, there was an extremely vulgar display of feelings and affection that day at Satherby Abbey.

The publishers hope that this book has given you enjoyable reading. Large Print Books are especially designed to be as easy to see and hold as possible. If you wish a complete list of our books please ask at your local library or write directly to:

Magna Large Print Books
Magna House, Long Preston,
Skipton, North Yorkshire.
BD23 4ND

This Large Print Book, for people
who cannot read normal print,
is published under the auspices of

THE ULVERSCROFT FOUNDATION